Ribbon of Light

Claire Yezbak Fadden

ISBN: 978-0-9988645-2-5

Editor: Barb Wilson

Book Cover: Diolinda Monteiro

Published by: Brightwood Books

Disclaimer
This story is a work of fiction. Names, characters, and
incidents are either products of the author's imagination or
are used fictitiously. Any resemblance to actual events,
locales, organizations or persons, living or dead, is entirely
coincidental.

Dedication

Always for Nick.

Shawn, Jake, Seth, Lisa, Rachel, Windley and Grace, my first and best fans.

Acknowledgments

My deepest appreciation goes to my critique partners Sharon C. Cooper and Trish Wilkinson who were there from the very beginning, swimming for me when I couldn't manage another stroke. I treasure them for loving this story through its endless revisions and ever-changing titles.

A writer is only as good as her early readers and I've been blessed with the best. Thank you Julie Bawden Davis, Frances Escandon, Cathy Escobedo, Margaret More, Esther Pearson, Carol Schoenherr and Kim Yezbak. You've waited a long time to see this story in print. Each of you contributed to bringing Julie to life on the page. She's a compilation of the strengths, goodness and passion shining in each of you.

Special thanks to Cara Chacon-Bent who taught me about manufacturing in China. Your wealth of knowledge is beyond my comprehension and I'm grateful for your generously shared expertise.

Lastly, this novel is a work of fiction. Any errors, mistakes or missteps are solely my own.

Dear Reader,

It's true! The first shall be last.

Ribbon of Light is the final novel in the *Begin Again* series, but I wrote Julie Rafferty's story first. Julie, the oldest Jameson sister, is the daughter her mother leaned on the most after their father deserted. Now a mother herself, Julie can't imagine anything worse than being a struggling single parent. She's carefully crafted her life to avoid that fate. But sometimes destiny moves you along another path, challenging your faith and self-confidence. Luckily, Julie has a stockpile of faith.

If you enjoy Julie's story, they you'll want to meet her sisters Monica Morgan and Kate Wiley, each with a story of inner strength, family bonds and deep faith.

Email me at claire@clairefadden.com for book discussion questions, to share your thoughts about Julie or just to say hi.

Happy reading!

Claire

Chapter One

Julie Rafferty slipped off her linen jacket and placed the wrap next to her, wishing she had worn something less boardroom to the basketball court. Sandwiched between her two daughters, she didn't mind the school's hard wooden bleachers. Her son Jason's junior varsity basketball game provided the perfect distraction from her workday responsibilities. She had left the office early—something she rarely did—excited to join her husband Trevor in cheering for Jason and his team. Today was a chance for the five Raffertys to spend time together as a family.

She caught Emily's eye and planted a quick kiss on her seven-year-old's chubby cheek. Nicole, on the verge of tweenhood, scooted quickly away, mortified Julie might kiss her in public.

"Your mother loves you." She kissed Nicole anyway.

"Mom, not here." Nicole dragged her palm across her skin, wiping away lipstick traces. "Not in front of Ethan."

So, he's the boy you have a crush on this week.

"Did you get your homework done during afterschool care?"

"I didn't have any homework," Emily answered, her blue eyes brimming happily.

Nicole frowned. "I have a chapter to read in history. I'll do it later."

"Yes, you will. Right when we get home. I don't want your grades slipping because you're spending time impressing Ethan."

"Mom." Nicole voiced her disdain. "Not so loud."

"Just kidding. Where's Dad?"

"Not here yet, I guess," her oldest daughter snapped, clearly annoyed at her mother's presence in her orbit.

"Maybe he's not coming because you came," Emily added.

"What does that mean?"

"Usually he's here and you're not. Maybe he's taking a break."

Just like him to complain that I'm the absent parent and then not show up. And after the big scene he made this morning about how I'm missing our children growing up.

Julie was familiar with solo parenting. Her mother couldn't attend many of Julie's or her sisters' events. So, when Monica and Kate looked to the sidelines of a soccer game or into the audience at a school play, she was the one they saw clapping.

Julie proudly possessed many of their single mother's strong qualities, but the one trait she didn't want to imitate was being an absentee parent. Her endless commitments as the founder of FunWorks, a fledgling software toy company, had quickly turned her into the role she had feared most. But not today. Today she arrived at the gym early, making certain Jason saw her. She wanted Trevor to see her, too. *Where was he?*

She unfastened the top two buttons of her silk blouse and fanned out her collar a bit, hoping to capture a sexy wife look. She wore the oversized bib necklace, a gift from Trevor, even though the clasp rubbed relentlessly against her skin. As soon as she opened the box on Christmas morning, Trevor hurried to put the jewels around her neck, saying, "I couldn't resist. I knew how beautiful the gold and turquoise would look with your blue eyes and auburn hair."

Why had she not worn that necklace before today?

The gymnasium's noisy commotion and high energy served as a welcome contrast to her workday, riddled with suppliers and shipping companies. She wanted nothing more than to watch her son make layups and free throws.

Julie marveled at the strength of Jason's legs, hairier than she remembered. With his knees bent slightly, her son kept his wrist loose and swished in both free throws before searching the stands for his dad. Julie did a quick scan of the gym. Still no Trevor.

The buzzer signaled the end of the first half. Julie cheered, hoping her enthusiasm would make up for Trevor's absence. Jason rewarded her with a steely glance and joined his teammates on the bench guzzling water from a squirt bottle. Her throat tightened at her son's disappointment. Trevor hadn't seen a single basket scored today.

Things weren't going well between her and Trevor, even after they had hired Teresa Desmond to help around the house. Grateful for Teresa's many talents, she had been the only plus to emerge from one of Julie and Trevor's many fights.

Old-fashioned, Trevor wanted his wife to meet him at the door at the end of his workday, the way his mother did. Be the goddess of the home. That wasn't Julie's plan and she told him so. Their blowout several months ago started innocently enough. Nicole couldn't find toilet paper. Somehow that was Julie's fault.

Emily jammed an elbow into her mother's side. "Jason has eight points now."

"What?" Julie shouted, not realizing the third quarter had begun.

"Jason. He just made another basket. Weren't you watching?" Nicole chided in her preteen, know-it-all voice.

"Yeah, I saw. Way to go, Jason," she shouted as an afterthought. "Where's your dad? He missed the first half."

She checked her phone. No message. Was he mad about her not being in the mood last night? How could he expect her to feel romantic toward him after the cruel way he had spoken to her? She had laid nestled against him, escaping in his kisses from the day's stress, treasuring his embrace. And then he told her he wanted to sell FunWorks. All the passion and love warming her body seconds earlier erupted into icy shards.

"Can I have money for the snack bar?" Nicole asked, ignoring Julie's inquiry.

Julie handed her a five-dollar bill. "Get a little something but don't ruin your appetite. Mrs. D will have dinner ready when we get home." The sisters scurried down the stands, racing toward nachos and licorice.

Minutes later, Nicole plunked down next to her mom, spilling cheese sauce on her tailored jacket. Emily slid in next to her sister, one hand holding a soda and the other a candy bar.

"Oh no! Sorry Mom. I didn't mean—"

"That's all right. That's what I get for wearing work clothes to play." She was as much at fault as Nicole for the accident. She wasn't about to let spilled cheese sauce ruin the evening. She reached for a napkin, poured water on it, and gently blotted the fabric. "Don't worry. The jacket can be cleaned."

Nicole held the nacho-filled cardboard bowl toward her mother, smiling. "Want any?"

Julie slipped a tortilla strip into her mouth and grimaced at the mixture of salty and stale. The cheese sauce coating the chips staved off her third-quarter hunger pangs.

She gazed around the gymnasium, hoping for a sign of Trevor. During the timeouts, she spied Jason's blue eyes scanning the stands, searching for his father, too. His broad shoulders and solid frame reminded her of a young Trevor. Her firstborn, a full head taller than most of his teammates, knocked hard on the door to manhood, seemingly overnight.

Trevor was staying away on purpose, she realized, her eyes misting over. His way of getting even because she was leaving on a business trip.

"Hey." A familiar hand touched Julie's shoulder, causing an electrifying charge to pulse through her body.

"I was wondering if you were going to show up," she said with more bitterness than she meant.

She was relieved to see Trevor. She wanted to be near him, touch his face, hold hands like they used to. Instead, she made a snarky comment, driving another wedge between them. Seemed like inflicting hurt and pain became the goal of every conversation they shared recently. Somehow their loving, supportive relationship had turned spiteful and vindictive.

Julie couldn't put her finger on when things changed, but she knew why. Trevor hated the time she devoted to growing FunWorks. He never understood her need to stand on her own two feet and take pride in something she created. He would never understand how her company gave her a sense of security he never could.

She moved her jacket to make room for him. Instead, he squeezed in between the girls. "Don't start with me. I work too, you know. I got here as soon as I could."

"What's Rickman got to do with you missing half the game?"

"He wouldn't stop rambling about nailing down sales figures before next week's shareholder meeting. Man, that guy is paranoid."

"Hi, Daddy. Want some nachos?"

"Sure, sweet cheeks." Trevor hugged Emily and Nicole before grabbing a chip. "Finally, I told him I had to leave. What did I miss?"

"Jason went on a scoring run. He has twelve points, eight from free throws." Julie allowed her pride to slip out. "Guess all that time you spent in the driveway teaching him how to draw a foul paid off."

"Someone has got to be home with our kids," Trevor said, his words dripping with judgment.

"Nicole, Emily. Go wash that sauce off your hands," Julie ordered.

"I can just lick them clean," Emily said.

Nicole stood. "Come on, Em. Let's go. I think they're going to fight again and Mom doesn't want us to hear."

"We're not fighting," Trevor said. "Just go wash your hands like your mother asked."

She watched the girls head toward the bathrooms. "They're right, you know. All we do anymore is argue."

"Not true. You're not at home long enough. I can't believe you have another weeklong business trip."

"I have a commitment to the company and the people who work there," Julie said in hushed tones. "If you can't or won't accept that, then there is nothing I can do to make things better between us."

"Can't or won't?" Trevor slid closer, swiping at a lock of his sandy blond hair. "When we were first married, all you talked about is how your dad deserted you and your sisters. How awful life was growing up without a father. Well, growing up with a mother who'd rather be somewhere else is just as bad. How do you think the kids feel about you never being around?"

"You're going to start that argument here? Now?"

"You're more like your dad than you realize."

She trembled at the insult. "Don't say that. I'm nothing like him. Our children never want for anything."

"There's all sorts of abandonment, Jules. Money isn't everything."

Julie gathered her jacket and purse. Her anger boiled on the edge, ready to topple out and scald Trevor. "I thought for a change we could skip the fighting, but I was wrong."

"You've got to take your foot off the gas pedal before it's too late. Our kids are growing up and you're rarely here for them...or for me."

"Things will improve after this product rollout. I'll be around more. I promise."

"Just answer this: Is it really that awful to be married to a man who wants to be with you?"

"Trevor, don't do this now. Just when the company is about to move to the next level."

"Yeah. The next level. And then the next."

Emily bounded toward her mother, displaying her hands for inspection. "Are these clean enough?"

"Perfect." He shifted enough for Emily and Nicole to slip between him and Julie.

"I've got to return a few calls and answer some emails. I'll see you at home after the game," Julie said to Trevor.

He shook his head in disbelief. "Gotta love this tag-team parenting."

"Obviously we need to talk, but not here." She leaned toward him. "Later tonight, at home. You know that place you want me to be."

"I can keep wishing," he said, now facing the basketball court, more interested in Jason's breakaway. "Drive to the basket. Drive to the basket!" He leaped up and shouted, "Yeah! Nice bucket, Jason."

Julie clomped down the bleacher steps, the sound of Trevor's cheers echoing in her ears. She didn't turn back, fuming at him for ruining the evening. She wanted them to be on the same side for a change, cheering together. Instead, he insisted on playing games, manipulating her to get what he wanted. She had witnessed her mother endure those same tricks.

Trevor had grabbed the final thread holding their already faltering marriage together and yanked hard, like a child wanting to unravel a wool sweater.

A harsh realization slithered through Julie's chest and took hold. *We can never weave these strands back together. Things will never be the same.*

Julie straightened her frame to her full five feet six height, convinced of her wisdom in investing herself fully in her company. Her strides lengthened until she reached the exit.

Outside the gym, she leaned against the wall, her chest exploding in anguish and despair instead of vindication. The reality shattered her heart, but at least she and her children wouldn't endure poverty the way she and her sisters had done.

***

Twenty minutes later, Julie turned into their driveway, still steaming at Trevor for ruining what she had hoped would be a family evening. Imagine him blaming his boss Joe Rickman for his own tardiness. Trevor had rambled on about how Joe wanted to nail down sales figures before next week's shareholders' meeting.

Something about a hostile takeover or some such nonsense.

Julie didn't care. She wanted what she wanted. And tonight, what she wanted most was for her and Trevor to be the perfect parents; at least in appearance if nothing else.

Wallowing in her self-pity, she nearly missed Zeke, Teresa's son, parked a few houses away. He leaned against the hood of his car while his mother stood at the curbside, her back toward Julie. Even in the dusky light, she could read Zeke's body language, see his faded T-shirt, torn jeans, and uncombed hair.

Julie crept to the front of the house, outside of Teresa and Zeke's line of vision, but close enough to watch Teresa reach into her apron pocket and hand an envelope to her son.

Zeke, Trevor's boyhood friend, grabbed the thick envelope, kissed his mother hurriedly, and slipped the packet into his jacket pocket. With his mission accomplished, he started his car and raced away, leaving his mother's slumped silhouette behind.

Her heart ached for Teresa. Being a single mother of an adult child was no easier than the hard life Julie's mother had shouldered. Teresa's only child drifted from job to job. After her husband's death, she had used what little money left from the life insurance policy to bail Zeke out of financial trouble, spoiling him at every turn.

Zeke could never seem to pull the pieces of his life together and Julie suspected the reason why.

Teresa stepped from the curb and quickly wiped tears with the corners of her apron.

Julie met her on the concrete path to the front door. "I see Zeke's back in town."

"For a little while," Teresa said.

"What did he want?"

"Oh, nothing. Some mail came to the house," she replied, moving away.

"Is he in trouble again?"

"He's getting out of trouble."

Julie recognized her tone—the same one Julie had used minutes ago when she tried to convince herself of something she hoped for rather than believed.

"Marilyn threw him out," Teresa continued, her eyes staring at the Rafferty doorway as though the answer laid just inside the opening. "Told him if he wants her back, he has to stop gambling."

Julie wrapped her arm around Teresa's shoulders and pulled her close. The tension in her body released slowly as they headed toward the door.

"He's joined Gamblers Anonymous. This time he'll make it, you'll see."

Julie nodded, never breaking her stride. Every parent wanted to believe their child's story, no matter the evidence to the contrary. Teresa was no different.

She wished Teresa's motherly conviction would be strong enough to change Zeke, but in her gut, Julie saw only more heartbreak ahead.

***

"Can I stay in your room for a little while?" Emily's squeaky voice emanated from Teresa's open door into the dark hallway a few hours later.

"Sure, sweetie," Teresa responded, arms opened wide. "Did you have a bad dream?"

Emily nodded and clutched Horace Hardbuckle, her scraggly rainbow-colored stuffed animal, a bit tighter.

"Well, you and Horace come sit with me for a minute." Teresa threw back the blankets and scooted over to make room.

Emily didn't hesitate to jump into the bed. Teresa cuddled the child and gently rubbed her arm. For the third time in two weeks, Emily had turned to her for late night comfort. The child's warm body curled against Teresa.

"You're shaking. Was the dream that scary?"

"I wasn't asleep." Emily wiped a kernel of sleepy sand from her eye. "They're fighting again. About Daddy missing the basketball game."

"Your parents are just talking, honey. That's how adults talk."

Emily shook her head. "They say mean things. They try to whisper, but I can still hear."

Teresa agreed. In nearly sixty years, she had never witnessed such vitriol and cruelty between a married couple. During the past five months, she sought every chance to defuse the mounting pressure building between them. She wasn't always successful.

Their arguments boiled down to the same thing: Trevor wanted Julie to be home. That meant selling FunWorks. Teresa knew that wouldn't happen, even if keeping the company cost Julie her marriage.

In recent weeks, Julie and Trevor's volatile relationship escalated to heightened levels. Each day only magnified the fact that Teresa's extra help around the house provided an inadequate bandage on a festering wound. Trevor and Julie's love affair needed a much stronger remedy than what Teresa could offer.

"It's late and there's school tomorrow," Teresa reminded. "How about you stay here tonight. We'll have a sleepover in my room, okay?"

Minutes later Teresa heard Emily's gentle snores. If only she could solve her own problems this easily.

Chapter Two

"Julie Rafferty! Gosh, I'm happy to see you," Mort Gunther gushed, hugging Julie awkwardly. "It's been what, three years?"

The two stood near the midway of the New York Toy Fair convention's grand hall weeks later, surrounded by exhibitors, vendors and potential customers, all pushing and prodding their way to success.

"Mort, where have you been keeping yourself?" Julie smiled and pulled the peplum of her jacket back into alignment. "Haven't seen you since you sold MaxOut Toys."

"No reason for me to freeze in this city if I don't hafta." He grinned, revealing a picket fence of newly capped teeth.

The Mort Julie remembered lived for the banter and barter streaming through the convention hall. He always seemed distracted, hurrying from one appointment to the next, savoring the deals he'd garnered for his company. The inventor/entrepreneur dressed the part of a creative genius, right down to wrinkled out-of-style jackets, no tie, and stretch-band slacks, a stark contrast to today's tailored suit, complemented with a vest and a Windsor knot crowning his necktie. Julie had ignored the rumors that Mort was forced out of his company, but perhaps selling his business was the right move after all.

Julie motioned for Mort to sit. "I'm glad retirement agrees with you. What brings you around this year?"

"Guess I missed the hustle and bustle a bit."

"You miss this?" She waved an arm at the chaos surrounding them on all sides. Every oversized plaything imaginable, and some that had no chance of coming to market stood larger-than-life in booth displays as far as the eye could see. "I'm beat from working all week. I've been on my feet since eight this morning. Can't wait to leave this craziness and catch a flight back home."

"I'm sure Trevor and the kids miss you."

Julie nodded. No use explaining what's going on at home, even to someone as generous as Mort had been during her novice years, showing Julie the trade show ropes. She would forever be grateful.

"The other reason I stopped by was to introduce you to—"

"Me, ma'am. Bennett Burnside." A squat-shaped fifty-something man, now standing behind Mort's chair, stepped forward and extended his hand. "Introduce me, Mort," he commanded.

"Seems like you already did that, Bennett."

"So I did." Burnside, dressed as impeccably as Mort, held Julie's hand a moment too long, his diamond signet ring digging into her skin. Cigar smoke, mixed with a musky cologne, emanated from his clothes. Julie appraised him quickly, noting his eyes and skin color gave him a Germanic look, but his coarse black hair, now graying, hinted of Italian heritage.

"Mort here tells me you have a real winner with your paper doll company. I hear there's even talk about featuring your characters in an animated movie. I might have a client interested in purchasing."

"That would be wonderful," Julie replied, reaching for an order form. "What is the retailer's name?"

"Oh, I'm sorry, ma'am. You misunderstand. They want to buy the company, not order a few cases of your product."

Julie straightened and took a deeper look at Burnside, realizing he now reminded her of an aging Spock from Star Trek without the quirky charm.

"What Bennett means," Mort hurried to explain, "is maybe it's time you sell like I did. Take more time with your family. You know. Enjoy life, like me."

Julie stepped back, shocked at her former mentor's suggestion. After months of enduring Trevor's threats to sell, her resolve to make FunWorks a success was even stronger.

Did Burnside really think she'd fold because of her friendship with Mort? Didn't matter. Cases of PlaytimePals were the only items up for sale.

Julie yanked the collar of her jacket and drew herself to her full height. No one, not even Mort, could force her to give up her dream. "I appreciate your interest, Mr. Burnside, but FunWorks is not available for purchase. I could make you a great deal on a gross or two of PlaytimePals, though."

Burnside whispered in Julie's ear, "Looking forward to doing business with you." He shoved his business card into her hand and smiled.

Julie, as though cemented in place, remained quiet at Burnside's surreal expectation. She watched as he and Mort disappeared into the crowd. His hot breath left a lingering aura around her, much like walking through a cobweb, clingy and disturbing.

She turned the card over to read: *Call me when you change your mind.*

She knew this wasn't the end of Bennett Burnside. His scribbled words signaled the beginning of looming trouble.

The next day, Julie settled into the narrow coach seat for the long flight back to Los Angeles. Her home, a suburb north of the airport, would soon be a mere forty-five minutes away.

For the first time in her adult life, Julie felt secure, having survived a tumultuous five years of growing her tiny business to one of the most talked-about toy software companies in the country.

Though proud of her accomplishments, she missed her kids. And her husband.

Julie rubbed her arms as if wiping away the Big Apple's chill, already anticipating the San Marcel sunshine soaking her with warmth. The extended trip to the Toy Fair had been worth the sacrifice of being away from the kids. Julie would make the time up to them once she got home.

The six days had passed slowly, missing her teenaged Jason; Nicole, the family rule-setter; and Emily, her baby, her joy. Spending hours in airport terminals and days at trade shows added up. Although a poor substitute for being there, Julie called every night. All part of the family sacrifice to get ahead, she reminded herself. Still, she regretted not being home in the evenings like most moms. Yet another way she resembled her own mother.

Orders from this year's toy fair would nearly triple last year's sales, but the news offered a mixed blessing. Julie doubted Trevor would share her happiness. Instead, he'd complain about how much more time she'd be away from him and the kids.

Her marketing director, Derek Gable, jabbed her with an elbow, pointing to an ad in the in-flight magazine. "3D paper dolls could take FunWorks to the next level. These printers will be everywhere."

Julie clicked her seatbelt in place and took the magazine.

"How soon can we get the prototypes in from China?" He pulled a list from a stack of files on the seat between them. "I promised some of the buyers from the larger companies samples before the end of this quarter."

"You shouldn't have done that. We're still in unit testing." Julie shot him a glare, wishing he hadn't promised anything so proprietary. "We won't be ready for at least six months." Even though software developers routinely released early versions of their products, Julie ignored this industry standard, reluctant to get the 3D PlaytimePals software in the hands of beta testers too soon.

"It won't be ready in time for Christmas?"

"No." Julie pushed off her high heels and briefly rubbed her feet. "It's a brand-new concept, so don't promise anyone anything. This Christmas we're pushing Celebrity PlaytimePals." She slid her shoes under the seat in front of her, leaned back and closed her eyes.

If Derek thought she'd listen, he'd talk halfway to the coast. But she needed sleep. A few minutes later she lowered the window shade and rested her head against the cool plastic, grateful for a nonstop flight. For once she'd be home in time for dinner.

Julie shifted in her seat, searching for a comfortable position. Sleep eluded her.

"There's nothing to be afraid of," a man's voice drifted toward her from the row in front of hers. "See, over there is Manhattan, where Uncle Dave works. Wave to Uncle Dave."

"But Daddy..." a tiny voice pleaded. "It's scary up so high."

"I'm right here. There's nothing to be afraid of."

"Oh look. There's the Brooklyn Bridge. See it?"

"Umm-hmm. The water looks greeny-blue," the girl answered, the edge in her voice smoothing.

Julie's thoughts circled back to an afternoon nearly thirty years ago.

"What's that you're working on, little ladybug?" her father had asked. The bow-back chair he straddled creaked as he leaned forward to pick up the doll.

"A blouse for Emmylou. Mommy brought her home from Dell's," Julie answered, referring to the restaurant where her mother waited tables.

Stuart Jameson ran a finger across the fraying lace randomly stitched along the doll's hem. "She's nice." He returned the moppet to Julie and kissed her cheek.

Julie rubbed where his stubble scratched her skin. Her nose twitched at the smell of beer.

"You're doing a fine job, ladybug. I've never seen a better dressed doll. Where did you get all those clothes?"

"I made them," Julie said.

"Wow," he continued, "I know you're beautiful, but when did you become so talented, too?"

Julie's chest expanded at the pride in her father's words. On those quiet afternoons, while her mother worked, Julie's passion to design and create grew.

Weeks passed and the late-night yelling increased, well after she and her younger sisters, Monica and Kate, should have been asleep. Julie pulled a pillow over her head to muffle the painful din.

The fighting escalated until one day the battle stopped. Her father had left for good.

Her number one supporter, the person who made her believe in herself, had vanished. Along with her hopes, Julie threw her dolls into a discarded trunk, slammed the lid closed, and locked her dreams away.

Julie blinked open her eyes in time to see a burst of smoke as the jumbo jet's tires hit the runway. "Guess I dozed off," she said to Derek.

"I'll say. You slept the entire flight. Even missed the meal service,"

"Dodged a bullet there." Julie winked. Airplane food ranked just above hospital fare in her mind.

"We landed!" the little girl shouted. "The ride wasn't scary at all, Daddy."

"Told you," he said. "Get your backpack. Grammy will be waiting for us."

Julie yanked her coat out of the overhead compartment and shuffled off the plane. Derek followed, still buzzing in her ear about the 3D product line.

She turned to shoo him away and glimpsed the father and daughter walking hand-in-hand, the little girl practically skipping across the concourse. Occasionally her father lifted his arm swinging her forward, each time receiving a reward of gleeful giggles.

Not every dad abandoned their family, Julie thought, following them toward the baggage claim. Maybe there were a few men who would stick around. Kind of like finding that rare pearl in an oyster.

Thank God Trevor was one of those guys. He'd never leave. His children meant the world to him.

Chapter Three

Trevor Rafferty clicked the two gold-tone latches closed and propped his acoustic guitar case against the wall inside Mulvaney's Bar. "Things were fine before Julie started her own company," he complained to Russ Wheeler, the band's keyboard player. Trevor's long-time friend was one of the few who listened anymore. He dragged a microphone stand from the stage. "I was important to her then."

Trevor winced, hearing the self-pity in his words. "Sorry, Russ. I don't want to keep harping on this stuff. It's just that Julie's work schedule keeps her so busy." *I practically have to schedule an appointment to make love.* "She's always worried about earning more money. She misses the little joys in life," Trevor continued, "the ones I fell in love with her for."

"Like being our prettiest groupie," Russ volunteered.

"Yeah. She used to be the first one at our shows, no matter how seedy the dive."

Russ unplugged his keyboard. "Haven't seen her in a while, though."

"She's flying home now from a sales trip. I guess she sold a lot more toys."

Trevor fought to keep from sounding disappointed at his wife's success. He and Julie were two different people. She loved being in charge, calling the shots, taking on more risk and responsibility.

He, on the other hand, never let his job interfere with his personal life. His position as a mid-level brand manager for Cook's Finest, a prepared foods manufacturer, helped pay the bills and left plenty of time for his true passions—Julie, their kids, and his music.

He wished his wife could see her career the same way but he suspected her insatiable desire for financial security grew after her father deserted the family. Throughout their twenty years of marriage, Trevor never quite managed to convince Julie of his devotion.

"You're in for half, so what's your beef?" Russ asked, referring to California's community property laws.

"She's always working." Trevor wound the amplifier cords and stacked them together. "There's no time for anything else."

"I hear ya. Women, who knows what they want anyway? Let's go get a beer."

"Not today, man." Trevor tapped his watch. "I have to get home and change before I pick her up from the airport."

"Fanning those flames, huh?"

Trevor fist-bumped Russ. "Always, man." But bringing Julie back into his arms would take more than a romantic evening.

He needed to change her view of him, of their family life. But how?

***

Julie shoved three twenties into the cab driver's hand and hurried to the front door. She dragged a rolling suitcase behind, enjoying the late afternoon warmth brushing against her skin. Being up early to catch the nine a.m. flight out of LaGuardia seemed like a good idea. Even though she slept during most of the trip, she still felt worn out.

The aroma of onions and peppers cooking—the fragrance of Teresa's homemade sauce—greeted Julie as she opened the door. The familiar sound of Nicole practicing that week's piano lesson lilted in the background. Julie dropped her purse and an airport gift bag full of toy-sized-apologies on the oak bench in the foyer.

She heard Emily's voice before she saw her. "Momma? Is that you?" Her youngest daughter bounded from the kitchen and didn't stop until her thin arms wrapped around Julie's thighs. "What'd you bring me?"

"Not a thing." Julie lifted her.

In a brushstroke, Emily's face changed. "But you went to a Toy Fair." Her tiny voice emphasized the word toy.

"There's a bag over there." Julie pointed, and Emily squirmed out of her embrace and ran to the bench, her pigtail swinging.

"Hey, Mom." Jason stepped into the hallway. Had he grown another inch? Julie stood eye-to-eye with her teenager.

The music stopped and Nicole barreled in behind him. "You brought us stuff?" She grabbed the gift bag from Emily.

"Have I ever not brought you back something?" Julie brushed a dark brown ringlet away from her older daughter's eye. "Is your dad home?"

"Up here." Trevor leaned over the second-floor railing. "You're home early."

"You noticed." Her smile stretched like a too-tight T-shirt. "I finished the buyer meetings last night and caught an earlier flight."

"Why didn't you call?" Trevor asked, irritation and hurt mixing in his voice. He hurried down, his blond waves bobbing atop his solid six-foot frame. "I was on my way to pick you up."

Why hadn't she called? She pondered his question. What was she afraid of?

She peeled off her gray shawl-collared coat, tossing the designer jacket on the couch. "Something smells good."

"Spaghetti." Jason removed a price tag and pulled his new Yankees ball cap on his head backward.

"Great." Julie pecked Trevor on his cheek, put her arm around her son's shoulder and herded everyone toward the kitchen. "I'm starved."

Teresa, now standing to the side of the kitchen doorway, motioned Julie to her. "Do you have a moment?"

"Of course." Julie sent Jason ahead, following Trevor into the kitchen and turned to Teresa. "Is everything okay? Were the kids misbehaving?"

"No. Nothing like that. They're all angels." Teresa pursed her lips before continuing. "There's been a bit of an emergency come up. I wondered if you could give me an advance on my salary?"

"I don't see why not. What do you need, a few hundred dollars?"

Teresa picked at a hangnail, avoiding eye contact. "Closer to a few thousand. Actually, I need ten thousand. In cash."

"Wow. What kind of emergency costs that much?" Julie asked, unprepared to provide such a large sum on short notice. "Did you talk to Trevor?"

"No, I figured he'd tell me to ask you."

"Oh. That's probably true." Still, Julie wondered what disaster had befallen her Teresa toting a jumbo price tag to match. Before she could reiterate her question, Teresa spoke.

"It's the house. They've found a leak in the bathroom. The whole thing must be remodeled. If I pay cash, they'll give me a discount," Teresa added quickly.

Julie wanted to help, but Teresa's story didn't ring true. As far as Julie knew, Teresa had paid off her home and lived comfortably on her deceased husband's pension. She agreed to nanny for them to fill her empty days.

"Have you gotten a few bids? I know a guy—"

"I already have everything arranged." Teresa clipped her words. "I'll pay you back."

"It's not that, Teresa. I don't keep that much money on hand." Julie tried to hold Teresa's gaze, but she looked away.

"I'd have to move a few things around. And I need to check with Trevor. How soon would you need the money?"

"By the end of the week. Sooner if you can swing it."

An awkward silence stretched between them before Julie replied. "Let me see what I can do. Might take a couple of days."

"Thank you." Teresa hugged Julie before joining the family at the dinner table.

Julie recalled seeing Zeke and Teresa a few weeks ago after Jason's game. When she had mentioned it to Trevor, he only commented that Zeke had moved back home.

Could he be the real reason Teresa needed cash? Had her son damaged Teresa's property and now she was covering for him?

Julie needed to find out before she handed over any amount of money to Teresa.

Julie shoved three twenties into the cab driver's hand and hurried to the front door. She dragged a rolling suitcase behind, enjoying the late afternoon warmth brushing against her skin. Being up early to catch the nine a.m. flight out of LaGuardia seemed like a good idea. Even though she slept during most of the trip, she still felt worn out.

The aroma of onions and peppers cooking—the fragrance of Teresa's homemade sauce—greeted Julie as she opened the door. The familiar sound of Nicole practicing that week's piano lesson lilted in the background. Julie dropped her purse and an airport gift bag full of toy-sized-apologies on the oak bench in the foyer.

She heard Emily's voice before she saw her. "Momma? Is that you?" Her youngest daughter bounded from the kitchen and didn't stop until her thin arms wrapped around Julie's thighs. "What'd you bring me?"

"Not a thing." Julie lifted her.

In a brushstroke, Emily's face changed. "But you went to a Toy Fair." Her tiny voice emphasized the word toy.

"There's a bag over there." Julie pointed, and Emily squirmed out of her embrace and ran to the bench, her pigtail swinging.

"Hey, Mom." Jason stepped into the hallway. Had he grown another inch? Julie stood eye-to-eye with her teenager.

The music stopped and Nicole barreled in behind him. "You brought us stuff?" She grabbed the gift bag from Emily.

"Have I ever not brought you back something?" Julie brushed a dark brown ringlet away from her older daughter's eye. "Is your dad home?"

"Up here." Trevor leaned over the second-floor railing. "You're home early."

"You noticed." Her smile stretched like a too-tight T-shirt. "I finished the buyer meetings last night and caught an earlier flight."

"Why didn't you call?" Trevor asked, irritation and hurt mixing in his voice. He hurried down, his blond waves bobbing atop his solid six-foot frame. "I was on my way to pick you up."

Why hadn't she called? She pondered his question. What was she afraid of?

She peeled off her gray shawl-collared coat, tossing the designer jacket on the couch. "Something smells good."

"Spaghetti." Jason removed a price tag and pulled his new Yankees ball cap on his head backward.

"Great." Julie pecked Trevor on his cheek, put her arm around her son's shoulder and herded everyone toward the kitchen. "I'm starved."

Teresa, now standing to the side of the kitchen doorway, motioned Julie to her. "Do you have a moment?"

"Of course." Julie sent Jason ahead, following Trevor into the kitchen and turned to Teresa. "Is everything okay? Were the kids misbehaving?"

"No. Nothing like that. They're all angels." Teresa pursed her lips before continuing. "There's been a bit of an emergency come up. I wondered if you could give me an advance on my salary?"

"I don't see why not. What do you need, a few hundred dollars?"

Teresa picked at a hangnail, avoiding eye contact. "Closer to a few thousand. Actually, I need ten thousand. In cash."

"Wow. What kind of emergency costs that much?" Julie asked, unprepared to provide such a large sum on short notice. "Did you talk to Trevor?"

"No, I figured he'd tell me to ask you."

"Oh. That's probably true." Still, Julie wondered what disaster had befallen her Teresa toting a jumbo price tag to match. Before she could reiterate her question, Teresa spoke.

"It's the house. They've found a leak in the bathroom. The whole thing must be remodeled. If I pay cash, they'll give me a discount," Teresa added quickly.

Julie wanted to help, but Teresa's story didn't ring true. As far as Julie knew, Teresa had paid off her home and lived comfortably on her deceased husband's pension. She agreed to nanny for them to fill her empty days.

"Have you gotten a few bids? I know a guy—"

"I already have everything arranged." Teresa clipped her words. "I'll pay you back."

"It's not that, Teresa. I don't keep that much money on hand." Julie tried to hold Teresa's gaze, but she looked away. "I'd have to move a few things around. And I need to check with Trevor. How soon would you need the money?"

"By the end of the week. Sooner if you can swing it."

An awkward silence stretched between them before Julie replied. "Let me see what I can do. Might take a couple of days."

"Thank you." Teresa hugged Julie before joining the family at the dinner table.

Julie recalled seeing Zeke and Teresa a few weeks ago after Jason's game. When she had mentioned it to Trevor, he only commented that Zeke had moved back home.

Could he be the real reason Teresa needed cash? Had her son damaged Teresa's property and now she was covering for him?

Julie needed to find out before she handed over any amount of money to Teresa.

***

Hours later, after the kids were asleep, Julie unpacked. She heard Trevor in the master bath brushing his teeth.

He spat into the sink. "It took you a full week to get a contract from Bull's Eye?"

"Only six days," Julie snapped, a defensive tone coating her reply. *He's making polite conversation, not criticizing me,* she assured herself, realizing six days might as well be a week.

"How many pieces?"

"One hundred thousand," she explained, worried her enthusiasm at the size of the order would annoy Trevor. "They're testing us in two hundred stores. If the sample stores perform strong, Bull's Eye will roll out the dolls to all their locations in time for Christmas shoppers." Julie's chest pumped with pride. "I got a good vibe from the buyer. She has two young daughters and they both loved the original PlaytimePals, so selling her on the celebrity ones came easy."

"You and boy wonder scored again."

Julie's smile waned, unable to ignore the disdain in Trevor's tone. "I wish you wouldn't call him that." She slammed her valise on the chair a little too hard. Trevor's sarcasm hit the intended mark.

She removed a leftover sample and held the paper doll as though the toy were her lifeline. Every girl could be a fashion designer when using her software that combined the simplicity of paper dolls with the high-tech magic of computers.

She opened the package and gripped the sturdy plastic cutout. Her finger followed the curves and texture of the shape.

A new-found sense of worth surged through her veins as she recalled the possibility of a movie deal. Even though she wanted his advice, she carefully chose her words, fearful that he would go off the rails, again, claiming the film idea was just another way to keep her away from him. She wanted Trevor to be proud of her, the way her father once had been. Instead, she shared her excitement, her goals, and hopes with Derek.

"The contract still has to be approved by Bull's Eye's legal department," she finally said to the partially closed bathroom door, downplaying the deal's significance.

Trevor mumbled something indecipherable as he rinsed. Sounded like congratulations. "Thank you, hon—"

The click of his electric shaver drowned out the rest of the sentence.

Julie set the doll on her dresser and shed her bra and panties. For a moment, she considered the black lace negligee folded in a drawer, then pushed the teddy aside and slid into an ankle-length cotton nightgown. She pulled on fluffy pink slipper socks to combat traces of the New York chill still penetrating her bones.

By the time Trevor finished in the bathroom, she had tucked herself under the covers in their queen-size bed, curving her body away from his side. She'd ask him about Teresa's loan tomorrow.

The bed dipped when Trevor climbed in and Julie curled into a tighter ball. She pretended to be asleep, not responding to his hand trailing along her back, his warm breath against her neck.

She loved Trevor. Why couldn't he be happy and encouraging about her success? At the very least, try to understand her commitment to FunWorks. How could he not know that building a business takes sacrifice? Be aware how competitors snatch away your dreams if you let up for a moment.

"Julie," he whispered. "Baby, you still awake?"

She smelled the woodsy cologne and wanted to wrap her body around his, soak in his warmth, tap into his strength. She'd looked forward to this reunion, but his every complaint, jealous remark and snide comment destroyed her passion.

After what seemed like an eternity, the bed frame creaked as Trevor rolled toward his side. Minutes later, she heard his gentle snores.

Not able to quiet her mind, she slipped out of bed, picked up Emma, the paper doll designed to look like Emily, and padded to the bedroom's bay window. She grabbed a nearby quilt and curled herself into the odd angle of the seat. Comforted inside the restricted space, she stared into the blackboard-like darkness.

The wind rustled through the trees as a car pulled into the driveway next door. Five minutes before midnight. The neighbor's teenage daughter scurried inside the door just in time for curfew.

Not long ago she'd been that teenager hurrying home. Filled with ideas, hopes, aspirations. She would show everyone how she didn't need a man to succeed. Julie held Emma against the window pane, lapsing into her old game of pretend. *See how successful I am, Mom? I'm making my own way. You'd be so proud.*

The bed creaked. Julie jumped. Trevor, still asleep, lay turned toward her now, his face softly illuminated by the street lamp. The face she loved for two decades. Still loved. Julie stifled a yawn, her gaze tracing Trevor's features. A sense of strength flooded her veins, diminishing her despair.

Julie's fate was her own. Like the dolls she manufactured, she could be anything she wanted to be. The choices were infinite.

She placed the paper doll on to the window seat cushion and headed back to bed. For their marriage to survive, Trevor needed to help or get out of the way.

She wouldn't sell her dream. Not for him. Not for anyone.

***

Early the next morning, Julie headed to work, grateful her recent trip offered a respite from bickering with Trevor.

Her mood lifted as she rushed toward her office, Derek's excited voice permeating the air.

"You should have seen the boss lady," Derek boasted. "A contract for 10,000 pieces here, 50,000 there. And they're talking about a PlaytimePals animated movie next summer."

"Wow, a movie deal. That will boost our off-season sales," Leanne Ford said.

Inside the safety of her office, she could savor her successful negotiations. What a contrast to her home life where she masked her enthusiasm.

Julie rounded the door to find Leanne standing a little too close to Derek. She wondered if her assistant's beaming smile came from an improved sales forecast, or if another, more personal reason, accounted for her glow. Julie's gaze locked onto Derek, and Leanne quickly stepped back, leaving space for Julie to pass.

"Ah, here she is." Derek sent a double finger point in Julie's direction. "Future movie producer."

"You exaggerate, Derek, but thanks anyway." Julie lifted the pile of mail from the corner of Leanne's desk and started toward her office. She licked her chapped lips, a souvenir from New York's arctic chill. The payoff in contracts and connections outweighed the cost of a little extra lip balm.

She flipped through the mail, stopping at an envelope from the law offices of Weinstein and Wallace. She ripped open the seal and read the wording twice, hoping she'd misunderstood. "I don't believe this," she murmured. Her pulse hammered against her eardrums. "This is crazy."

"Don't believe what?" Derek asked, entering from the doorway.

"How can they do this?"

Derek scanned the sheet in Julie's shaking hand and frowned. "They're claiming we infringed on a Game Masters patent?"

"This is bogus." Julie's heart rate increased. She read the letter again. "Who is Game Masters? I've never heard of them, much less taken their idea." She sucked in a deep breath and shoved the letter into Derek's hand. "Someone's out to make a quick buck. We didn't steal anything."

"Everything's going to be okay," Derek reassured. "I'll go and fax a copy of the letter to Gary now," he added, referring to Gary Carlson, the company attorney.

Julie waited for Derek to leave before rifling through a stack of business cards she collected at the toy fair. Was Burnside connected to Game Masters? The niggling fear in her stomach expanding like an overinflated balloon. His card had to be there.

Derek stormed back into Julie's office a few minutes later. "Gary thinks this is just posturing on their part. He'll get to the bottom of their complaint. Not to worry. These things happen all the time. It's probably just a nuisance claim."

Julie grunted, still pawing through the pile.

"What are you looking for?"

"This." She handed him an embossed business card.

"Who's Bennett Burnside?"

"Someone who wants to buy FunWorks."

"What? You're selling?"

"Of course not. Mort Gunther introduced us."

"Are you talking about the old dude with the graying goatee Mort was introducing to everyone at the toy fair?" Derek asked.

"He's the one. The San Marcel Hospital pediatric wing is named after him."

Derek's eyes opened wider. "That takes some cash."

"Even though Burnside is well-known here in San Marcel, I'd never met the man, until the toy fair."

"What did that snake oil salesman offer?"

"He creeped you out, too?" Julie crossed her arms and ran her hands over her skin as if pushing away goose bumps. "He acted as though his only reason for being there was to meet me."

"Maybe it was," Derek said.

"He got angry when I told him selling FunWorks would be like selling one of my children."

Derek plopped into the chair in front of Julie's desk. "How much did he offer?"

"I didn't ask. He shoved that card into my hand and said to call him when—not if—I change my mind. Should I be worried?"

"No reason to go off the deep end."

"Not yet anyway." Julie glanced at the crisp, neatly typed complaint and hoped Derek's college buddy could combat Game Masters and their maneuvers.

"Look," Derek said, "we haven't done anything illegal. Gary will straighten the matter out."

Julie didn't answer immediately. The knot forming in her stomach foretold a different scenario. FunWorks was in danger.

Chapter Four

Julie planned to be home hours ago, in plenty of time to read Emily a nighttime story and listen to Nicole's recap of her friend's sleepover. But the lawsuit and Bennett Burnside's offer to purchase were too coincidental. She stayed at the computer researching Game Masters, losing track of time.

Her Google search of Burnside only revealed more of what she already knew. From the press's viewpoint, he sized up as a good and generous guy. Somehow, she didn't think so.

Knowing everyone would be asleep, Julie tiptoed into the kitchen for a bottle of water to put on her nightstand.

"Working late…again?" Trevor asked.

Julie nearly tripped over Jason's backpack tossed by the doorway. "You startled me. Why are you sitting in the dark?" She dropped her briefcase and clicked on the lights.

"Turn them off. I think better in the dark"

"Thinking about what?" she asked, eyeing the whiskey tumbler in his hand.

"Just things." He took a swallow. "Were you with Derek?"

"You're not starting that again. Look, Trevor. I'm beat." She stretched her arms and yawned.

"Just tell me, Julie."

"Tell you what?" *That you're not the only one who wants me to sell Fun Works.* "I'm too tired to fight. I'll see you in the morning." She headed to her bedroom without the water and perhaps pushing Trevor's heart farther away from hers.

"How ridiculous," she mumbled, climbing the steps to their bedroom. "I'd never be romantically involved with Derek." *He is too young, too immature. He's not the man who stole my heart so many years ago.*

***

"He's left me." Julie slid a dog-eared square of paper left on her pillow days before toward Leanne and watched her unfold the stationery.

Julie had memorized every word.

I can't live the rest of my life waiting for you to be successful enough. Always hoping you will be satisfied with your latest venture. Wondering if this newest paper doll will make enough money so you'll have more time for the kids and me. I'm tired of watching you chase a target that will never stop moving.

I'll talk to Jason, Nicole and Emily, but I think they'll be relieved not to hear us fighting anymore.

I love you, Julie. I always will. I just can't live with you.

Trev

The last words hit Julie the hardest. Her deepest fear came true. Trevor deserted her. No different than being abandoned by her father.

Julie slapped the cover of her portfolio closed and turned to Leanne. "Whoever said women can have it all was full of it."

The pair had spent hours the following week holed up in the conference room, debating the final designs for the '70s, '80s, and '90s paper doll lines. Julie struggled to keep her focus. With each passing day, the life she feared most—raising her children without a dad—became her new reality. She wanted to escape to a kinder world. One where men kept their promises and no one ever left. For better or worse.

"I never expected to be a career woman with kids only to pay someone else to raise them." Fear plummeted to a new depth as dread pulsed through Julie's veins. She quickly swiped the tear seeping from the corner of her eye. "I know how awful that feels. After Dad left, Mom worked around the clock just to keep food on the table."

Stuck in the memory, Julie sniffled and caught another runaway tear. Mom did the very best she could, better than a lot of kids whose mothers were home all day.

"You're not doing that. You have Mrs. Desmond. It's like having your own mother home with them."

Julie leaned back in her chair. She could leave her family. Run away from the hurt, the pain, the disappointment. But then she'd be no better than her father. No, she'd stay and fight. Julie would be the anchor, just like her mother taught her to be.

Leanne scooted closer, setting the note on Julie's desk. "You're going through a rough patch. And this litigation isn't helping. We both know that Trevor loves you."

"When I told him about the lawsuit, he seemed happy. Like the end of FunWorks would be good news."

"Maybe he's jealous. You know men and their egos," Leanne said. "Does he feel like he still wears the pants in the family?"

Julie's eyes widened. "You think I've emasculated him?"

"No. I'm sorry if I said something I shouldn't have. It's just that..."

"It's what?"

"Nothing Julie, really." Leanne pointed toward the doorway. "Derek asked me to run a three-month sales report. I'd better get started."

"Sure, get Derek the reports. We can go over these sketches later," she said, but Leanne had already left.

Julie sat in the quiet emptiness of her office, staring at the space Leanne occupied moments before.

Her efforts to provide security for her family had resulted in the ultimate self-fulfilling prophecy. She leaned her forehead against the windowpane and closed her eyes, letting the smooth, cool glass soothe her.

Her actions had forced Trevor out of her heart, her bed, and now her life. What else could he do but leave?

Their breakup was her fault. Julie lifted her head and opened her eyes. Tears gleamed in her reflection. She used the heel of her hand to wipe them.

How could Trevor not know how much she loved him? She thought he understood how growing up without a father and the challenges her single mother faced had damaged her. She had to fix this, win him back and make their family whole again. But how? If she chose Trevor, she lost FunWorks. And if she lost FunWorks, what would she have? Who would she be?

Her determination to protect herself had summarily stripped Trevor of his manhood? She never wanted that. She would never intentionally hurt Trevor but somehow building her business resulted in injuring the man she loved most and devastating her marriage.

I must make Trevor see how important he is to me. But how?

***

Trevor clicked open his guitar case on a cocktail table near the stage of Mulvaney's Bar. The Bob Seeger lyrics echoed through the bar's sound system.

Trevor strummed along with the song.

"Can we end practice early?" he asked, not looking at Russ Wheeler. "It's my night with the kids."

"Again? You cut out early last week," the lead singer answered.

"Can't be helped." Trevor tightened a couple of strings on his Gibson Firebird and hooked the neck in the guitar stand. Ever since he'd moved out of the family home three weeks ago, he had less time for the band. And a layoff rumor at work had him working longer hours, so that left little time to spend with the kids.

Russ slammed his beer glass down on the bar top. "Man, I know you're having troubles, and I'm sorry. But where's the commitment to us? Are you in this band or not?"

"Yeah, dude. I'm in the band. Have been since you had pimples and couldn't grow a mustache."

Russ folded his arms. "Funny."

"Look, cut me a little slack here." Trevor found himself clenching and unclenching his fists, trying to control his anger.

"I did," Russ said. "The last four times you left early. We need to practice."

"I'm here now. Let's get started." Trevor's throat tightened.

He didn't need Russ giving him a hard time. Since leaving Julie, he lived in a vise, all his options narrowing, constricting, and shrinking. He had to do something soon to save his marriage before he snapped.

It seemed to him that Julie hardly blinked when he moved out. He still hoped she'd beg him to come back and restart their marriage, but as days passed and she never called, he faced the reality that money took his place in her heart. Time to move on.

Russ plugged in his keyboard. "Your body is here, but your mind, dude, it's somewhere else."

"Look, things are weird right now for Julie and me, but we're working through our stuff." Trevor lied. He regretted leaving his wife. His dad wouldn't have let things get this out of control, but his mom never wanted a career, much less her own business. She baked cookies, for God's sake, and took him and his brother to baseball practice. His mom loved being around the house. Julie barely made time for the kids. And when it came to their relationship...a meeting, a convention, and any sales call took precedence.

Russ grimaced. "You missed an entire riff because you forgot the notes."

"It won't happen again."

"I hope not. The guys are asking if we should replace you."

"Do what you gotta do," Trevor said, as the side door opened, and sunlight streamed into the dark room. The drummer, Clay Miranda, and guitarist Ryan Leonard strolled in.

"Hey, dude." Ryan shook Trevor's hand and set his guitar case on the stage. "Great to see you."

Clay nodded. "Ryan, help me get the rest of my equipment out of the van."

Trevor watched the two head out the door.

Russ nudged his keyboard into place using his potbelly stomach and wiped his hand along the back of his neck through his shaggy hair. "Zeke's mom still watching your kids? I haven't seen her since the funeral. How is she doing?"

"Adjusting to being a widow, I guess."

"Man, that's tough."

Trevor unwound a cord and plugged in his guitar.

"Zeke still living in LA and playing the ponies?" Russ asked.

"Nah, he moved back. As far as I know, he's got his gambling under control. Teresa told me he'd joined Gamblers Anonymous. He and Marilyn are working things out."

"Only a saint would stay married to a guy who gambles away his paycheck every week."

Trevor shook his head as he strummed a few chords. "Hopefully attending the GA meetings is helping, but I don't really know. His mom doesn't say too much, and I don't ask."

Russ plunked a few keys, nodding satisfaction at the tone. "How you doing in your new place?"

"Okay, I guess. You'll have to stop by for a beer." Trevor continued to hope his absence would force Julie to choose him over FunWorks. Instead of her rushing into his arms, he found himself alone most nights in a drab one-bedroom apartment, too small to fit him and his children at the same time. On the refrigerator, a pizza parlor magnet held a photo of last year's Grand Canyon family vacation.

What bothered him even more was that he had to hear from Teresa that Julie was being sued.

With something so serious that not only affected the business but their family as well, why hadn't she turned to him for help? Instead, she dug in deeper, putting in longer hours to learn everything she could about patent infringement law.

"Truth is, things aren't working out." Trevor noted the irony of the breakup song now playing in the background. Maybe it was time to move on.

"Things take time, buddy."

Trevor fingered his strings. "Yeah."

That's what worried him. Julie having too much time without him.

And with Derek.

Ninety minutes later, Trevor put his guitar case in the trunk and slammed the hatch closed, the forlorn melody still haunting him. He turned up his jacket collar against the cool night air.

Stars dotted the pristine sky, reminding him of the many nights he and Julie used to spend stargazing from their bedroom deck. While she sipped a glass of red wine, he'd point, pretending to know the constellations. A couple of times the kids had joined them after sneaking out of bed.

But tonight, he and Julie wouldn't be searching for Andromeda in the night sky. The only woman waiting for him was their housekeeper.

Chapter Five

"Yes. I can be at Victor's by twelve-thirty." Julie's heart pounded from the invitation to lunch at the little Italian restaurant she and Trevor once frequented early in their marriage.

"We need to talk," Trevor said.

"I agree," Julie replied, hoping *talk* was code for 'I want to come home.' When Trevor rented an apartment a month ago, she convinced herself that this was a stunt. He'd return to her and the kids as soon as he came to his senses.

Today could be that day.

She ditched a late-morning meeting with Derek and Paul Kramer, the head of Bull's Eye's purchasing team. Twenty minutes later, Julie claimed a small table by the window and spied a couple strolling, hand-in-hand.

Julie's chest tightened. Seeing two people smiling, laughing, and seeming to enjoy spending time together only magnified what was missing in her marriage. She continued watching. Were they a new love or had they been together for years? The couple laughed again as the wind buffeted their clothes. The woman pulled back the hair blowing across her face and whispered something to her partner and he kissed the tip of her nose.

Julie turned away. New love, she decided. Definitely new love.

She checked her watch. Half past one. *Where is Trevor? He's never late.*

She glanced around. The restaurant's familiar red-and-white checkered tablecloth, old black and white photos gracing the walls, and Dean Martin crooning "Volare" in the background brought back memories of happier times. A time when she and Trevor would gaze into each other's eyes, feed each other, and share their dreams.

Thinking about dreams reminded her of what happened just before she left work minutes ago. Derek had waved a purchasing agreement in the air before tossing the contract on her desk and announcing a meeting within the hour to confirm a storewide rollout of Celebrity PlaytimePals. Although she had anticipated this news, today a multimillion-dollar sale didn't seem important.

She glanced down at the narrow strip of gold circling her ring finger. The brilliant-cut diamond Trevor proposed with barely weighed a fifth of a carat. The size screamed budget. Still, Julie loved the jewel, almost as much as she loved the man who had placed the ring on her finger.

"Something to drink?" Ida asked, startling Julie back to the present.

"No. I'll wait for Trevor. He should be here any second." Julie fidgeted with her napkin and glanced at the door. "Actually, can you bring a bottle of the house wine? You remember, the Chianti Trevor used to order?"

"Oh, of course I do. Are you sure you want that stuff? Only the college crowd orders that rotgut anymore. Maybe you'd like—"

"No, the house wine will be perfect. We'll order lunch as soon as he gets here."

Ida returned with a squat-shaped bottle encased in a straw basket. She poured Julie a glass of the ruby-tinted wine, shook her head and sashayed away.

Julie closed her eyes and took a sip, remembering the first time she tasted the tart *sangiovese* grape. The snappy acidity of the Tuscan wine puckered her lips.

"Hey."

Julie turned at the sound of Trevor's voice.

"Well, you look great." The words tumbled out awkwardly as Julie set her glass down.

"Thanks." Trevor greeted his wife of twenty years with a quick peck on the cheek.

"Your call surprised me. And that you wanted to meet for lunch, especially here."

"They have fast service and it's close to my office."

"Oh." Julie slid her wineglass closer, sensing conversation and lunch would be strained if his dry responses were any indication.

"I need to get back soon, so we should order." He opened the menu, blocking her view of his face.

"You're in a hurry?"

"I've been working through lunch so I can take off early these days."

"Really?" She said to the back of his menu. "Are you saving time?"

"Not saving so much as using my time differently." He lowered the menu. "I want to be available for the kids. Which leads me to one of the reasons why I wanted us to meet. We need some sort of schedule."

"I thought your leaving was temporary until we could work a few things out." Julie swallowed, hoping to smooth the screech leaching into her voice. "Setting schedules sounds permanent."

"They need some stability, Julie. Don't you think?"

"I don't understand what you mean." The words scraped Julie's throat, dreading the answer they'd evoke.

"I have other commitments now. That's why I want a schedule."

Her hand shook as she lifted the wineglass. "What kind of commitments?"

"Like tomorrow. The band is playing at Mulvaney's."

"What's the band's name now? Free Willy?"

"Close." Trevor grinned and Julie's heart leaped. God, she missed the sexy way the left side of his full lips tilted up. "Free Wheelin'. After Russ."

"Crazy Russ Wheeler. I can't remember the last time I saw him. What's he doing now?"

"Same things. You know, work, wife, kids. He's trying out a new diet." Trevor's hand brushed hers as he reached for the menu again. "You really should come check us out."

"What time? Maybe I'll stop by."

"That would be great," he said. "The first set starts at nine. And we're not as bad as you might think."

Julie set her glass on the table and leaned in, surprised by Trevor's accusation. Staring into his fiery green eyes, she knew he was serious. "I never thought you guys were bad. You're great. It's just that—"

"You thought playing in a band was a waste of time." Trevor finished her sentence.

Julie blinked and jerked back. "What?"

"The band didn't make any money; in fact, it took money out of the family budget, remember?"

Julie lowered her head, embarrassed to hear those angry words mirrored back at her. The words she'd spoken during one of their many arguments. "I'm sorry."

To Julie, any step toward the band equaled a step away from her. As a new bride, she hadn't wanted to compete for Trevor's attention. Guitar strings and amplifiers had strained their limited budget. Mostly, she wanted Trevor by her side to support her dream, never considering the same might be true for him.

"Look, I don't want to go there again." Trevor's jaw set, his green eyes clouded. "We need to order. Where's Ida?"

"I'm sorry if I acted like your band wasn't important." Julie laid her hand on his forearm and his muscles stiffened. "We were young. I didn't know how to share you."

"You didn't know how to trust me, you mean," he countered, challenging her defense.

Julie shrank against the chair. Maybe he was right.

"You still don't." He tossed the menu down and drew in a deep breath. "Look, I didn't come here to fight. Lord knows we've had enough of those. I wanted to make sure everything was okay with you and the kids."

"I don't want to fight, either. I came here thinking you wanted to talk about getting back together. Don't you want to come back?"

"Hey, Trevor. Where have you been lately?" Ida asked, order pad in hand. "Do you want your usual? And two forks?"

"Uh, not today, Ida." He handed his menu to her. "Get me a torpedo sandwich to go."

"To go?" Julie slid an empty glass toward him. "I ordered wine."

"Yeah, I see, but I gotta get back to the office. Maybe next time."

"I'll have a small antipasto salad," Julie said, wondering if the hurt and disappointment showed in her eyes. He wasn't coming back, and she had no one to blame but herself.

Arriving at work, Julie rushed into her suite of offices. "Have a few minutes now to go over those sketches?" she asked, slowing at Leanne's desk. "We never finished and I promised Kelly we'd decide before the end of the day."

"Yeah, sure." Leanne popped up from her desk and grabbed a notebook, hurrying behind Julie. "Now's a great time."

Leanne had avoided her since their conversation yesterday. Julie knew there was no foundation for Trevor to be insecure, still, she was glad Leanne shared her thoughts. Just because Julie didn't want to rely solely on a man shouldn't be interpreted as a knock against his ability to provide for her and their family. Or should it?

Leanne took a seat at the conference table across from Julie. "I'm sorry about what I said yesterday regarding Trevor."

Julie lifted her hand. "Don't worry. We're friends. You were sharing your opinion, that's all," Julie said. "That was your opinion, right? Not anyone else's?"

"What do you mean?"

"Nothing. I wondered if you and Derek.... Oh, never mind."

"What about me and Derek?"

"You two seem to be more than coworkers, that's all."

"I like him. Too soon to tell if it's going anywhere." Leanne blushed. "Is there a company policy about dating coworkers?"

"No, of course not. It's nothing like that," Julie said, alarmed she hadn't thought of their relationship as a personnel matter. Two of her key people might be falling in love and she didn't care.

She folded her hands to quell her paranoia. Did Derek and Leanne discuss her marriage, judge her relationship, blame her for its failure?

"I wondered if the emasculating comment came from a man, that's all," she added.

"Men do like to be right all the time." Leanne chuckled. "But no, Derek didn't say anything about you and Trevor, at least not to me."

"We'd better get back to work, or I'll never get home tonight." Julie slid on her reading glasses.

"It's too soon for '90s PlaytimePals to be retro," Leanne said.

"To a ten-year-old girl, anything older than last year is retro." Julie shuffled the art boards splayed across the oval table. PlaytimePals targeted girls aged five to twelve, so the company marketed with the nine-year-old in mind.

Five years ago, the idea for do-it-yourself paper dolls came to Julie by necessity more than enterprise.

"All you think about is that baby," Nicole, barely four, had whined, her chubby arms crossed. *"You love her more than me."*

Julie sensed her daughter's steely eyes as she nursed Emily. Nicole didn't like sharing her mother with a crying, pooping baby. Especially a colicky infant, who demanded twenty-four-hour attention. Julie lifted Emily to burp her and laid her in the bassinet. She then sat on the couch and buttoned the front of her blouse.

"Nicole." She motioned her daughter to her. *"I could never love anyone more than I love you."*

Nicole squirmed, scooting her bottom onto her mother's lap. *"You never play with me,"* she grumbled. *"See,"* she pointed to her kid-sized table. *"All the dollies are waiting for our tea party. You promised yesterday."*

"Sometimes babies don't let us keep our promises." Julie kissed Nicole's forehead. *"I'll tell you what. When Daddy gets home from work, he and Jason can watch your baby sister and we'll play."*

"When will that be?" Nicole sounded skeptical.

"Shhh," Julie warned, pointing to the sleeping Emily. *"Let's go into the kitchen and start our party now."*

Nicole tugged Julie by her pant leg in the opposite direction. *"But the dollies are in here."*

"Don't worry, we'll make our own," Julie replied, unsure how to achieve the promise.

Once in the kitchen, she quickly searched for anything that might work as a crafting supply. If they were lucky, Emily would sleep for an hour before she'd demand her mother's undivided attention again.

Julie pulled the wax paper liner from inside a cereal box and set the bag and its contents aside. Then she grabbed a paper towel roll, some school glue and a pair of scissors.

"What are you doing, Mommy?"

"We're making paper dolls."

Nicole let out a harrumph. *"With an old box and some napkins?"*

"Sure. This is what your Nana and I used to do when I was your age. Get us something to color with."

Nicole fished in the junk drawer and found a few stray crayons and a yellow highlighter. Julie cut two paper doll bodies from the cereal box cardboard and danced them around the tabletop.

"What do you think of our playtime pals, Nicki?"

"They're naked." She giggled.

"Then let's dress them." Julie unwound several panels of paper towel and began designing clothes. She raided her sewing basket for additional notions and handed Nicole the treasures.

Nicole glued pieces of ribbon, rickrack, and stray buttons on her mother's designs. Julie topped each doll with yarn hair and watched the concentration on her daughter's face as she worked with sticky fingers to outfit the dolls.

"This is a lot more fun than a tea party," Nicole said, showing her latest progress.

Julie nodded approval.

"I'm naming this one Ginger and that one is her best friend Emily, after the baby."

"Those are beautiful names," Julie said.

"Can we make more, Mommy?"

"You bet. I'll have to empty another cereal box, though."

Nicole grinned and then went back to gluing. "I think we should have two boys."

Ninety minutes later, Nicole leaped off her chair to greet Trevor and Jason and introduce her dad and brother to Ginger, Emily, Jason, and Scotty—four prototype PlaytimePals dolls. Miraculously, Emily didn't stir, sleeping peacefully through the commotion.

That day Julie knew making toys would be her future and she never vacillated on which direction to take FunWorks. That part was easy. Her daughters, now seven and eleven, were a live-in focus group. Nicole and Emily tested every new product idea. So far, the strategy worked.

If only she understood Trevor as well as she knew toys. The time to fix their marriage was now. Hopefully, her night at Mulvaney's would be a step in the right direction.

Chapter Six

Zeke laid his cards on the Raffertys' kitchen table. "That's how you win at five card stud. All spades."

Teresa wanted to enjoy Zeke's unexpected late afternoon visit, but uneasiness swirled in her gut. He claimed to be turning his life around. Getting a job, holding regular hours. "Just a matter of time until I'm back with the wife," Zeke had claimed earlier.

Teresa ached for this to be true. She missed her grandbabies and prayed daily for Marilyn to take Zeke back. She understood the odds of that happening were about the same as one of Zeke's many job offers coming through— astronomical.

Teaching the Rafferty kids the art of card playing seemed innocent enough, but Teresa had survived so many of Zeke's poor decisions, she knew entertaining children, even his own, fell to the bottom of the list. She busied herself in the kitchen, waiting for him to tell her the real reason for his visit.

Instead, he kept dealing cards.

"I'm running out of matchsticks," Emily lamented.

"Me too," Nicole said.

Zeke grinned. "How about one more hand, and then I gotta get going. This time we'll play seven card draw, deuces wild. Everybody antes up." He dropped two matchsticks in the middle of the table. "Ma, you got dinner ready for me?"

"Another twenty minutes," Teresa said.

"I don't got twenty minutes."

Teresa furrowed her brow. "I can't make the meat cook any faster."

"The pot right?" Jason asked, referring to everyone's wager.

"Yep," Zeke said.

"Can you teach me how to do that?" Emily asked, her eyes glued to Zeke's hands as though he were performing magic.

"What, this?" he asked, showing off a riffle shuffle, letting the cards cascade together.

She nodded.

"When I have more time. Here we go." He dealt five cards to each of the Rafferty children.

"Emily, honey, you understand what 'deuces are wild' means, right?" Teresa asked from her spot near the stove.

"Kinda."

"Just show your hand to ol' Uncle Zeke and I'll tell you what to do. I help my little girls all the time."

Teresa wondered if Zeke had seen his daughters recently, but she didn't dare ask. The last time she questioned him, he had stormed into her bedroom and dumped everything out of her closets. "How do you like it when someone digs into your personal stuff?" he yelled, throwing her clothes, jewelry, and shoes around the room. "If you don't want me to do this to your crap, stop asking me so many dumb-ass questions."

She wanted to defend herself but knew the effort would be useless. Once Zeke got wound up, nothing but time would mollify his anger.

"I'll help her." Teresa tucked in behind Emily and placed a hand on her shoulder. "Why are you here anyway?" she finally asked her son.

Zeke fingered the growing pile of matchsticks in front of him. "Just stopped by for a visit."

"You never stop by without a reason, so what is it?"

"Do I win?" Nicole asked. "All my cards are red. That's a flash, right?"

"You mean a flush," Zeke corrected. "All the cards need to be from the same suit. You have two diamonds and three hearts. Nice try." He winked before turning to Jason. "Whatcha got, big man?"

"Three fours." Jason displayed his cards with pride.

"Nice. Nice. And you, Princess Emily?"

Teresa turned over Emily's cards. "A full house, fives over sevens."

"Wow, that's a great hand, little girl, but not good enough to beat old Uncle Zeke. A full boat, eights and tens." Zeke laid his cards on the table and raked in the pot.

"Why are you here?" Teresa asked again, a sharper edge to her question.

Zeke pushed away from the table and walked toward the living room, gesturing for Teresa to follow. "Really Ma, I just wanted to see you and thank you for the envelope you gave me the other night."

"Are we playing cards or what?" Jason yelled from the kitchen.

"Be right back, dude. Hold yer horses." Zeke turned to Teresa. "Their dad should be the one teaching them how to draw to a straight."

Teresa put her hands on her hips. "Hard to do when you're earning a paycheck. And speaking of working, when are you going to find a job?"

"I have a few things hanging. Just waiting for one of them to come through. Where's the bathroom?"

"That way," Teresa pointed.

"Great. Tell the kids to deal another hand."

"Where's Zeke?" Jason asked when Teresa returned alone and opened the oven door. The tang of barbecued chicken filled the air.

"He'll be right back." Teresa slid the tray out and brushed sauce onto the meat. "Dinner should be ready soon."

"It's my turn to pass out the cards," Emily said, doing her best to imitate Zeke's fancy shuffle.

Teresa slammed the oven door and scurried toward her bedroom, remembering she'd left her purse there. *How stupid of me. I should have known. He's here for more money.* She raced through the doorway. Zeke had stolen from her before.

Instead, she found him standing in the living room, holding a photo of the Raffertys.

"What are you doing?"

"Just looking at pictures of this nice family." He returned the photo to the mantel and moved toward the kitchen. "Is that chicken done yet? I'm starving."

"Dinner will be in a few minutes." Teresa retrieved her purse and quickly scanned her wallet. *Cash and credit cards untouched. Car keys accounted for.* She clicked shut the clasp and grimaced.

An uneasy feeling crept up her spine. Zeke never did anything without a reason. He didn't come to steal her money, so why was he there? She would wait in fear for the answer, knowing that whatever Zeke was up to would certainly cause more heartache.

***

Hours later, Julie inspected the fit of her skinny jeans in her bedroom mirror. Her boots would go great with them, she thought. Julie enjoyed acting like a high-school girl dressing for the homecoming dance, wrapped up in anticipation of what might happen tonight. Trevor had invited her and that's all that mattered.

She stood at the top of the staircase and hollered down, "Teresa, have you seen my new black suede boots? I want to wear them tonight."

"You mean those high-heeled, painful-looking stilts with the zippers on the sides?"

"Yep, those are the ones."

"I thought they were Nicole's," Teresa said. "Check her closet."

"What eleven-year-old wears high-heeled boots?" Julie jogged to her daughter's room. "Found them," she called out moments later, as though they were first prize at the county fair. "See?" She jiggled the boots at Teresa trudging up the steps.

Teresa surveyed the discarded blouses, pants, and a black spandex dress piled on Julie's bedroom floor. "Where are you going tonight that you're in such a tizzy? I've never seen you so excited."

"To see Trevor's band." Julie sucked in her stomach, already snug against the waistband.

Acting a little like a groupie, she slithered into a tight, low-cut red sweater she'd found in the back of her closet. She turned back to the mirror and tossed her head a little, pleased at the oversized silver earrings dangling from her earlobe. Then she twisted open a tube of Crimson Kiss and painted her lips. "They're at Mulvaney's tonight. I'm hoping they'll play 'Smoke on the Water.' Trevor always sings that song for me."

Teresa scrunched her face. "Oh, I remember that tune. Many nights I thought the walls of my garage would vibrate into rubble." Teresa began hanging Julie's clothes back in the closet. "Zeke loved the drums. Did I mention he stopped by today?"

"No. What's going on with him?"

"Said he was in the neighborhood. He played cards with the kids and grabbed a quick bite," Teresa remarked. "I'm hoping he's settling down. That he and Marilyn get back together."

Julie nodded but didn't reply. From everything Trevor shared about his long-time friend, Zeke would never be the son Teresa deserved.

"Bert and I were glad when the group found another place to practice." She laughed. "I wish Zeke had kept up his band friendships. I'm glad those kids are still playing together."

"They're forty years old; hardly kids."

Teresa set a blouse she finished folding on Julie's dresser. "They'll always be kids to me."

Julie grinned into the mirror, checking for lipstick smudges on her teeth. "Trevor invited me during lunch today."

"You two had lunch? That's a good sign."

"He wants to talk about us getting back together." Julie figured if she said the words, they'd come true.

Teresa put her hands on her hips. "Did you tell him about the lawsuit?"

"A little." Julie ground her teeth. "He doesn't like hearing about FunWorks."

"Well, you better tell him how serious this whole thing has gotten."

"I will, just not tonight." Tonight, she wanted him to see the woman he fell in love with, not a business owner. Julie adjusted her bra and fluffed her hair.

"This might not be the best timing," Teresa tugged a loose thread on her sleeve, "but I wondered if you thought about that loan? I—"

Emily sailed in and plopped on the bed, trampoline-style. "Mommy, why are you dressed like that? Your clothes are too tight."

"I'm going to see Daddy's band tonight." Julie yanked at her plunging neckline and sat beside Emily.

Emily bounced higher. "Can I go, too?"

"You're too young." Emily stopped jumping and Julie tugged her daughter's caramel-colored braid that reached halfway down her back. "Be good for Mrs. D, okay? I'll tuck you in when I get home. I love you." Julie kissed the tip of Emily's nose and stood to leave.

"Don't worry about the kids. There's an Indiana Jones marathon on one of the cable channels tonight."

Julie grabbed her purse and leather coat and took a quick glance in the mirror. "I won't be late, Teresa. We'll talk about the loan tomorrow. I'm sure we can work something out."

Julie hugged the woman quickly. "You're shaking."

"I'm a little chilled," Teresa answered, swiftly moving to Emily. "Hope I'm not coming down with a cold."

"Get a good night's sleep," Julie said, before practically skipping to the door. She stopped at the foot of the stairs. Teresa had been shaking and her face held a pale, grayish color. Maybe she was getting sick.

Or maybe she needed the loan for something important, something critical. Otherwise, she would have never asked for the money.

With the threat of divorce and patent infringement litigation, Julie was reluctant to take on any other financial commitments, even for Teresa. She spent the week avoiding the topic, worried about having the necessary funds for her own family's expenses, let alone her housekeeper's.

Julie drove to Mulvaney's while pondering if Teresa's real reason for needing this money involved Zeke. Would she go into debt for a son who only brought her sorrow? According to Trevor, Zeke was involved with drugs, illegal gambling, and petty theft. And that was when they were in high school. Had Zeke graduated to more serious crimes?

Julie broke into a laugh. *There goes your old paranoid self, sticking its nose where it doesn't belong.* Ever since the patent mess had started, her mind wandered to the worst-case scenario.

She parked, checked her makeup in the rearview mirror and headed toward the bar.

Tonight is for new beginnings, not suspicions. She forced a deep breath. *Still, I wonder why Zeke's around so much recently.*

Julie entered the sparsely lit bar to Lynyrd Skynyrd's "Free Bird" floating through the air. Halfway through their first set, Free Wheelin' knew how to entertain an audience. Trevor's energetic singing and mischievous smile served as strong evidence of his love of music and playing with these guys.

Despite Mulvaney's smoke-free policy, Julie struggled to focus her eyes in the darkness of the neighborhood pub. After her vision adjusted, she recognized Trevor on stage, singing and strumming his guitar. Russ kept his familiar steady beat on the keyboard. She thought she knew the other guitarist, but didn't recognize the drummer, Zeke's most recent replacement.

She found a small table in the back, ordered a Jack and Seven and let Trevor's voice wash over her, savoring the sultry tones he once purred into her ear years ago. She stirred the whiskey, closed her eyes and sipped, allowing the smooth, smoky sweetness to invade her body.

The Friday night regulars crowded inside, edging their way to the bar. Though conversations, clinking glasses, and boisterous laughter competed for attention, Trevor's voice charged the air.

After another song, the band took a break. Trevor still hadn't seen her.

Julie flagged a waitress. "I'd like to buy the lead singer a drink."

"Oh, you mean Trevor?" She cracked a wad of chewing gum. "He only drinks water during sets."

"Really?" Julie said. "Well then, send him the finest bottled water you have. Be sure to let him know it's from a fan in the back of the club."

"Sure, honey." Her tone was snarky. "I'll add some Perrier to your tab."

Julie waited, expecting Trevor to grab the water and join her. But he never came. In fact, she craned her neck and saw him near the stage, chugging the sparkling water. He sat with three women who laughed as if whatever he'd said was the funniest thing they'd ever heard. Russ ambled up, beer in hand and joined in their laughter.

After what seemed like an eternity, Russ nudged Trevor to get ready for their next set. Trevor squeezed the shoulder of a shapely blonde, smiled, and headed toward the stage, never glancing in Julie's direction.

The realization stung Julie like a backhand across the face, leaving her cheeks hot with anger and pain. Her hands shook as she threw some bills on the table and hurried to the door.

He wanted me to see my replacement. That's why he invited me tonight.

Her marriage was over.

Head down, Julie ran into the chest of a man on his way in. She stumbled from the impact. He grabbed an elbow to steady her.

"Whoa. Are you o… Julie? Hey, it's Rick. Come by to see the guys?"

"Yes." She nodded a quick hello and rushed past Russ's younger brother before the flood of tears exploded, reducing her to an incoherent mess. Her heart tightened so sharply she could barely breathe.

And the other woman.

***

The next morning, Julie hunched over the Saturday newspaper and stared blankly at the headlines. An hour earlier, Teresa had placed a hot cup of coffee in front of her and started a conversation about the night before. In no mood to relive another disappointment, Julie grunted a meager response, sending Teresa off to another part of the house to guess about Julie's most recent calamity.

Julie didn't bother with makeup to conceal the dark circles under her eyes or use a comb to smooth any tangles in her wavy hair.

Jason had hitched a ride to the game with his basketball coach hours ago. The girls, still in their room, were probably conspiring for a trip to the mall. There was no one at home she needed to impress.

"Look who's here. Found him standing on the front porch." Teresa rolled her eyes. "Says he needs to talk to you. I told him you were under the weather."

"Derek. I'm surprised to see you." She turned to Teresa. "You remember my marketing director—"

"I know who he is." Teresa's folded arms rested solidly across her chest.

"Hey, Julie." Derek, his hair still wet, bounded past the housekeeper, a portfolio in hand.

"You've been a slowpoke around here all morning, still in your PJs." The corners of Teresa's mouth turned down. Her disapproving scowl reminded Julie of a half-eaten donut. Teresa moved toward the counter and took a mug from the cabinet. "I'll pour Derek a cup of coffee while you go upstairs and change."

Julie clutched the lapels of her chenille bathrobe and pulled them together. "It's okay. You can go. Derek can get his own coffee."

"Are you sure?" Teresa questioned. "Doesn't look like you touched the cup I poured for you. Let me warm it up."

Julie placed her hand over the rim, blocking Teresa's reach. "No. I'm fine. Thanks anyway."

Derek set a folder on the table. "I was on my way home from the dive school and thought I'd drop this off. But if I've come at a bad time, I can leave."

"No. Stay. How'd your lesson go?" Julie took several swallows of coffee, ignoring the icy taste. For weeks, Derek and Gary Carlson had trained for their diving certification. She never got the excitement of extreme sports, but she admired Derek's passion for everything from rock climbing to wingsuit flying.

"Awesome. Today we practiced sharing the air supply. Next week we tackle the buddy system."

Teresa handed Derek an empty mug. "I can stay a few more minutes and keep Derek company while you change."

"There's no need for you to change your plans." Julie fluttered her fingers at Teresa as though she could make the woman disappear with the wave of her hand. "Derek needs to update me about yesterday's meeting. I'll see you later."

Julie looked away, preventing Teresa's piercing scowl to achieve its usual effect—guilt. Instead, she turned to Derek. "Sorry, I haven't checked my phone this morning. How did the negotiations go?"

Derek slurped from his overfilled mug. "Remarkably well. They're totally behind this. Television, radio and print ads, promotional tie-ins, contests, events...the whole enchilada!" He became quiet as if waiting for her excitement to catch up with his.

Julie shifted in her chair, holding her coffee mug in front of her face like a shield.

"All two thousand stores. This is big time."

"And what are we giving them in return?"

"Just what we agreed to—exclusive distribution in their stores through the Christmas season." A defensive tone invaded Derek's words.

"Sounds like we're putting all of our eggs in their basket."

Derek dragged his chair closer, his eyes wide with expectation. "For a limited time. But it's not just any basket. This is Bull's Eye. The largest toy retailer in the country."

"But this agreement prevents us from selling to the DollaRites and Sav-Marts, right?"

Derek slumped back in the chair. "Uhh, yes. You knew that before I set the meeting. Why the question now?"

"Guess I'm a little sensitive this morning."

Because I'm getting squeezed from all sides. First Trevor, now you. Julie's teeth clenched, her defense against the mounting stress building inside.

"This is a giant step forward for us." Derek locked Julie in his gaze. "I really believe this is the right direction for FunWorks."

Julie turned away and shook her head. *I can't think about this now.*

"Here's the proposal." He slid the slim red folder with a Bull's Eye logo closer to Julie. "You need to sign the marketing contract before they'll approve the purchase agreement."

Instead of opening the file, Julie dragged herself to the coffeepot for a refill.

"What's going on? I know you're stressed about that stupid lawsuit, but you've never passed on a chance to meet with a toy retailer. Especially not one as big as B.E."

Julie sat back down, cupped her hands around the mug and let out a sigh. "I trust you. If you think this is the best way to go, then I'll support your decision fully. To be honest, Derek, I'm going through a tough time." She swallowed, tightness in her throat growing. "Trevor left me." The words seeped out like poison leaking from a vial.

"I knew something was wrong." Derek leaned closer, a smile slowly formed, bright and understanding, a grin guaranteed to melt any woman's heart. She'd witnessed the magic, most recently on Leanne.

Julie stared at Derek through a veil of tears. She should be pouring her heart out to one of her sisters, but Monica was busy with her four sons, one of them seriously ill. Baby sister Kate was too young to shoulder this load. Should she confess her heartbreak to a single guy with no clue about marriage? His only commitment was a yearly gym membership.

Julie inhaled sharply. She had to talk to someone and Derek was here. Derek was always here. "I thought we'd patch things up, but—"

He patted the back of Julie's hand. "It's okay."

The tears flooded as she told him about Trevor ignoring her at the bar last evening, omitting the part about him fondling another woman.

After she finished, Derek clasped her hand. "What can I do?"

"Take care of the Bull's Eye deal."

Derek pulled her hand to his lips and kissed lightly. "Trevor must be crazy not to see what he has. I'll keep our toy ship afloat, but there is something else I need to talk to you about. The Game Masters' lawsuit. It's been nearly a month since FunWorks was served."

Julie tightened her jaw, making it difficult to speak. "I wondered when that was going to come up."

"Gary hounded me at our lesson this morning. We need to respond."

Julie yanked her hand away and stiffened her back. "Your friend needs to talk to me about these things, not you."

Derek stared at his notepad. "I know, but since I brought him on, I feel responsible. We have to do something."

"I'm not going to be pushed around," Julie declared. "If they think they have a case, let them sue. They'll lose, big time."

"Maybe, but they're moving forward with their patent infringement claim anyway. If they don't hear back from you, Gary says they will file a declaratory judgment action, and..." he glanced at his notepad, "...ask the court to determine the validity of the patent asserted in the cease-and-desist letter."

"This is a sham." Julie stared past Derek. *How do I prove I invented PlaytimePals? How do I start my life over without Trevor?*

"This could be the end if we don't act quickly. Gary is worried you don't realize how serious this lawsuit is."

"The same guy who dismissed it as a nuisance claim? Now it's a serious lawsuit?"

Derek frowned. "BAB Enterprises, one of the largest conglomerates in the country, owns Game Masters. They have pockets deep enough to keep FunWorks drowning in litigation until our cute paper dolls are yellowed with age."

"So that's the bottom line? You and your pal discussed this between dive lessons?" Julie complained, incredulous that her marketing director discussed such sensitive issues with the company's legal counsel.

"They want to buy the company. Maybe you should consider their offer."

"If I sell, you'll be out of a job."

"If they win the suit, I'm out of a job, too. At least this way you walk away with something. Gary says they'll pay me a generous severance."

Julie slammed her mug on to the table, coffee slopping down the sides. "That's just great! If I don't sell at their price, these sons-of-bitches will use the courts to run me out of business. Pardon me if I don't have stardust in my eyes about this deal."

"We need to take an objective look at this thing. Then talk to Gary. If you want to fight to the death, then that's what we'll do. But odds are, we will lose."

"According to?"

"Gary says he's seen this kind of takeover before."

Julie's fingernails clicked against the ceramic mug. "Why would a mega-conglomerate care about a little company like ours?"

"I have no idea. But with the holiday season coming up, we don't want our product line locked in litigation."

Julie's mind raced. This phony lawsuit hadn't just happened; someone, maybe Bennett Burnside, was the driving force. Julie needed time to think, to focus, but her disintegrating marriage had to take priority. Maybe it wasn't too late to win Trevor back. Maybe if she pulled herself together, sold FunWorks, he'd return to her and the children.

Derek scooted his chair closer to the table. "Gary says we have forty-five days from when we were served to file a written response with the court. We've been sitting on this for nearly a month, so now we're down to two weeks to respond."

"And if we don't?"

"Game Masters may get a default judgment against us."

"Default judgment? What's that?"

"As in game over. We lose. A default judgment wins their case, and the court will not listen to our side." Derek clasped Julie's hand again. "Consider the alternatives. FunWorks is my future, too. I've sunk my reputation into this business."

"I know," Julie said, wishing Trevor, not Derek, was the one to help sort through the options.

"Over the weekend, think about how you want to handle this so we can meet with Gary first thing Monday. If we make the wrong move, they'll bury us so deep we'll both end up with nothing."

"I can't make a decision right now. I need to talk to Trevor."

"Gary says these guys mean business. To Game Masters, buying us is like buying popcorn at the movies."

"Derek, I just don't see how—"

"Hey, Mom? Where are you?" Jason called from the hall. "You missed my game." His sneakers squeaked as he made his way into the kitchen. "Dad's here."

Trevor appeared behind his son.

"Hi, Jul…" His voice trailed off. His stare bounced from Julie and settled on Derek. "Have I interrupted something?"

Julie pulled her hand away from Derek's and tugged the belt of her robe tighter. "Derek just stopped by to tell me about an agreement he approved yesterday."

"I see." Trevor fiddled with his car keys, his gaze steady on Julie. "We wondered where you were. I guess now we know."

Julie hurried to Jason. "I needed more sleep. I'm sorry I missed your game, honey. How did you do?" She pushed strands of sweat-laden hair from her son's forehead.

Jason moved out of her reach and toward the refrigerator. "We won. I shot the game-winning basket again. What's to eat? I'm starving."

"I'll make you a sandwich."

"Nah." Jason chomped through a leftover fried chicken drumstick. "I'm gonna take a shower."

"Trevor, please stay for lunch," Julie said. "I need to talk to you…about FunWorks."

"Not today. I've got other plans."

Julie watched a bitter snarl form across Trevor's lips, and her hopes for a civil conversation evaporated.

"Ask Derek. He looks eager to help," he added before following Jason out of the kitchen.

But Derek's not my husband, Julie started to say. Still, there was no point talking to someone's back. A few seconds later, she jumped at the sound of the front door slamming. A sudden coldness flashed behind her eyes. Trevor had left. Again.

"Now what do I do?" Julie asked the question, but she knew the answer. Learn to live as a single mom and take care of her children.

Now more than ever, she needed to save her business—the only security she could hold on to.

***

"Daddy!" Emily shouted as Trevor reached the front door. "Can you take Nicole and me to the movies?"

Trevor spun to face his youngest daughter, now standing at the foot of the staircase. "What?"

"You said you would take us to the movies, remember?"

"No, honey. I forgot. Today's not a good day."

"Why not?"

"It just isn't. Okay?" He stooped to her eye level. "We'll plan a movie date on another night. I promise. Daddy has to go now." He kissed Emily on the cheek and rushed out, slamming the front door behind him.

Trevor smashed the flat of his hand against the portico column.

I didn't see that coming. She's sleeping with Derek. And with our kids in the house. I thought by now she'd want me back. What a fool I've been.

Chapter Seven

Julie gazed up at the Burnside Building. The onyx-mirrored glass and steel structure stretched to the sky. She'd envisioned FunWorks someday having such a prestigious address, but now nervous goosebumps coated her skin at the immense building. Selling to Bennett Burnside would be better than being sued by Game Masters. And it might give her a second chance to be the wife Trevor wanted.

Glad she hadn't invited Derek, Julie could have her say and make a deal with Burnside. Having anyone in the middle would only belabor the issue at hand while they argued some meaningless point. In her mind, sacrificing her company to buy back her marriage was a fair trade.

Julie ignored the unsettling feeling that crept up her arms as she stepped inside the revolving door leading to the lobby. For a moment, she was a little girl on a downtown adventure with her mom. She fought the urge to take one more spin inside the glass cylinder as she and her younger sisters used to do until their impatient mother would finally reach between the turnstile wings, grab them by their wrists, and haul them out. Julie's life now spiraled out of control, just like being stuck inside a spinning door.

As she stepped across an endless stretch of marble tiles to a bank of elevators hidden behind a floor-to-ceiling aquarium, Julie realized the anxious tone in her mother's voice hadn't been from annoyance at her children. Bridget Jameson's life had spiraled out of control back then, much as Julie's was now.

Julie pushed the button for the top floor. When the doors opened, she came face-to-face with Burnside's secretary.

Margie introduced herself and offered an outstretched arm as she pointed down a light-flooded hallway. "Right this way."

Julie admired the gleaming hardwood floors interspersed with oblong carpets. The intricate patterns reminded her of hand-knotted Persian rugs she and the kids had viewed at a traveling exhibit at the San Marcel Museum of Modern Art; except Burnside's display was better.

Through expansive windows, Burnside's office showcased a panoramic view of the prettiest parts of San Marcel. The high-gloss finish on his ash desk cast a blinding glare. Eclectic pieces of pottery—no doubt tastefully placed by an interior designer—dotted the credenza and nearby bookshelf. In the corner, a ficus tree basking in the sunshine only added to Julie's mounting apprehension. She took in the squared edges, the exact centering, pens lined up by height. Nothing in the room was personal. No photos, no diplomas, no awards, no coffee cup. Not even a dust mote hung in the air. All elements signaled a driven, controlling man.

Was calling this meeting a mistake?

Burnside entered the room through a high-ceiling panel doorway that, moments before, had appeared to be a stationary wall. The dramatic entrance struck Julie as a bit too much like a Las Vegas magic act; one you probably got free tickets to somewhere off the strip and would go to only if you ran out of money.

Though a man of average height, he filled the room with his presence, carrying the confidence of someone who covered every angle. A tailored pinstripe suit and erect posture aided to his image.

Smokescreen, Julie thought. She'd seen it before. A big illusion for a lesser man.

"Ms. Rafferty."

The sound of his voice made her shoulders twitch, much like the instant back arch of a frightened cat. That creepy feeling she first experienced at the Toy Fair returned, crawling slowly up her arms.

She closed the space between them. "Thank you for agreeing to see me."

He directed her to a chair. "Would you like something to drink?"

"No, thank you." She fought to keep her voice steady. "I'm here to follow up on our conversation at the toy fair. We didn't get much time to discuss your offer."

Burnside shifted to sit behind his desk. "You weren't interested then. What changed?"

"I've had more time to consider the possibility. And I discussed our meeting with my husband," she lied. "He thought I should listen to what you have to say."

Burnside reached inside his jacket for a cigar. He rolled the panatela between his fingers for a moment before snipping the end. He took his time lighting, then drew in a few puffs. "My client has reconsidered acquiring your company. At least through traditional channels."

Julie straightened. "I don't understand."

"I now represent Game Masters."

Julie stared, nonplussed. Burnside had been so friendly at their first meeting, conspiratorial in fact. "I have a client who will pay top dollar for your company," he had said. "They love everything about your product line."

"Game Masters?"

"I believe they're suing you." He placed his cigar on an ashtray, leaned forward and licked his lips. "In fact, I know they are. I filed the paperwork."

"Did you?" She dug her fingernails into her palms to subdue the tremor in her voice and the anger brewing inside. "You're behind this phony lawsuit?"

"Not me. My client. I told you they want FunWorks."

"Enough to make a false patent infringement claim? That's crazy."

"There's nothing false about their filing." Burnside tapped his finger against his cigar, loosening the ashes. He took another puff.

The pungent, earthy smell nauseated Julie.

Burnside handed her a document. "We can still work out a deal."

Julie scanned the sheet. "This is twenty percent of the company's value. And that's before we roll out our new celebrity line." She tossed the sheet back at him.

"No, you keep it."

"This isn't a bona fide offer."

"As bona fide as you can get." He met Julie's glare. "Margie has the paperwork ready. If you sign now, the lawsuit goes away and you leave with a big check."

Julie stood, rage now replacing her disbelief. "I have no intention of giving my company away. I'm here to find out what your clients are offering."

"Now you know." Burnside grinned. "And a very fair offer I must say, considering the serious litigation your company is facing. I'll be waiting for your call."

Julie gathered the papers, shoved them into her purse, and yanked the leather strap onto her shoulder. "You'll be waiting a hell of a long time, Mr. Burnside."

She strode toward the elevator, not allowing Burnside the satisfaction of seeing how his demands rocked her foundation. Game Masters wasn't slowing down their attack. If anything, they were ramping up the assault.

Moments later, she spun through the revolving door, not stopping this time to reminisce. She needed to get back to the office and do something. But what could she do? Who could perform the exorcism to end this nightmare? She hoped Derek or Gary would have an idea. Or maybe Trevor.

Anger coursed through Julie's veins as she phoned Gary Carlson on her drive to the office.

"Hey, Julie. I was planning to call you today," Gary said when he picked up.

"You need to find a way out of this. Some legal maneuver to stop Burnside," she yelled into the receiver after revealing what had transpired in the meeting moments ago.

"Let me dig deeper and I'll get back to you." Gary clicked off, leaving Julie shaking behind the steering wheel. She had taken the bait and now flailed as Burnside reeled her in like a helpless trout. How stupid she'd been not to see setup written all over this.

Stay calm, she thought. *Think smart now.*

Derek confronted Julie the moment she returned to her office. "Gary called. I don't understand why you saw Burnside without me."

"I wanted to straighten this mess out by myself. Now I know I shouldn't have. You're the one who said listen to what the guy had to say."

"Yes, I said listen."

"Well, I listened. Without you." When Derek pushed, Julie pushed back harder. No one was going to pressure her into a corner. Selling or waging a fight to save FunWorks was her decision alone. She wouldn't let any man dictate her choices.

Julie's mind flashed back to a fight with Trevor about starting the company.

"We're not living in Toyland. We have three kids and a mortgage," he had shouted before walking out, and slamming the door.

Now Burnside had slammed another door. Limiting her options.

Derek stopped abruptly in front of her desk. "I wanted to be there, too. In on some of the decision making."

"I wouldn't have made any decisions without talking to you first and running the deal by Gary." Julie glared. "Here's their offer."

Derek scanned the paper. "You're not seriously considering this?"

"Hardly, but they expect me to. It was no accident I met Burnside at the toy fair. He was setting the stage."

"That sounds very cloak-and-dagger."

"What else could it be." Julie folded her arms across her chest, thinking. "He knows we'd never accept such a lowball offer."

"We need to take a serious look at this. Right now, I'm headed to the research facility. Our focus group starts in thirty minutes." Derek tapped his watch. "I'll check in with Gary to see how his strategy is coming."

Julie nodded her agreement. Having their lawyer handle things was the smart move.

"You're right. Let him take care of the legal ramifications. You deal with the focus groups and make sure we still have customers when all of this is over. Like you said, this Game Masters' lawsuit will turn out to be nothing more than an inconvenience."

Julie wanted to believe that, but the gleam in Burnside's eye signaled that the game was just beginning.

***

The next day, Julie, Derek, and Leanne reviewed shipping counts and inventory numbers from Leung Jun, the contract manufacturer in China. She compared the figures to placed orders. Despite some minor cancellations, FunWorks would post a record-breaking year. Julie couldn't shake the sense that Bennett Burnside had pored over these same figures while wringing his hands menacingly a la Snidely Whiplash.

"Can you believe it?" Leanne asked. "With all this craziness, PlaytimePals are still holding their own."

"The positives from the focus group are through the roof," Derek added.

Julie kept her gaze on the spreadsheets. "That's why we're in this situation. If nobody bought our stuff, Burnside and his merry band of thieves wouldn't be after us."

Derek chuckled half-heartedly. There wasn't anything funny about a lawsuit and nothing *Comedy Central* about the bunch from Game Masters. "Why is Burnside coming after us so hard? There have to be other companies with healthier bottom lines he could savage."

Julie tilted her head back. "I've been thinking a lot about that. Why are they going to extreme measures to scare me into selling? It's not adding up."

"What are we missing?" Leanne said.

"Beats me." Derek rolled his chair away from the conference table.

"Gary said he'd have something for us by the end of the day. In the meantime, let's get these orders in to the plant. We've wasted enough time worrying about Bennett Burnside." Julie handed the sheets to Leanne and turned to Derek. "Where are we with the celebrity PlaytimePals rollout for next season?"

"I have confirmations from everyone, except Dana March, and I should get that today," he remarked about the sixteen-year-old sitcom star, the centerpiece to the new line. Everything she touched flew off the store shelves. Model Korey Yves Brandt and England's singing twins Silas and Simon rounded out the four teen idols—guaranteed top sellers into a demographic FunWorks hadn't reached before.

"The date has been cleared with Bull's Eye for the kickoff reception," Derek continued. "Since they have a six-month exclusive, they have already put a media buy in place and a publicity plan to make sure we get great coverage."

With the retro PlaytimePals line barely out the door, Julie pushed hard on the celebrity ones. She had hand-selected the pop icons and movie stars who were positive role models for her target market and put them through the Nicole-Emily Test: *Would I want my daughters playing with these celebrity characters?* If the answer was no, their likeness would never be on PlaytimePals.

"We should surprise them with a preview of the hologram version," Derek said.

"Okay, but no mention of the 3D designs yet." The idea of three-dimensional paper dolls progressed slowly. Julie didn't want to promise the toy world more than she could deliver. On the other hand, Derek loved to overpromise and see Julie sweat to meet the delivery schedule. Like the time he guaranteed more product than their plant could produce if the crew worked around the clock for a month.

Julie groveled for an extension on the delivery date, risking cancellation if Bull's Eye's management declined. If Paul lost confidence in their ability to meet their commitments, the word would spread to other buyers that FunWorks wasn't a reliable supplier.

Derek had put her in that situation once. She would never make that mistake again.

Chapter Eight

The morning craziness drained what little patience Julie managed to salvage from the week's troubles.

Nicole had thrown a fit because the hem of her favorite skirt unraveled. Nothing would satisfy her except Julie stitching the seams back together. Jason methodically dribbled his semi-flat basketball against the tile floor, reminding Julie that the last needle to the air pump was bent and she had forgotten to buy new ones. Sweet Emily walked around the house shuffling playing cards, hoping someone would notice.

Julie ached for Trevor, not that he would have been much help with a needle and thread. Still, he would have inflated the basketball and commented on Emily's attempt at being a card shark. They would divide and conquer. Seeing her stressed, Trevor would have wrapped his arms around her until she took a slow breath, sending whispered reminders of the important things.

When he left, he took Julie's true north, her compass pointing her in the right direction. With him as the wind under her wings, she easily pulled off confident and self-sufficient. Since their separation, the least little blip on life's screen tossed her off-kilter.

So later that morning, when Leanne practically clipped Julie's heels following her down the hall inside their suite of offices, Julie knew her last strand of sanity would be ripped out.

"Have you seen today's paper?"

"No, I didn't have time." Julie dropped her purse and briefcase on her desk and braced for the worst. "What's going on?"

"I guess the bad news is out." Leanne handed her the early edition of the *San Marcel Mercury News*.

Julie took the folded newspaper, Leanne's stare boring into her. She turned away and read the headline:

FUNWORKS SUED FOR PATENT INFRINGEMENT
Lawsuit seeks monetary damages and injunctive relief from local toymaker

Julie's stomach dipped, as though she had fallen through a hole. Dread soaked her insides. She wondered what their next threat would be. Now she knew. Burnside wanted to make things public using the media as bomb throwers. She continued reading.

By Roberta Perkins, Staff Writer

In a court filing earlier this month, FunWorks, Inc., a San Marcel-based toy software firm, was accused of using Game Masters' patent-protected technologies without a proper license.

Game Masters seeks unspecified damages and court orders to block all sales of FunWorks' popular PlaytimePals paper doll software and all other products named in the suit that Game Masters claim violate their patent.

The complaints were filed with the US International Trade Commission, which has the power to block imports of products and parts made

with contested technology and U.S. District Court in Wilmington, Del., which can award damages and order FunWorks to stop sales...

"Who is Roberta Perkins? She talks as though we're already guilty."

"Are you okay?"

Julie tossed the paper onto the desk. "Not really." Her stomach churned. How would she fight this?

"You've received a few calls from business-beat reporters. They said they'd call back. Should I put their calls through?"

"No!" Julie snapped. "Not yet." She needed time to think. Now that the suit was public record, all her customers would know. The loan officer, too.

"Has anyone from San Marcel Commerce called?"

"No. I don't think so."

Julie let out a quick sigh. "Good."

"What can I do?" Leanne asked.

"Nothing...except get Derek."

"Anything else?"

"Nope." She waited for Leanne to leave, then dialed Trevor. He'd be happy to hear this news. He'd been hoping for the end of FunWorks. But before the call rang through, she hung up, afraid to hear his response.

Derek stormed into Julie's office moments later. "Bull's Eye canceled their order. The PR, promotion, everything. I can't believe this." His hands sliced the air to emphasize each point. "They don't want to proceed until they know the outcome of this lawsuit."

The timing couldn't have been worse. Julie was waiting on a bank approval for a $500,000 working-capital loan to avoid manufacturing delays. Without the loan, FunWorks would plummet into a financial hole.

Derek dropped into the chair in front of her desk. "They read about the lawsuit in the morning paper. According to

Paul, they can't take a chance on believing the grievance will be resolved quickly and in our favor. He claims he's sorry."

"The hell he is," Julie grumbled. "They don't want to fight Game Masters. Can we sue them for breach of contract?"

"I'll ask Gary, but that will take time." Derek twisted the papers in his hands into a tight coil.

"We can't make payroll." Julie had counted on the Bull's Eye deal to keep the company afloat during the expansion. "We can't pay the manufacturer."

"I don't see how we can hang on until this lawsuit is thrown out." Derek shifted in his seat, disbelief hung on his every word. "Maybe selling isn't such a bad idea."

"Selling is a horrible idea." Julie rubbed her neck, attempting to soothe the muscles bulging with tension.

"We don't have enough capital behind us."

"I know." Julie's options evaporated like water on a hot skillet.

Game Masters had turned off the spigot, narrowing her choices to only one—a fire sale to them. The reality stung. They had been successful in tightening the tourniquet around her assets. That kind of success might embolden them, reducing the already meager offer even more.

"Game Masters still wants to make a deal. Maybe we should meet with Burnside again. See what they have to say."

"I'm not selling." *Not yet.* The space behind Julie's eyes throbbed. "I can't sit by while those vultures swoop in for the kill. They'll claim we've infringed on their patent, immerse us in litigation and not prove a damn thing."

"I know, but we have to respond." Derek shook the baton of canceled contracts at Julie. "This isn't going away."

Julie blinked back tears. "There must be something else we can do. Maybe we can talk Paul into delaying the cancellation until we get our game plan together."

"I'm on my way to his office now to beg for a few days," Derek said.

"I'll go, too," Julie said through a mixture of anger and disbelief. Her chest tightened making her breath shallow and labored.

A variety of solutions—none she wanted to pursue—streamed through her mind. She rushed to keep up with the changing landscape. There had to be an answer; one that kept her as the owner of all she'd built.

***

Trevor took a swig of his third beer but didn't enjoy the effect. He and Russ hung around Mulvaney's after band practice. The alcohol did little to remove the vision of Julie, wrapped in her bathrobe while holding hands with Derek. He wanted to believe their marital problems didn't drive her into the arms of a lover. And a younger one at that.

"When she met me for lunch at Victor's, I hoped that things had changed," Trevor told Russ, fingering the foam on the rim of his glass. "She seemed open to the idea of working on our marriage. On us. That's why I invited her to see us play. I never thought she'd trade me in for that dude." He took another swig of his draft. "Isn't that what guys do during a midlife crisis, find someone else?"

Russ propped an elbow on the bar but remained silent.

"I thought she'd show on Friday just for old times' sake. Spending the night with Derek must have been more important than watching her middle-aged husband act like an over-the-hill rocker."

"What did your kids say about Uncle Derek spending the night?"

"I didn't bring the subject up."

Russ called the waitress over to order another round. "I can't believe Zeke's mom is letting Julie play house with that guy."

Trevor stared at the drops of condensation slowly sliding down his beer glass. Everything seemed to be slipping away. The life he worked for, the woman he loved, evaporating like early morning dew under a blistering sun.

"Heck, when we were in high school, Mrs. D wouldn't even let us hold hands in her living room," Russ snorted. "She'd never allow this. Just doesn't add up."

"Oh, everything adds up." Trevor took a swig and licked the suds from his lips. "I'm not part of the equation. I deserted Julie. Teresa thinks this is what I deserve. You should have seen that jackass Saturday morning. Sitting at my kitchen table like it was the most normal thing in the world. And Julie, in her nightie, entertaining this thirty-year-old jerk."

"Julie was in a nightie?"

"Well, not exactly." Trevor swished the beer glass, took a swallow and handed the empty to the waitress before accepting a full one. "Her flannels, I think, wearing her ratty bathrobe."

Russ shook his head. "Dude, Julie dresses like she just walked out of a photo shoot for some fashion magazine. She wouldn't entertain company in flannel PJs."

Trevor wrinkled his forehead. Russ was right—Julie liked the high-powered exec look: tailored suits, expensive purses, stiletto heels. Her fancy leather briefcase, an import from Italy.

"Maybe all this success has gone to her head." Russ set his glass on the bar. "But you two have loved each other for as long as I can remember. Man, you gotta talk to the woman before giving up."

"Yeah."

"You left *her*, remember?" Russ admonished.

"I had to do something to get her attention. I never thought I'd opened the door for that chump to steal my wife. We were a team."

"Tell her that. Stop playing this stupid game, waiting for her to ask you to come back. She probably thinks you're right where you want to be."

"She knows me better. At least I thought she did."

"Maybe, maybe not. Either way, you need to find out."
***

Julie paced Mercy General's ER, hoping a doctor or nurse would walk by with good news about Derek.

Leanne's call two hours earlier, spliced with details about a scuba diving accident, had sent Julie racing to the hospital. In between Leanne's panicked sobs, Julie surmised Derek's condition remained unchanged—alive and unconscious.

The previous day, Derek had rambled on to Julie about the predicted ocean conditions. The day slightly warmer than the sixty-five-degree water; calm water, no wind, bright sun. A perfect day for a dive.

Thankfully, Trevor's wild side peaked at a bike ride around the park. But Derek craved a different adrenaline rush. Without a family to shower money or attention on, he opted for danger. Last year parasailing fed his adventurous habit, the year before, he rappelled off cliffs.

Gary cocooned himself in a plastic chair in the corner of the waiting room. His pale, sun-starved coloring now echoed a clammier shade of white Julie didn't think possible. His ghost-like translucence contrasted sharply against his nearly blue lips. His dive shirt and board shorts were still damp.

When she arrived, Gary told her that he and Derek were tethered to each other via a buddy line, when Derek's tank malfunctioned. Diving with a pal improved a diver's chances of avoiding accidents.

Things certainly hadn't worked that way this time.

Leanne sat next to Gary, her coloring nearly as pale as his. She wore a rumpled top and a pair of jeans, her face free of makeup. She seemed more upset than someone would be about a coworker, confirming Julie's suspicions that their relationship had pushed past the boundaries of business associates. Derek didn't have any family in the area. No surprise that Leanne's name came up as his emergency contact.

Leanne blew her nose into a tissue. "He said you had his back. Tell me again what happened."

Gary stared at the floor. "The dive master anchored the boat near a deep drop-off and reminded us to maintain shallow depths."

Julie let the weight of her body drop into the chair across from Gary. "And?"

Gary rubbed his hands along his thighs. "We did. Our depth gauges read about sixty feet. His tank had plenty of air. I don't understand what went wrong."

Leanne poked Gary with her finger. "But your air supply was perfectly fine? Derek might die, but his best pal is in robust health. How the hell could this happen?"

"I swear I don't know."

Leanne's eyes filled with tears.

Julie shifted closer, placing her arm around Leanne. "Scuba diving with his buddy. That's all I heard before he left work yesterday," Julie said. "This meant the world to him."

Gary sighed. "I've been going over every step in my head. He gave me the thumbs-up and then swam toward a starfish on a coral formation. I turned away for a second and the next thing I knew, he was waving his arm up and down. It looked like he struggled to breathe."

Buddies kept track of each other for the entire dive, Derek had told her, maintaining a distance that could be easily closed within a few seconds. So why hadn't Gary reached Derek sooner?

"I thought maybe he was suffering from nitrogen narcosis, but we weren't deeper than seventy feet. Then he signaled he was out of air." Gary made a slashing motion across his throat. "I gave him my alternate air source as soon as I reached him, hooked my arm under his and swam to the surface."

"You checked his tank?" Julie asked.

"Yes. We checked each other. That's the idea of the buddy system," Gary said. "You're not alone."

Julie extended her hands toward Gary, including him in the hug. Closing her eyes, she whispered a prayer for Derek.

With Trevor gone, she had no one to turn to. Her heart pounded and her head throbbed. She scrunched her shoulders to relieve the tightness, but the stretch didn't help.

Derek might die.

Could this have anything to do with Game Masters?

She slid her gaze to Gary.

Had Burnside gotten to him? Had he sabotaged Derek's tank?

She let out a deep sigh, aggravated at the wild thoughts her mind seemed to propose these days.

Chapter Nine

Two days later, Julie exited her office elevator and walked straight into Gary's path.

"Hello, Julie." Gary greeted her with his hand extended.

Julie retreated toward the closing elevator doors outside her office suite. "After our conversation at the hospital, I'm surprised to see you," she said. "I don't want to discuss anything with you until Derek is out of danger."

The nerve of this guy.

"I know."

They headed toward her office.

Then why was he following her?

Julie continued to her executive chair but didn't sit. She glanced at her watch. Barely nine o'clock.

"I thought we could get this response to the lawsuit taken care of." Gary set his briefcase on Julie's desk and clicked the latch open. "Review Game Masters' offer and—"

"Your best friend is barely breathing and you want to talk business?"

Derek had been unresponsive for four days before the doctors finally removed the endotracheal tube and allowed him to breathe on his own. Both Julie and Leanne took turns visiting the hospital ICU, hoping for good news on his progress. The neurologist offered very little hope, supplying vague answers to Julie's questions.

"His organs are functioning," the doctor had said, "but Derek's brain was deprived of oxygen. This anoxic brain injury caused some of his brain cells to die. Everything seems to be improving as we expect." Everything except Derek's brain.

The doctor droned on with more medical gobbledygook.

Julie had asked whether he would regain consciousness. Though the doctor was encouraged, he couldn't say for sure.

He finished his lecture by encouraging Leanne and Julie to talk to Derek. "Converse about anything and everything. Hearing words or sounds, triggers circuits in the brain and scientists believe that hastens recovery."

Julie wondered if Derek heard her during those brief moments while she sat at his bedside discussing the weather and watching sitcoms. Sometimes she'd ask his advice about the lawsuit or how to win Trevor back. Derek had remained still, not even blinking, as she sobbed about the unfairness of life, oceans of guilt engulfing her at the possibility that she was ultimately responsible for his condition.

"He's improving, right?" Gary sounded hopeful.

Julie folded her arms across her chest. "Depends. He's not dead."

She didn't care that her deep disdain for Gary showed. She suspected he knew something about the accident—something he wasn't revealing. Julie vacillated between thanking him for saving Derek and blaming him for the near-death catastrophe.

Julie knew the courts waited for no one. Still, she treaded water just to keep the doors of FunWorks open. How would she outmaneuver the legal grenades Burnside had lobbed in her direction?

"Okay. Get on with it," she relented.

Gary pulled a stack of papers from his briefcase and handed them to Julie. "We can get some smaller details out of the way. This litigation mostly affects you, anyway. You and your husband."

He moved to her side of the desk, motioned for her to sit and leaned over her shoulder. The heat of his breath touched the back of her neck. Staring at the *wheretos* and the *herewiths* as Gary explained them made her head spin.

He shoved a pen at Julie. She noted beads of sweat collected on his upper lip. "This is our response to the suit. I recommend you accept their very fair offer."

Julie squared her shoulders. "Have you read their offer? It's anything but fair."

Any hopes that this lawsuit would magically correct itself disappeared, staring at Gary Carlson's hollow eyes. Shards of naïveté, gullibility, and happy endings pierced her brain, temporarily freezing her thought process. She missed Derek's insight. She relied on him as a friend and confidante. When would he speak again…offer his advice…tell one of his horribly corny jokes…continue his budding romance with Leanne?

She squeezed her eyes closed at the realization stabbing her brain. She'd allowed Derek to fill the roles rightfully belonging to Trevor. Her husband should be by her side, not her employee.

"The law doesn't care about anything but the law," Gary continued. "We need to move forward or you will be in an even worse situation. We'll lose all our legal arguments."

Julie placed her hands on her desktop and leaned forward. "I know you're right. I haven't decided how I want to proceed. I need some time to weigh my options."

"There aren't many," Gary explained, "and only one that would end positively for you and FunWorks."

"I don't want to discuss this now. Give me a day to think," she told him in a way that defied further comment.

I need to formulate my own strategy, Julie thought, regretting that she had allowed Derek's accident to sidetrack her actions. Gary was right. She needed to do something, but she'd be damned to let him or anyone paint her into a corner.

"I can't have this meeting right now," Julie said. "We're waiting until Derek is out of the hospital and back to work." She pushed away from her desk and stood to emphasize the point.

"I understand how you feel. I'm worried about my best friend too," Gary said, "but delaying will only prolong the process and may cost you in the long run."

"What do you mean?"

Serious doubts about Gary's competence continued to bubble like water boiling in a pot. She needed time to find another attorney. One with her interests in mind.

"Game Masters will withdraw their offer to purchase and pursue the lawsuit. They'll run you out of business." Gary closed the gap between them. "You'll be left with nothing but steep legal bills. I don't want to see that happen."

Julie remained silent.

"Let me just point out a couple of key factors."

She shoved the papers at him. "Didn't you hear me? I'm not making any decisions without Derek. Now, excuse me." She pointed to the mounds strewn across her desk.

"But we don't know if or when Derek will be…"

Leanne glowered from the doorway as she held Julie's office door open.

"We'll be in touch, Gary." Julie walked to her credenza and opened a drawer, ending their conversation.

"But—"

"You heard the lady," Leanne said, emphasizing each word. She slammed the door as soon as Gary stepped into the hallway.

Julie turned to Leanne. "Are you okay?"

"Yeah. I'm just so mad."

"Derek means a lot to you."

"We were just getting past the 'wanna-have-a-cup-of-coffee' stage."

"You have feelings for him?"

Leanne smiled as though considering the possibilities. "He asked if he could list me as his emergency contact when he started taking scuba lessons."

Julie nodded. "Any word today?"

"No change. That's all the nurses will tell me."

Julie hugged Leanne. "He'll wake up, asking for a cold beer and everything will be back to normal."

Julie said the words her heart hoped would come true. Maybe life would go back to normal for these young lovers. She wished the same for herself and Trevor.

***

Julie's second meeting with Bull's Eye purchasing manager took longer than she expected. She hadn't spoken to Paul Kramer since Derek's accident. After three hours of pleading and promises, he agreed—as a courtesy to their long partnership—to wait another week before he formally canceled his company's Christmas order.

One week until she would have to lay off employees and abandon her production schedules in China. One week until her foundation, her security, her identity collapsed.

Julie scurried past Leanne's desk. "Follow me. I need to bounce an idea off you."

If Bull's Eye pulled their orders, she might as well switch off the lights. She had to tackle Game Masters head-on.

She pursed her lips, waiting for Leanne to sit. "I can't delay this until Derek is back."

"I know." Leanne sniffed. "This morning the nurse said he could regain consciousness tomorrow, or next week or next year. Or never."

"We have to believe he will recover fully. And I must make sure FunWorks is still around when he does. That's why I want to talk to you about Gary. I have a bad feeling about his visit yesterday."

"It's like he wants to isolate you. Hurry you into a bad decision."

"That's what I think. Has Derek ever talked to you about Gary? You know, if he trusts him? What kind of man he is?"

Leanne shook her head. "They're friends as far as I know. Good friends."

"Nothing has changed between them recently?"

"What do you mean?"

"Ever since we were served, Derek seemed to lose patience with Gary, questioning his expertise. I got the feeling he regretted recommending him."

"He didn't talk to me about that."

"Game Masters can't prove their case. We're the company with the valid patent. The way Gary talks, you'd think I'm the one who did something illegal. He's pressuring me to settle for next to nothing."

Leanne stared at the carpet for several seconds before returning her attention to Julie. "I don't like what's happening either. Once you sell, I'm out of a job, but what else can you do?"

"Maybe there is something I can do," Julie said.

Leanne looked confused but remained still as Julie continued, "You can't have too many legal minds working for you, right? Like when you're sick, you get a second opinion."

"Yeah, so?"

"I've decided to consult a patent infringement lawyer."

"Who?"

"I have no idea." She grinned, feeling more encouraged than she'd felt in weeks. "But I'm sure the two of us can come up with a great candidate."

Leanne popped up with the enthusiasm of a cheerleader and headed toward the door. "I'll have a list of names to you within the hour."

"And references. Who they represented, past and present."

"Boy." Leanne turned to Julie, a grin spreading across her face. "Gary won't like this."

"Too bad."

"What happens if he complains?"

"I'll fire him." Julie enjoyed the decisiveness in her voice. "Either way, we're getting to the bottom of this."

"Excuse me." Leanne reached for the ringing cell phone hidden in her jacket pocket.

"Hello. Yes, this is Leanne Ford." She placed her hand against her chest as though bracing for bad news. Tears filled her eyes. "He's what? Oh, my God. I'll be right there. Thank you."

Julie blinked back her own tears. "Well?"

"That was the ICU nurse. Derek's awake."

***

Julie hated the smell of hospitals. Antiseptic and death-like. The long halls and dingy white walls, the nurses and the institutional lighting swept her back to the final days of her mother's life.

She and her two sisters, Monica and Kate, had kept a constant vigil, but in the end, Bridget Bowden Jameson's heart gave out. God had needed another angel in heaven.

Julie walked into Derek's room, several hours after the phone call. Leanne left the office immediately, barely saying goodbye. Just as well. The couple deserved time alone and Julie welcomed a few moments to unscramble her own thoughts.

"I'm surprised at the lengths you'll go to get a few days off." She planted a quick peck on Derek's cheek before setting a vase of carnations on a nightstand.

Derek touched her hand lightly. His body, covered with a hospital-issued blanket, appeared thinner. His usually inquisitive, challenging eyes were dull and flat. She searched for the obstinate fire that made him her trusted friend. Instead, she found listlessness, apathy, and despair.

Julie nodded to Leanne and sat, a new tension coursing through her veins. *Please, God, let this be a temporary condition, a side effect of his strong meds.*

"The doctors say your recovery is nothing short of a miracle."

"I shouldn't be here at all," Derek strained to speak. The endotracheal tube had left his throat hoarse and his voice raspy. He clenched his fists, struggling with each word.

91

Julie swallowed hard. "Maybe you had a strong reason to recover." Her eyes moved to Leanne's concerned face.

"I saw a guy near the tanks before we dove." Derek took in a slow breath. "Not a part of our group."

"You need to rest." Leanne patted his hand. "Don't get worked up again."

"Someone messed with my tank." Derek's gaze flicked between Julie and Leanne. "It wasn't Gary."

"Of course not." Leanne turned to Julie. "The Coast Guard is investigating. So far everything points to a routine malfunction. No one at fault."

Obviously, Derek and Leanne had discussed the possibility of attempted murder during the hours before Julie's arrival. Her stomach gelled into panic as she realized Derek thought someone tried to kill him.

Was the accident a result of bad luck, or something more sinister?

She dismissed the incident as an unfortunate turn of events, like when she chose the slow line in the grocery store. It was no one's fault. Life just happened. But Derek's observation stripped her of a rational answer and confirmed her suspicion of foul play.

"On a happier note," Leanne continued, "If Derek's breathing remains stable for the next forty-eight hours, the doctor says he can go home."

"That's great news." Julie hoped the words camouflaged her paranoia.

"It will be longer before he can go back to work, though," Leanne added.

"Of course," Julie said. "FunWorks will be waiting for you."

Derek used the heels of his hands to sit up. "Leanne says you're hiring a new attorney?"

Julie explained her plan.

"I'll be back soon and I can help."

Julie enjoyed the glimmer of spirit returning to Derek's face. "Take care of yourself first."

Leanne settled Derek back against the pillow. "I know," he whispered before falling asleep.

"I'll see you back at the office, Leanne." Julie turned to leave. Maybe her prediction of happily ever after would come true for Derek and Leanne.

Still, Julie couldn't quell the anxiety mounting in the pit of her stomach; the threat of approaching trouble couldn't be denied.

According to Derek, a stranger was near their boat that day. Had he disabled Derek's tank? Was Derek supposed to die in the mishap? Or only be harmed enough to scare Julie?

Someone purposely caused this tragedy, leaving Julie with a haunting thought—who would be hurt next?

***

A day after Derek regained consciousness, Julie met with Gary in her office.

The two had crossed paths in the halls near the ICU that morning, but she refused to talk business with him. She needed a clear head to make smart, emotionless decisions and not let Gary prevent her from seeing the whole picture. Gary could be the root of her problems.

Staring at Derek still connected to monitors and IV drips left her with a deep desire to seek revenge. Maybe that would come later.

Gary sunk deeper into the leather couch cushions after hearing she would be hiring a second attorney. The normally quick-witted lawyer regained his composure slowly.

"It's nothing against you," Julie said, bridging the silence. "We're missing something. I want a fresh perspective."

"But two lawyers will double your cost," Gary replied, finally stringing a sentence together. "Didn't Bull's Eye cancel?"

"They've reinstated their holiday orders," Julie lied. "You don't have to spend more to get this matter resolved."

"Yes, I do." Julie injected firmness in her voice. "I'm the client. I want you to team up with the second attorney. Work together to check out the facts and advise me."

"That's what I'm doing now. Advising you."

"I want a second opinion."

"You're right. I don't know everything about patent law." Gary's voice sounded squeaky, high, as though a pin had pierced him, releasing a slow leak of air. "We have patent law attorneys on staff. I'm sure you can get a discount on our services by staying with our firm."

"Right now, I'm not thinking about cutting corners." Julie's voice rose with each word. "I know you understand. Why are you pushing against me?"

"I'm working with you, not against you." Gary stood.

Julie waved her hand, dismissing his claim. "I don't have the time or interest in debating this any longer."

"Julie, I know a good deal when I see one. And this is a great deal. Game Masters' execs are willing to drop the suit and pay two million to buy your company outright."

Julie wanted to order him out of her office. Instead, she went to the window and watched a flock of tree swallows take flight before answering. "You don't seem to grasp what's going on, do you?" she said, still facing away. "I'm. Not. Selling."

Gary joined her at the window. "You're being a bit melodramatic, don't you think?"

She spun on her heels and met his steely stare. "The only thing keeping me from firing you right now is your friendship with Derek."

"They want to end the lawsuit and buy FunWorks…for a lot of money."

"You think two million dollars is a lot of money? Do you know the current value of our business?"

"Well, not actually, but—"

"There's another reason I should terminate you as our lawyer. FunWorks' worth is the first thing you should have researched."

"I'll get right on the valuation analysis." Gary hurried to his briefcase and scribbled on a legal pad.

"Always late to the game, huh, Gary. Here's another thing you can research. If they're sure they can win, why do they want to buy us out?" Julie baited, hoping to get Gary to tip his hand. He was behind this latest crisis, or at least he knew who was. She crossed her arms and stood with her feet apart, tapping her toe. "Well?"

"Because they don't want the negative publicity."

"Then explain this." Julie shoved the newspaper with Roberta Perkins's article into Gary's chest. "I want another lawyer—one familiar with patent litigation—and definitely not one who gets a paycheck from Ryder, Rush & Ryder like you do."

Sweat trickled down Gary's face, despite the cool room temperature. He swiped his hands along his trousers. In spite of his efforts, Julie watched his briefcase slip when he reached for the handle. "I've always worked in the best interest of you and FunWorks," he defended.

"This isn't about you." Julie inhaled sharply and guided him toward the door. "I'll notify you once we've hired the second attorney. In the meantime, file the necessary paperwork for a continuance. I don't want to mess with any of this until after the Christmas orders have been filled and Derek is back at his desk."

Julie waited for Gary to leave the room. She squared her shoulders.

Take that, you conniving rat.

Chapter Ten

Getting the kids off to school the next day was harder than usual.

Jason grunted one-syllable responses to Julie's questions. Emily idly swirled her spoon in her cereal before reluctantly taking a bite. Nicole stared at an empty bowl, apparently too disinterested to pour a pile of corn flakes.

"Is this the week you find out what California mission you'll be doing your report on?" Julie prodded.

Nicole tilted her head.

"Is there one in particular you want to learn about? Jason did San Luis Obispo for his project. Maybe you'll get that one." Julie turned toward Jason. "Do you still have all your notes?"

Jason gave her the exaggerated eye roll every teenage boy manages to perfect before they turned driving age and slammed his binder closed. "Mom, you're talking four years ago. I probably threw them away."

His goodbye kiss missed Julie's cheek and landed somewhere in the air. He snatched his backpack off the floor, shoved a sticker-covered white binder inside and bolted. "I'm going to Chet's. He's giving me a ride to school today and then to basketball practice."

Even for Jason, that was an abrupt exit.

"Mrs. Stevenson is outside honking," Nicole added, taking the remaining lunch bags from Teresa. "Don't forget to pick me up from piano lessons," she shouted over her shoulder as she and Emily ran out the door.

Julie stood for a hug, but before she reached her feet, both girls were gone.

"Not even a kiss from Emily." She turned toward Teresa. "Did my three children just blow me off?"

Teresa mumbled an undecipherable comment and busied herself at the kitchen counter.

"What's going on here?"

"Something about Derek being here Saturday morning and you still in your bathrobe, holding hands." Teresa glanced over her shoulder. "I told the kids I never left the entire time."

"They can't possibly think—"

"Jason blames him for the separation. Him and your job." Teresa set a glass of orange juice on the table, but Julie didn't sit. "Have you spoken to Trevor since Saturday?"

"Well, no, I haven't." Julie tried to hide her surprise. "Trevor left me, remember?"

Teresa started unloading the dishwasher. "You asked for my opinion."

"No, I didn't. I asked you what was going on, not for gossip."

Julie exhaled and stared through the sliding glass door, wishing she could run away from the hurtful truth that now defined her life.

Teresa put her hands on her hips. "Well, you're going to get my opinion anyway. You can pretty much do whatever you want. You're an adult, even though you're not acting like one. Making bad decisions, screwing up your life. Fine with me, but don't take your family down with you. Get your priorities in order. If not for your sake, then for the sake of these three little ones."

Teresa's tone slid Julie back to when she was a quarrelsome teenager, knocking heads with her mother every chance she could. The righter her mother's argument, the angrier Julie's words in retort. She wanted to storm out of the kitchen after shouting, 'You're not the boss of me.'"

Instead, she held her gaze, taking in the blanket of lilac-colored flowers from her jacaranda tree littering the backyard. The season had changed from summer to fall without Julie noticing.

"When your business took off, you asked me to work longer hours, and I did. I watched you change from a full-time homemaker to a full-time business owner in minutes. You fought to get PlaytimePals in all the best stores. When buyers told you they'd never heard of your product, you dug in your heels and convinced them they needed your paper dolls on their shelves. Where's that fighting spirit now for your marriage?"

"This is different. I can't make Trevor want me."

"Didn't things go well Friday night?"

Tears brimmed in Julie's eyes. "He has a girlfriend."

"Who? Trevor?" Teresa let out a snort and rolled her eyes. "I don't believe it."

"I saw her. At Mulvaney's in the front row."

Teresa pointed to a chair. "Sit down."

Julie inhaled a shaky breath. If she kept Trevor's affair a secret, she could pretend there wasn't one. Telling Teresa made the cheating real.

"There is someone else. A very young, very pretty someone else."

"Our Trevor's seeing another woman?" Teresa raised her eyebrows.

A rapid drumbeat thumped in Julie's chest. "He said he wanted to separate for a while so we could work on our marriage. But I saw the real reason, and she has blonde hair, tight jeans, and perky breasts."

Teresa put her arm around Julie. "Trevor would never be that cruel. He wouldn't have you stumble into a scene like that. What did he say to you?"

"I didn't stay to talk to him. I saw what I saw and left." Julie blinked back tears.

Teresa shook her head. "The least you could do is ask him. I know Trevor. He loves you and the kids. You both need to take a serious look at what you're doing and how it's affecting this family."

With those words, Teresa opened a wound Julie had plastered over.

After her dad had left, Julie spent weeks fashioning new doll dress designs. She wanted to show them to her mother or brag about the first-prize ribbons she'd won at the county fair for doll clothing and creative stitchery.

Instead, she made certain Monica and Kate finished their homework and brushed their teeth while Bridget worked a double shift at the diner. Julie vowed then she would not end up like her mother. She wouldn't rely on any man for security the way her mother had done.

"You're a woman who knows how to get what she wants." Teresa touched Julie's hand. "You don't give up."

"It's this lawsuit. I'm so worried, I don't know where to turn. Derek was my sounding board in unraveling all the legalities. And now he's recovering from an attempt on his life. I can't prove foul-play, but still, I know it's true. The kids don't understand. This is my future. *Their* future. I can't let everything I've worked so hard for slip away. Do they really think I'm that heartless?" Julie swiped at tears with both hands.

"No, honey. You're their mother. They love you. I'll keep praying for you."

"Prayer. That was Mom's solution to every problem. But I never saw a single Hail Mary make anything better."

"You've always said your mother's faith pulled you and your sisters through the tough times."

"She believed, so I believed. Now, I'm not so sure."

Julie's face tightened, realizing the family hadn't gone to church since Christmas. Had she lost her spirituality? Was that why she'd stopped going to mass on Sundays, opting for sleeping in and having lazy breakfasts at home? "Doing the right thing doesn't always work out the way you plan."

"Maybe your version of the right way isn't the same as God's."

Julie laughed. "Yeah. He's got his own agenda and He doesn't clear His plan with me before throwing catastrophe and heartache in my path."

"You have your mother's strength and her passion for family. You'll get through this rough time, if for no other reason than for your kids."

Julie turned to leave. "I'd better fix my makeup. I have a full day at the office. New toy lines, sales promotions, national tie-ins and, oh yeah—a little matter of being sued. God's working overtime lining up crosses for me to bear. Oh." Julie recalled her promise to talk about Teresa's loan. "With everything going on, we haven't talked about the money you need."

"I didn't want to add to your burden, but if you don't have the cash, would you cosign a ten-thousand-dollar loan for me?"

"To repair a bathroom leak?" The words spilled out before Julie could stop them. Teresa obviously didn't want to disclose the real reason she needed cash.

"The water caused more damage than they originally thought," Teresa answered, her head bowed.

"I'm sorry," Julie said, angry at insensitive questioning. "It's none of my business what you spend your money on. How soon do you need an answer?"

"Within the week would be great," Teresa said, still staring at the floor.

"If I can help, I will. I'm a little stretched right now. I don't want to bore you with my troubles, but I am supposed to hear from the bank this week about a working capital infusion. If my loan comes through, I should have no problem backing yours."

"I understand. That's why I haven't asked recently."

So wrapped up in her own troubles, Julie had failed to recognize the suffering painting Teresa's face. This woman who had been a strength to her, much like her own mother, was hurting. Something was terribly wrong for Teresa to need thousands of dollars. Julie hoped Teresa's health wasn't forcing her into debt.

"Normally this wouldn't be a strain, but with…"

"Don't worry. I know things will work out." Teresa blinked quickly. "It's really not that important."

Julie heard the words but didn't believe Teresa for a moment. "Look, Jason doesn't have practice tonight. Let's go out for a family dinner. The kids like that all-you-can-eat buffet place."

"The one where he eats ten kinds of pasta and Emily doesn't stop until she's tried every combination at the ice cream bar?" Teresa sighed, apparently relieved the subject had changed. "Trevor likes that place, too. He's a fan of their sliced roast beef."

Julie smiled. "You're so subtle. I'll call and see if he's available to join us."

Maybe Teresa was right. She should have asked about the bleached blonde.

Sadly, she knew why she hadn't. The pain of his answer would have been too hard to bear.

***

Before Julie placed her purse on the desk, Leanne handed her three phone messages, two from Gary and one from a local reporter.

"Oh, and I thought you might want to read this," Leanne handed over an article printed off the Internet. "After your meeting with Bennett Burnside, I remembered reading this from two years ago."

The story recounted the case of a family from Georgia. The parents of a ten-year-old had won $100,000 in compensatory damages and $9.9 million in punitive damages in a lawsuit against MaxOut Toys. The suit claimed their son permanently lost partial use of his right hand after playing with BlastAway, a handheld video game manufactured by the start-up company. The article read in part:

"Because of their negligence, this young lad is unable to perform any of the normal activities a boy of ten would enjoy," their attorney said, arguing that MaxOut management knew the dangers of overuse of their product and was required to provide consumer warnings. "Young Benji is now designated as a special needs student. On the Little League field, Benji can't pitch, play first base, or even bat properly."

Julie remembered Mort Gunther's appeal to the ruling. An appellate court upheld the original judgment, forcing the fledgling toy manufacturer to file for bankruptcy.

Funny. She hadn't seen Mort since he lost his company…until he introduced her to Bennett Burnside.

Leanne handed Julie a copy of another news item dated months later from the Global Business Briefs section of the *Wall Street Journal,* announcing Game Masters' acquisition of bankrupt MaxOut Toys for an undisclosed amount.

An icy surge ran down Julie's back. She set the papers on Leanne's desk and clenched the journalist's phone message in her hand.

Roberta Perkins, San Marcel Mercury News. Please call before 2:00 p.m.

Julie recognized the name and the same byline on the patent-infringement lawsuit article.

While placing the call, Julie licked her lips, a nervous habit she had since a child, waiting for the phone to connect.

"Ms. Rafferty, thank you for returning my call." Roberta Perkins's monotone voice replied. Julie pictured her more as a Helen Thomas-style journalist than a wide-eyed Lois Lane.

"An unnamed source on the San Marcel Narcotics Task Force claims the US attorney's office is requesting a court order to confiscate your company files. Would you care to comment?"

Julie collapsed in her chair, her legs no longer able to support her. "What did you say?"

"Is FunWorks actually a front for money-laundering?"

"I don't understand the question," Julie said, her voice shaking.

"It's the first step before the Narcotics Task Force initiates an investigation," the reporter said in a matter-of-fact tone.

Nervous energy soared through Julie's veins. "The Narcotics Task Force? What is this all about?"

"The task force received a tip that FunWorks launders money for drug traffickers."

"What a ridiculous allegation." Julie's pulse quickened, and her hand flew to the silver crucifix dangling on a thin chain around her neck. She fingered the cross and took in a deep breath.

"May I quote you?"

"Quote me? For what?"

"For the article I'm working on. You did know you are under investigation?"

Julie didn't respond.

"In my experience, allegations of federal law violations are taken very seriously by the United States Attorney, especially Del Evans's office," Roberta said, suddenly sounding supportive. "If I were you, I'd call my attorney."

"I have no comment about the allegation," Julie managed to say. "I will remind you, though, that a libel suit can be very expensive. In my experience, newspaper publishers fire irresponsible writers whose sloppy work costs them money." Julie disconnected the call and threw the cordless phone across the room.

Now those jerks had gone too far.

She retrieved her phone.

Twenty minutes later, after waiting on hold, a clerk in US Attorney Del Evans's office informed her that Mr. Evans was unable to take her call. The clerk couldn't say anything about the allegations, but she confirmed that contacting a lawyer would be a good idea.

"How long do these investigations take?" Julie asked.

"Hard to say," the droning voice replied. "Every case is unique. When it's connected to money, sometimes the IRS and the DEA get involved."

Julie held the phone receiver near her ear for a minute or two listening to the dial tone.

The IRS and the DEA?

Burnside wanted FunWorks so much, he sicced the Feds on me. Why?

Chapter Eleven

"He's still locked in that all-day planning meeting." Trevor's secretary said. "I don't think he's had a chance to check his phone for messages." Julie had spoken to Peggy three times in two hours. By the conciliatory tone in her voice, Julie wondered how much she knew about their breakup.

"Thanks anyway." Julie clicked off and tossed her cell phone onto the desk. Even all-day meetings stopped for bathroom breaks. And Trevor always checked his phone. He could have called if he'd wanted to.

Determined not to get stuck in the office, Julie slid the product design sketches into her briefcase and snapped the latch closed. She retrieved her phone and dialed again, this time leaving a message. "We'll be at the all-you-can-eat buffet on Marshall around six o'clock. The kids would love you to join us." She paused. "I'd like it, too."

She flung her purse strap over her shoulder, grabbed the briefcase and headed out the door, with plenty of time to meet her dinner dates. Her heart sank, recalling the orchestrated freeze-out that morning. The sullen, angry looks on their faces, proof she caused their broken home.

How do I explain that it's their father who wants to change partners, not me? I would never leave.

***

Trevor and Bob Toomes trudged back to their offices, arms loaded with marketing plans covered by hastily scribbled notes.

Bruce Floyd, director of Cook's Finest snacks division, had his eye on a vice presidency. If he could increase profits by more than five percent, the board would give him the promotion; or so the rumor mill claimed. Bruce had been pushing his people like a demon for the past five weeks.

Trevor hummed the chorus from "Won't Get Fooled Again" as he collected his phone from the box and clicked on the power.

"What's with that guy?" Bob said. "Making everyone leave their cell phones at reception, so we wouldn't have any distractions?"

"Meet the new boss. He's worried the numbers presented at the shareholders' meeting next week won't be strong enough." Trevor's phone beeped. "We're turning a good profit. They'll get their dividends."

Trevor's screen flashed a missed message. "...the kids would love you to join us," he heard Julie say, then added, "I'd like it, too."

"At six," he shouted. "Crap, it's 6:20 now. Maybe if I call, they'll wait."

"Who'll wait?" asked Bob.

"Julie and the kids," Trevor answered as he dialed.

"Damn. She's not getting a signal inside the restaurant. Gotta go. See you tomorrow, Bob." Trevor's stride to the car turned into a gallop. Getting to the restaurant would take thirty minutes.

Don't let this be the night Nicole and Emily skip tasting everything at the dessert bar. Please God.

Breaking the speed limits cut his trip to twenty, despite rush-hour traffic and hitting red lights on the side streets. "Yes!" He sent a fist pump into the air when he spotted Julie's car parked a few spaces over.

He bounded through the front doors, paid the cashier the dinner fee, and searched for his family. Trays, plates, and silverware clattered. Conversations, laughter, and a mixture of babies' coos and cries filled the air. Trevor's eyes darted from face to face as he made his way through the maze of food stations.

Then he saw Emily near the ice cream, balancing a cherry on top of a chocolate sundae.

"How about a few more sprinkles and some extra whipped cream?" Trevor asked. Emily's eyes opened wide in surprise.

"Daddy! I knew you'd come." She dropped her dish onto a counter and hugged him. "I wish you could've gotten here sooner. This is my third bowl of ice cream."

"Your third? Your belly will hurt tomorrow."

"Oh, I didn't eat them. I stalled." She smiled, revealing a dimple deep in her chubby cheeks.

"Nice work, scout." He kissed the top of her head. "Where's Mommy…and everybody?"

"Over there." She pointed to the far corner. "Follow me." She skipped back to the horseshoe-shaped booth, nearly knocking over a grandfatherly gentleman standing at the carving station. Trevor gathered Emily's ice cream bowl and followed.

At the center of the booth, Julie and Teresa sat with their heads together, deep in conversation. Something serious from the looks on their faces.

"Hey, everybody. Sorry I'm late. Bruce's planning meeting took forever." Trevor set Emily's bowl of melting ice cream on the table. "I'm starving. The guy didn't even bring in lunch."

Trevor smiled at Julie sitting in the center of the booth. Her blue eyes seemed to light up. Tonight, an emerald glint played off the fuzzy knit sweater he had given her last Christmas. He loved the way the cashmere hugged her curves, giving her a playful, soft look; the opposite of how she dressed for work. His empty stomach performed a loop-the-loop when she smiled back.

Emily scooted in alongside Nicole and shoved her sister to make room. "I checked my messages about 6:20. That's when I heard about this little shindig." He beamed at Nicole and Emily.

"6:20? Why it's not even seven o'clock yet," Teresa said. "How could you get here that fast?"

"A little luck and a lot of speed." Trevor winked at Jason hunched over the remains of roast beef, mashed potatoes, and corn. Crumbs from a dinner roll decorated the corner of his mouth when he smiled back.

Trevor hugged Teresa and moved to the end of the booth next to Emily. "What were you and Teresa talking about? Something serious?"

"Just work." Julie's finger traced a drop along the side of her water glass. "I'll tell you later." Her eyes shifted to Emily slurping the ice cream concoction, then back to Trevor. "We're all glad you're here."

Trevor smiled, his insides sparking.

Teresa pointed a finger at the rows of food. "Go get something to eat."

"You're nearly done," Trevor said. "I'll catch a burger on the way home."

"But you had to pay to get in here." Teresa waved both hands, shooing him away. "Go get something while Julie finishes her coffee. I'll take the kids home, so they can get started on their homework. You drop Julie off when you're done." Without waiting for a response, she gathered her purse, slid out of the booth and stood. "Okay, kids, let's hit the road. *Hijinks High* comes on in thirty-five minutes, and I don't want to miss the beginning."

"Oh, yeah, *her* show." Nicole rolled her eyes. "We got her hooked on that stupid sitcom, and now everything revolves around it."

Trevor turned to Julie. "Is that okay with you? I mean, can I drive you home?"

She cocked her head to the side, the way she did when she wanted to appear aloof, noncommittal. Trevor had seen that maneuver many times when she attempted to hide or push aside her deepest feelings.

"That would be nice," she said.

He answered with a broad smile. *Yes, it would.*

***

Julie watched Trevor mow through a pile of thinly sliced roast beef and a side of spaghetti before turning his attention to a hot dog. Thankfully, he wasn't a picky eater, a quality Julie often credited for their marriage enduring.

"Does that taste better than my Tuna Noodle Surprise?" Julie cajoled, recalling how Jason and Nicole complained about that supper years earlier.

"I ate two platefuls."

"The kids hated that meal. They insisted on banning that casserole forever from the family dinner menu."

"Hey, I thought it was good. I liked the crunchy potato-chip topping."

"What topping? Those were undercooked noodles," Julie confessed.

"Whatever. I liked the way you cooked. Or, how you used to cook when you were home more." Trevor spread a dollop of brown mustard on his hot dog. "What did you and Teresa have your heads together about a few minutes ago?"

"The latest installment of 'As the Paper Doll Turns,'" Julie said. "I think our corporate attorney isn't representing my best interest."

"You mean Derek's college buddy? He seems capable. What does your boy-genius think?" Trevor shoved a French fry into his mouth.

Julie flashed a crooked smile. *Always a wisecrack.* "I haven't asked. He's just come home from the hospital."

"I'm sorry. I forgot about his injury. How is Derek doing?" Trevor ran another fry through the ketchup puddle and shoved the potato piece into his mouth.

"He's much better and should be back to work soon.

"So, what's the problem?"

"I didn't think there was one until Derek's scuba diving accident. As the days pass, the accident is looking more and more intentional." Julie searched Trevor's face for a clue. Was he interested, or merely being polite? She couldn't tell.

"Um hmm," he nodded, his mouth full.

"That's when the pressure ramped up." Julie dug through her purse and handed him the newspaper clipping.

Trevor scanned the article.

"Bull's Eye canceled their order right after that story was published. Derek and I met with the purchasing manager to beg for time to straighten everything out."

"Did he agree?"

"Yeah, but only for a few days. He won't wait any longer and run the risk of having empty shelves during December. After the meeting, I went to the office to plead with the bank for an extension."

"Sounds like the right thing to do."

"When I got back, Leanne handed me a message from a reporter. The same one who wrote that article." Julie stared at Trevor and exhaled a trembling breath. "She wanted my reaction to a possible investigation."

His eyes widened. "Investigation?"

"She claimed to be following a lead from an unnamed source." Julie's fingers formed air quotes around unnamed. "Apparently, the US District Attorney's office got a tip that FunWorks is a front for drug money."

"You? Laundering drug money?" Trevor laughed. "That's ridiculous."

Julie shot him a hard stare. "I'm glad you think this is funny."

Trevor cleared his throat. "Sorry. The idea is so ludicrous... Did you tell Gary?"

"No. I just found out. Anyway, I doubt there is an investigation." She hoped that were true. "I asked her when the article would appear, and her answers were very vague."

Trevor grunted.

"Weird stuff started happening after Mort Gunther introduced me to this guy at the toy fair who wanted to buy FunWorks."

"You never told me."

Julie leaned in closer. "I thought you'd want me to sell."

"Who's the prospective buyer?" Hurt laced his voice.

"Bennett Burnside."

"The guy who half of San Marcel is named after?"

"He's the one. I think he's involved in Mort losing his company."

Two weeks before Mort sold MaxOut Toys to an unnamed investment company, his teenage son suffered a drug overdose and nearly died. The recollection sent a spike of panic through Julie's body.

Trevor started to reach for Julie's hand, then pulled back, picking up another French fry instead. "You think Burnside and Game Masters are working together?"

"I know they are," Julie said. "He admitted as much when I met with him." She gagged, recalling the putrid scent of Burnside's cigar.

"Maybe this investigation is another way for Burnside to apply pressure."

Julie nodded. "There's no benefit to Burnside if a negative story is printed about a company he wants to buy. He wants me to give up. I've got to call his bluff."

"What's your next move?"

"Still trying to figure that out." Julie sipped her coffee.

"Are you keeping Gary on?"

"Not sure yet."

"You trust Derek. Derek trusts this guy, right?" Trevor made the proclamation without looking Julie in the eye, clearly annoyed to advocate for his rival.

"Not since the accident." She twisted her white napkin into a paper snake.

"That's tough. When you lose trust, everything goes out the window."

Julie searched Trevor's face. How had he meant that?

"What would you do?"

His brows peaked, spotlighting his hazel green eyes, now afire with curiosity. "You're asking me?"

"Yes. I want to know what you'd do. What we should do about our company."

Trevor slid his plate to the side, perched his elbows on the table and cradled his chin. "You've always been good at making adjustments, replacing things when they don't work or meet your needs. This is just another adjustment."

"You don't understand, Trevor. If one more contract gets canceled, we won't be able to pay our bills." Her hands clenched, pushing her fingernails into her palms. "Everything is happening too fast. I don't know who I can count on."

Trevor moved closer, placing her hand in his. "Look, it's simple. Having Gary Carlson as your attorney doesn't work. He is replaceable. You've made replacements before. I don't understand why it's so hard for you this time."

"Because this time I'm in over my head. This has turned into so much more than designing dolls!"

Oceans of resentment overpowered Julie's matter-of-fact business attitude. With her marriage crumbling, she questioned her own ambitions. She wanted Trevor to be her partner in every facet of her life. Why didn't he want that, too?

Maybe she had placed her business over the man she loved, never allowing him to really share her life. Was all this her fault?

"Julie, I want to help, but..."

"But what. Selling FunWorks is what you've always wanted."

"No. Not like this. Not when I see the fallout. I only want—"

"What's best for me and the kids. I know."

"Look, Julie." He patted her hand before letting go, as though releasing her from his life. "Things change. People change."

Julie heard the ache in his words. *You're the one who changed.* Their relationship had changed. She nodded, teary-eyed. "It's getting late and I have a million things to do tomorrow. Will you still drive me home?" She reached for her purse and scooted out of the booth.

"Of course. But Julie, we need to talk." Trevor reached again for her hand.

About your new girlfriend, I don't think so.

"I'm all talked out tonight. Another time, okay?"

Chapter Twelve

Julie spent most of the next day at her desk researching patent infringement cases. Of the fifty or so lawsuits, Bennett Burnside's name appeared eighteen times, pretty much the superstar of bogus patent litigation. His fingerprints were on some famous cases, all with large price tags.

She studied a two-year-old newspaper article announcing the opening of Burnside Willows Country Club to the public. The photo caption read: *San Marcel Mayor Allan Roper. US District Attorney Del Evans and Judge S. P. James look on as local philanthropist Bennett Burnside cuts the ribbon.*

Julie remembered walks alongside the golf course's greenbelt bordering the rolling hills, waterfalls, and deep ravines and the serenity that once accompanied those outings. Citizens of San Marcel recognized the Burnside name with honor and respect. Now, those syllables sent shocks of horror through her soul.

Del Evans. That was the name dropped by the reporter when Julie first learned about the Narcotics Task Force investigation. Evans and Burnside knew each other. Of course they did. Slowly the pieces collected, leading Julie to realize far more than FunWorks was being threatened.

"Wow, this is heavy." Leanne plunked a stack of printouts on Julie's blotter, the third delivery of nearly one hundred pages Julie had sent to the printer adjacent to Leanne's desk.

Leanne pointed. "I made some notations about Bennett Burnside. Some are more revealing than others, but most of them suggest he's a magnet for flimsy patent infringement cases." She puffed out a breath. "Of all the clients he's represented, I could only find one instance when a suit actually went before a judge."

Julie stopped reading and studied her administrative assistant. Ten years her junior, Julie appreciated Leanne Ford's uncommon gift for anticipating what needed to be done. She'd been surprised at how, over the past two years, their business relationship slipped comfortably into a trusted friendship. No wonder Derek had fallen for Leanne.

"MaxOut. That case you asked me to track down," Leanne said. "All the other cases settled one way or another before they got to court."

"The family in Georgia?" Julie stared at the sheets of paper. "That's the only case that went to court?"

"As far as I can tell." Leanne leaned over Julie's shoulder.

"An old case about a San Marcel plumber keeps popping up," Julie said. "His name is Ray Bolley. I'm trying to find more information about that one."

"A plumber?"

"Yeah, I know it's not toys, but all the other pieces match our situation." Julie ticked the facts off counting on her fingers. "One. He had a patent on a water-saving pump. Two. He made a lot of money until the patent infringement lawsuit hit. Three. Weinstein and Wallace represented the plaintiff and settled the entire matter out of court."

"Coincidence?"

"There are too many similarities for coincidence. See if you can find phone numbers for the Thorsons or anyone connected with MaxOut. I would call Mort myself, but the details of how he lost MaxOut are sketchy and after the way he acted introducing Burnside, I don't think he'd be very candid with me."

"Got it," Leanne said.

"I'll keep digging into the plumber's case and see if I can find any other cases tied to Burnside. I want to know what went wrong, and I sure as hell can't count on Gary to find out." Julie blew out a deep breath. "By the way, how's that list of patent attorneys coming?"

"I'll have the names for you this afternoon," Leanne headed for the door.

Patent law can't have that many practicing attorneys, Julie thought. Whoever we hire will know Burnside or know about him. She rubbed her hands across her face. A quick and disturbing thought skittered through her mind.

What if she couldn't find a lawyer willing to fight him? What if Burnside owned every patent law attorney within a hundred miles? *I might end up with someone worse than Carlson.*

***

Julie climbed the stairs leading to Emily's bedroom. Nine-thirty. Two hours later than she'd planned to be home. Too late to tuck her youngest daughter in.

"And God bless my brother and my sister." Emily's sweet voice stopped Julie in the hall. She rested her forehead against the door jamb, grateful for this moment of faith not unlike those she and her sisters had shared growing up.

If only Monica and Kate lived closer. She could trust them. Their judgment. Their support. Like most sisters, they spoke nearly every day or sent texts in between the events of their busy lives. Emails flew back and forth about Kate's upcoming baby shower or how Monica's son Bodie continued his recovery from leukemia. Next year he was certain to make the all-star team. Their communications contained upbeat messages, anticipating happiness, not drowning in sorrows.

Julie's sisters were there virtually. Not physically. She couldn't tell them in a text or an email how her life had hit rock-bottom. How Trevor no longer loved her. No. That kind of conversation took place in person.

Julie wanted to chase the lawsuit from her thoughts and escape the sensation of being worn down by a steady stream of water pelting a rock, grinding her strength to sand. After a moment, she peeked in on Emily kneeling, and Teresa standing nearby, their backs to Julie.

"All right, get under the covers." Teresa pulled back the pale pink and yellow quilt.

"Oh, I forgot." Emily bowed her head again. "And God bless Teresa. She's the best friend I have." *Teresa's her best friend, not me.*

"God bless Emily and send your grace upon the Rafferty family," Teresa added before blessing herself. "Nicely done. Now hop in."

Julie watched Teresa tuck the corners of the quilt around Emily and hand her Horace Hardbuckle. Emily cuddled her favorite stuffed animal.

Julie started to enter the room, but the tenderness of the scene froze her in place. An observer to Teresa's genuine love for Emily, Julie sent thanks for this stable force in her little girl's life. And in her own.

"You've got to be tired," Teresa said.

"Yeah, a little. The zoo was fun, though." Emily picked at Horace's scraggly rainbow-colored yarn hair. "We saw bears and koalas, and did you know elephants are the largest land mammal?"

"I'd heard that." Teresa joked and moved to the corner of Emily's bed.

"I sat by Brianna and Caitlin on the bus." Emily's voice turned serious. "Caitlin's mom and dad are divorced, too."

Teresa wrapped an arm around Emily. "Why did you say *too?* Your parents aren't divorced."

"It's just a matter of time. That's what Caitlin said. Her dad moved out and then her parents got divorced."

Julie's hands clutched, aiding her attempt to hold back a wall of tears forming behind her eyes. "She says that's what happens. The dad leaves, and the mom gets a divorce, and a boyfriend."

A boyfriend.

"Well, for your information, Caitlin isn't the final word on how people live their lives. I thought we had an agreement about this. Have you forgotten?"

"I remember." Emily hid behind Horace. Teresa tugged him away from Emily's face.

"What are these tears trickling down your cheeks. There's no need for waterworks."

"Daddy's still doesn't live here and Mommy's working more than ever. She promised to tuck me in tonight, but she isn't here." Emily sniffed. "She's always too busy."

This arrow shot through Julie's heart and she shook away a fresh tear trailing down her cheek.

"That's not true, Emily Bridget." Julie watched Teresa squeeze her daughter tighter. "Didn't we have a nice dinner, all of us last night, your dad included? And didn't your mom and dad hang out afterward and have some time alone?" Teresa tilted Emily's chin to meet her eyes. "Those are all good signs. Small signs, but good nonetheless."

"Jason and Nicole said that doesn't matter."

"Is that so?" Teresa said.

"And Caitlin says I'm a dummy to believe you." Emily took the tissue Teresa pulled out of her pocket and wiped her eyes. "She says, Mommy will get a boyfriend, and Daddy will get a girlfriend and they'll both be horrible." Emily sniffed hard through her nose. "That's what happened to her parents."

Julie squeezed her eyes shut, blocking Emily's words from her mind. *Oh, honey, that's not what's going on,* she thought, still unable to move.

"I don't know Caitlin's parents or their circumstances," Teresa said. "I'm sorry things didn't work out for them. But honey, that has nothing to do with your folks and your family. Their situation is completely different." Teresa squeezed Emily's hand. "You can't predict the future. What you can do is trust your mom and dad to do the right thing. I believe that, and I know you do, too."

Emily shook her head. "But Jason and Nicole—"

"Never mind those two. Maybe we have to crank it up a bit." Teresa smiled.

"Like that chef says in that cooking show you watch?"

"Exactly. 'Kick it up a notch.'"

"You mean, pray harder?"

"Maybe with more conviction. Show God you believe in your prayers. That you believe in your family and in Him. He'll show your parents the way."

Julie's heart ached for her baby girl. She should be the one comforting Emily, not Teresa, but her legs wouldn't move. Emily spoke the truth. She and Trevor would divorce. *He's already found my replacement.*

"Why does everything take so long?" Emily's whine stretched the sentence. "I've been praying forever and nothing's happened."

"Things don't work out as quickly as we'd like." Teresa pulled her in for a hug. "Or they don't always turn out the way we think they should."

"Mommy and Daddy might get divorced?" Emily asked.

Julie covered her mouth, hoping neither of them heard her sob. She shifted away from the doorjamb and propped herself against the wall for support.

"I don't know. If I could predict the future, I'd buy a ticket for Saturday's lottery." Teresa brightened. "I can tell you this: things work out for the best. Now close those sweet eyes and try not to worry. Your family is in God's hands."

Julie crept quietly away from Emily's bedroom door and slipped unnoticed into her room. Emily blamed her and maybe she was right.

Julie didn't bother to turn on the light. Instead, she unbuttoned her jacket, kicked off her heels and fell onto the bed. She stared at the ceiling, her hands folded. A prayer streamed from her lips. *Let everything be okay, God. Help me figure this out. Give me strength.*

She heaved a sigh. She hadn't prayed since her mother died. Now seemed like a good time to start.

***

Julie could barely see space between Leanne and Derek as she approached the couple, standing near Leanne's desk.

She grinned. Their romance was clearly on track. It was Derek's first day back at the office since the accident and for someone who had barely escaped death, his laugh was strong.

The boyish grin lingering on his face disappeared when Julie cleared her throat.

"What's so funny?" she asked, scanning the office for a clue.

Derek stepped away from Leanne and swiped his fingers through his brown waves. "We've been digging for information on Burnside."

Leanne blushed. "I read some old newspaper clippings about MaxOut Toys and tried to track down the plumber Ray Bolley like you asked. Derek made some lame joke about designing a working man's version of PlaytimePals." She raised her eyebrows. "The butcher, the baker and the plumber."

"I know the doctor cleared you to come in, but you could take a few days off and get your strength back," Julie said. "Or at least improve your jokes."

Derek snickered. "I never was any good at stand-up." He re-tucked his shirt into his waistband and seemed to stand a little taller. "Don't worry. I feel fine. I couldn't stay at home and think about losing everything. Besides, I spent enough time wondering if my best friend purposely sabotaged my tank."

Julie studied Derek. She'd suspected Gary of playing both sides but surely, he wouldn't have resorted to murdering his lifelong friend. Perhaps their scheme had gotten out of hand. Was Derek supposed to struggle momentarily for air, then have Gary ride to the rescue?

Finding no evidence of equipment tampering, the Coast Guard had cleared the scuba company and the instructor.

120

Still, the timing appeared too coincidental. Burnside's fingerprints were clearly evident on this ploy to cut off a main source of her company's oxygen. But instead of the fear Burnside hoped to instill, the accident left Julie livid. His manipulation only crystallized her resolve.

"I've been on the phone to the East Coast. This guy is a professional dismantler," Leanne said, returning to her computer screen. "Every company he's taken over has been split and sold in pieces for a fraction of the company's worth."

Julie pulled a few pages out from the pile next to Leanne and scanned them. "Burnside is an accomplished crook."

Derek handed Julie the spreadsheet he and Leanne had compiled. "Crook, thief, swindler, thug, hoodlum. You choose the label. But he's smart, ruthless, and very experienced."

Julie caught him glancing at Leanne, no longer wishing to mask his feelings for her.

Leanne cleared her throat. "I spoke to two people yesterday. They both left me with the impression that working with Burnside is tantamount to being run over by an eighteen-wheeler and afterward thanking him for the smooth ride."

Julie reviewed the spreadsheet. "What are our chances of proving any of this?"

"Not great. Burnside covers his tracks well," Derek propped against the desk, slumping. "It's dumb luck we've stumbled upon the few pieces of information we have."

"There's a laundry list of victims," Leanne said. "But none will say anything bad about the man who paid for Symphony Hall."

"Half of San Marcel is named after Burnside." Julie pinched the bridge of her nose. "These people are scared; terrified, in fact. They don't know if they can trust us. So far, our best lead is that plumber in South Carolina. I spoke to him yesterday. His case was settled some ten years ago. Since then his health hasn't been so good."

Julie handed Leanne a printout of his wife's obituary. "Myra died about two years ago. No children, so it's just him now. He's willing to talk, but not on the phone. Most of the others hung up as soon as I mentioned Burnside."

"Are we overreaching?" Leanne said. "Maybe these people don't want us in their personal business. I'm not sure I'd talk to you if you called me out of the blue."

Julie glanced at Derek who moved to a chair. "It's possible we're reading this thing wrong," she remarked, "but I don't think so. This guy specializes in getting big companies what they want. He zeroes in on successful, small independent owners like me. From what I've read, even if they fight back, he wins by drowning them in litigation until they have no other choice but to go out of business or sell cheap."

Julie stood, nervous energy firing through her fingers. She handed a stack of pages to Leanne and paced. "For now, let's focus on our leads—Ray Bolley and MaxOut Toys—instead of wasting time worrying about Gary Carlson."

"Can we convince some of those other business owners to talk?" Derek asked. "Maybe get a better idea of how Burnside works, so we don't go in blindly. Like maybe that plumber."

"We may be more prepared than the others, but I'm not sure that's going to save the day," Leanne said.

Julie put her hands on her hips. "Wrong! Preparation is everything. Leanne, take Derek home. He needs to rest."

"What are you planning?"

Julie shifted into a Wonder Woman stance, hoping the pose would infuse the confidence and capabilities required to win. "To fly to South Carolina to meet with Ray Bolley, of course. Bennett Burnside is going to be sorry he chose FunWorks as his next acquisition-by-intimidation."

Chapter Thirteen

Exhausted after the five-and-a-half-hour flight from Los Angeles to Hilton Head the next morning, Julie waited for a half-hour in the rental car pick-up line before beginning a forty-five-minute drive to meet Ray Bolley in Bluffton.

She adjusted her jacket and made her way toward the corner of the diner. She recognized Ray immediately. Late sixties, lean, and lanky. She guessed there would be no plumber's crack peeking out from the waistband of the pants clothing his spindly body. She could not help but grin.

Ray soaked in the last of the meatloaf gravy with cornbread and looked up from his plate.

"Hey, hello there," he greeted her moments later. "Julie?"

"Yes. Glad to meet you, Mr. Bolley." She extended her hand, but Ray waved away the formality and motioned for her to sit.

"Call me Ray."

She scooted into the booth across from him.

"Look at you in a three-piece suit with your leather notebook thingy. You should try to blend in with the locals." He let out a snort.

"I'm glad you waited," she said, ignoring his comment. "It took me longer to drive here than I expected."

"I would have stayed a bit." He smiled. "What do you have on your mind that would cause you to fly across the country to watch me eat meatloaf?"

"Well, Mr. Bolley—"

"Ray. Mr. Bolley's my grandpap."

"As I said on the phone, Ray, I'm trying to find out about Bennett Burnside. And your name keeps popping up."

He ran a hand over his stubble-covered chin. "I'll bet."

"I'm hoping you can help me."

"Help you?" Ray pushed his plate away. "How?"

"I see you got a friend," the waitress said, approaching their booth. "Here for dinner?"

Julie looked at Ray.

"You've been traveling most of the day. Go ahead and get a bite," Ray said. "I'll leave when I'm ready."

Julie quickly ordered a salad and an iced tea.

"Just call me if you need anything else. I'm Mabel," she said before sashaying away.

Julie leaned closer to Ray. "Why wouldn't you tell me on the phone how things ended with you and Burnside," she asked in a hushed tone.

"Let's say they ended the way he planned," Ray said.

"Why did you leave San Marcel?"

"My wife wanted to move back home, close to her family. She grew up near here. In Walterboro. When I retired ten years ago, we moved."

"You're retired?"

"Well, semi. I do a little work for some folks in town."

Julie wondered why Ray was being elusive. "Is that the only reason you left San Marcel?"

"This is a beautiful place. With those high bluffs that face the May River, we don't have a mosquito problem. It's home now."

"For you and your wife?" Julie asked, knowing the answer.

Ray didn't reply until after Mabel plopped Julie's salad down several minutes later.

"Myra died a couple years back. Now it's just me." He tossed his paper napkin onto the table.

"I'm sorry for your loss," Julie said, a sadness overtaking her. "Myra must have been a wonderful woman."

"She was." Ray paused, lost in thought before clearing his throat. "You didn't spend money on a plane ticket to talk about me."

"True enough." Julie offered a contrite smile. "I mentioned on the phone that I manufacture a line of software for children's toys, paper dolls in particular." Julie set two of the dolls on the table. "They're called PlaytimePals."

"So far this sounds about as opposite from plumbing as can be." Bolley gulped his coffee.

"You might think so, but we have one area of common ground." Julie set her fork down. "I know Burnside swindled you out of your water-saving invention."

"That he did," Ray grunted. "Thought I'd heard the last of that sorry excuse for a human being until you called. Sounds like he's back to his old tricks again."

"So, you know why I'm here."

Ray emptied his mug and set it on the table. "Guessing you're his newest victim."

"He's after my company." The words caught in her dry throat. "Burnside is suing me for patent infringement. And I'm hoping you might know some information that will help me combat his allegations."

Ray waved his arm at Mabel for a refill and stretched his long legs, apparently no longer in a hurry to get home. "Don't know how much this ol' hound dog can help, but yes, missy. I'll tell you what I know."

Julie reached for her pen, barely able to contain her relief. *Finally, someone would tell her about Burnside.* Her heart pounded against her chest as though looking for an escape. "Do you mind if I take notes?"

"Nah, go ahead. He came after my invention pretty hard," Ray continued. "At the time, I didn't realize the value of my pump, but Burnside sure did. He knew water rates were about to go up by ten percent because of an increase in the costs from the regional irrigation district. He must have had an in with the water board to find that out so early. The final straw came when Myra's oncologist claimed he no longer accepted our health insurance. Three days later, a newspaper article announced a large endowment to the cancer center from the Burnside Foundation."

A gray mist clouded Ray's eyes. "I sold the company to Burnside. The following week, a nurse called to schedule Myra's treatment, tripping all over herself with apologies. Some sorta mix-up with the billing department, she claimed. But we both knew the truth." Ray scratched his head. "Now, folks all over the country—heck, the world—use my pump."

Julie placed her hand on Ray's and they sat in silence.

"But look, that's in the past." Ray pulled his hand away and gulped his coffee, wiping the back of his hand across his mouth after he finished. "I have a good life here. Me and Myra lived happily. That wouldn't have happened if I was involved in selling a dang water pump."

"My entire life is PlaytimePals," Julie said, knowing those words were truer than ever. "The business supports my family. I'm glad things worked out for you, but I can't lose my invention. And definitely not to a crook."

"They're awful cute, your little dolls." Ray lifted one and moved the shape in a dancing motion. "I can see why you don't want to turn them over to someone like him."

"If you could do things over again, what would you do differently?"

Ray displayed a toothy grin. "Do different? Well, I don't think I'd do anything different. With Myra sick, and well..." He pulled in a deep breath. "No, no. Things worked out like they were supposed to."

"There must be something that still sticks in your craw. Something you regret."

"Well, before we moved to South Carolina, Myra did want me to talk to a lawyer. She found a good one near San Marcel. I just got to him too late."

"Too late?"

"Yeah, I signed all the papers. Burnside drew everything up all legal and proper. Handed me a check, slapped my back and sent me on my way. By then I couldn't see a reason to pay a lawyer."

"Do you think I should contact him?"

"Couldn't hurt."

***

Trevor gazed around the entryway of the home he shared with his family for nearly a decade. A silk plant stood in place of the tray where he once dropped his keys when he got home. One cord, instead of two, dangled from the outlet to recharge a cell phone. The Nikes he kept in a basket by the front door were missing, too.

Teresa handed a large paper sack to Trevor. "Nicole's backpack is by the door. Here are Emily's five things that begin with Q. She needs them for school tomorrow."

"What did you come up with?" he asked, pulling a rubber duck and a sack of instant oatmeal from the bag.

"A quarter, her baby quilt, Quaker oatmeal and a quill," Teresa said. "It's really a feather."

"And the duck says quack?" Trevor asked.

"You got it."

Trevor laughed, hiding the hurt of Teresa now being the one to help find stuff for the Letter of the Week. That used to be his job. Just another casualty of living away from home.

"Let's go, guys," he shouted. Nicole and Emily trotted down the steps. "Where's Jason?"

"In the kitchen with Zeke."

"Zeke's here?" Trevor asked, bolting toward the kitchen.

His childhood pal glanced up from the cards through bloodshot eyes. "Hey, guys." He jutted his chin in greeting. Trevor huffed out a breath, combating the lingering stink of cigarette smoke reeking from Zeke's clothes. "We gotta go, buddy."

"I'm all packed," Jason said. "He's teaching me how to play Texas Hold'em,"

"And he's pretty good, too," Zeke volunteered.

I don't want him to be good at gambling. Look how far that's taken you. "Terrific."

"Thanks, Zeke." Jason gathered his cards into a pile. "See you later."

"Yeah, see you later." Trevor herded Jason out the door.

"We'll practice again next week," Zeke hollered after them.

Like hell you will, Trevor thought.

"Tell Julie I'll see her at Jason's game tomorrow," Trevor said.

"Mom might miss my game. She flew someplace."

"South Carolina," Teresa added. "Something about the lawsuit. Can you bring the kids home after the game, or do you want me to pick them up?"

"I'll bring them, no problem. Uh, did Derek go, too?"

"I don't believe so."

Trevor released a breath. "When is Julie due back?"

"Late tomorrow, I think. Said she'd call if her plans change."

Why hadn't she told him?

"Okay. See you tomorrow, Teresa."

"Pizza or tacos for dinner?" Trevor asked as they walked toward the car, wondering if Julie felt the way he did about Zeke hanging around.

How could he tell Teresa her son was not welcome at the house, especially when he didn't live there anymore?

***

The next day Trevor banged his pencil against his desk to the downbeat of "Whole Lotta Love," mouthing the lyrics blasting through his earphones.

He placed his Led Zeppelin playlist on repeat as soon as he reached the office, a temporary shield against his crumbling life. The music infused strength and energy and helped clear his mind.

Julie purposely hadn't told him she flew to South Carolina. His wife had cleared him out of her life in big and small ways. *I'm watching my marriage evaporate and there's no one to blame but me.*

"Ready?" Bob Toomes asked, tapping his foot impatiently.

Trevor pulled out one earbud. "What?"

"You remember. Rickman and Floyd? The big shareholders' meeting Tuesday? Our presentations?"

Trevor turned off his music and squinted at his coworker. "That's today?"

"Yeah. In five minutes."

"What more can we do?" Trevor snapped. "We've worked overtime to finish the annual meeting presentation early. How many times does Rickman want us to run through the slides?"

"Beats me. I think we have to put up a good front. If he gets fired, they'll reorganize and who knows where we'll be working."

"I'm not dusting off my resume, at least not yet," Trevor said, his mind still fully engaged with thoughts of Julie. The memory of their impromptu family dinner a few nights ago kept his worries about joining Bob in the unemployment line at bay.

He couldn't shake her stunning image, just like the first time her warm azure eyes drew him in when they met at the San Marcel State college bookstore. In spite of new worry lines puckering around her lips, Julie possessed the same radiant, inquisitive face.

For a moment, he had thought she wanted him back. Then she started talking about Derek and his accident.

"Are you going to the planning meeting or not?"

"Yeah, yeah. I'm ready. Let me get my notes." Trevor slid the sales report to the corner of his desk, tucked his portfolio under his arm and followed Bob.

At 2:15, Bruce Floyd finally offered a break.

"He's so sure he's going to take over, he's measuring the windows in the CEO's office for new drapes," Bob remarked as he and Trevor approached the vending machine. "And

Rickman is so scared about losing his job that he thinks any idea is a good one."

Trevor fed money into the slot and retrieved a soda. "Yeah, Rickman's running scared and Floyd is using his insecurity against him. There seems to be a lot of management-by-threats and scare tactics recently." He fished in his pocket for more coins and dropped them in. "That's what Julie's up against with her company."

"Really?"

"Julie owns a product they want, and she won't sell it, so they're trying to drive her out of business. All legal and what appears to be proper, with attorneys, lawsuits, patent infringement claims."

"That sounds serious. What's she going to do?" Bob asked.

"She's trying to fight, but I don't think it's going well." The gravity of Julie's situation came into focus. The thought belatedly occurred to him that perhaps he should have listened more at dinner instead of turning off as soon as she mentioned Derek.

"Things better with you two?"

"We had dinner a few nights ago," Trevor flattened his tone, removing any sign of promise from his voice.

"That sounds encouraging."

"I thought maybe we could work things out." Trevor glanced at Bob. "The thing is, I never took Julie's business seriously. Spent most of my time jealous of her success and the attention she lavished on FunWorks and not on me."

"Your wife is successful."

"Yes, and I should be happy about that. Instead, I escaped by playing in the band or inventing profitable ways to sell cheese and cracker snack-packs. Then being mad at her for working late."

"That's tough, man. Especially with all the craziness going on around here, you might want to pack your salesman's bag of tricks and try them out in the toy world." He chuckled. "Take me along, too."

"If Julie still owns a part of the toy world."

Bob peeled the cellophane off his sandwich and took a bite.

"I don't know all the details," Trevor said. "Every time Julie talks about the lawsuit, she mentions her marketing guy, and I stop listening."

"How come?"

"Damn jerk." The metal cafeteria chair screeched against the tile floor as Trevor pushed away. The thought of Derek made his insides boil with a mixture of jealousy, anger, and betrayal. "I caught him at my house a few weeks ago after Jason's basketball game. Said he brought Julie some urgent paperwork."

"He's probably just protecting his interests."

"They were holding hands."

Trevor's mind tumbled to the first time he heard Derek's name. He had just clicked on the nightly news when Julie took the remote and handed him a sheaf of papers.

"I want to talk to you about starting a business," she had said, her voice electric with excitement.

He paged through the detailed business plan. "You've put some effort into this." Everything was there—prototype designs, customer demographics, test market segmentation, and distribution channels. "I don't see how we can afford this."

"I'll get a loan. A woman is considered a minority to the Small Business Administration." Julie sounded desperate.

"I love you babe, but I just don't think so."

Disappointment momentarily rippled across her face. When she spoke again, all signs of hurt had washed away. "It's a good idea, and I'm following through, no matter what happens."

Weeks later Julie slid a document from the Small Business Administration across the kitchen table. "This will get us started. Derek has already quit his job."

"Who's Derek?"

"Derek Gable. Remember, I told you about him. He believes in my idea."

"Man, you're scowling," Bob's words snapped Trevor into the present. "That's an angry look."

"What?"

"Your face says you wanna beat somebody up."

I do. Derek Gable.

"As a friend, I've got to tell you, lately you've been acting like you're on another planet. Like right now. Your body's here, but your head and your heart are with Julie," Bob said. "Start listening to your wife. Sounds like she really needs you."

Trevor tossed his half-eaten sandwich on the table. "You're probably right, but I've dug this hole so deep, I don't know how to get out." He rubbed his face with both hands as a fiery anger in his belly spread.

Bob lightly punched him on the shoulder. "Put down the friggin' shovel and get yourself a ladder, dude. Climb out of the hole. Try an apology and some flowers."

"Too late. She's got another guy."

"She tell you that?"

"Not exactly."

"It's time you stop guessing and find out where you stand. Get off your butt, buy dozens of roses, crawl on your knees and beg her to take you back."

Trevor didn't answer. He'd already played his hand, forcing Julie to choose between him and her career, and lost. He successfully pushed the woman he loved away, and he couldn't see a path back.

***

Julie stowed her carry-on in the overhead bin and dropped into the aisle seat, mulling over the meeting with Ray Bolley. His candor, outrage, and cautionary advice had shifted her into panic mode.

She quickly dialed Derek, forgetting the time difference. A groggy voice answered as she heard Leanne's sleepy voice in the background asking who was calling.

"Oh gosh, I woke you. I'm so sorry." Julie said, slightly embarrassed to learn her suspicions about their relationship were true.

"That's okay." Derek stifled a yawn. "What did you find out?"

"It's worse than I thought. Burnside practically put Bolley's wife in an early grave. He had to choose between her doctor bills and his water pump. Obviously not much of a choice."

"That's crazy," Derek began. "Maybe we need to—"

"Oops. I gotta go, they're closing the cabin door and the flight attendant signaled to me to turn my phone off. We'll talk more when I get to the office." She powered off her phone.

Burnside and his underlings were the evil behind everything bad happening, including the attempt on Derek's life. Julie shuddered at the stark truth. Ray's experience confirmed the depth of Burnside's duplicity. Once he locked onto something, he never gave up, Ray had warned her. Julie could count on more misery, increasing in severity until Burnside achieved his goal.

She chomped her gum, hoping her ears would pop. Once the plane reached its cruising altitude, Julie pulled her portfolio from her briefcase, released the tray table and set the notepad in front of her.

First things first. As soon as she got off the plane, she'd arrange for an appointment with Vincent Williams, the attorney Ray recommended.

Step two: Figure out who was Burnside's mole. Maybe Gary Carlson? Julie didn't think so, but perhaps Gary would lead her to the Judas in her midst.

Burnside followed a pattern, going point-by-point, plotting his intended outcome. Back-door deals, palms greased, and a traitor willing to be bought off. The ingredients to Burnside's success. Forcing her to scurry like a mouse in a maze, he closed off every pathway, systematically pushing Julie to his desired end.

Julie couldn't waste a moment. Her family's livelihood—and maybe their safety—depended on her decisions. She must uncover FunWorks' traitor.

Chapter Fourteen

The next morning, Julie snuck out of the house before dawn, heading for the office, her children still asleep. She rarely broke their morning ritual of eating breakfast together before sending her brood off to school. No matter how crazy the day became, she treasured those few moments in the morning.

Today, though, her world spun out of control, as though ominous clouds hung overhead, and she couldn't run fast enough to escape them. Today Teresa could cover for her.

On the drive, Julie contemplated the ad copy and the media buy proposed for the Christmas season. Kelly Samms, the art director, needed approval before fast-tracking the holiday marketing campaign. Julie liked the new slogan, *A Magic Time—PlaytimePals*. The lively vibrant palette of colors Kelly incorporated into the plan popped off the page. Still, Julie's mind kept drifting to the lawsuit and yesterday's conversation with Ray Bolley.

Her meeting with Vincent Williams, still a day away, left her anxious about what he would say. If he didn't have a solution that would save her company, Kelly's designs would be meaningless.

She grabbed the art boards from the front seat and headed to her office.

"What do you mean the deal's off?" She heard the words as she passed Derek's office. "We just signed contracts last week. Yes, I know, but… That's a breach. We'll sue."

Julie stopped in the doorway.

"Look, Gus," Derek yelled into the phone, "we've worked with you guys for five years. You can't do this to us. But… Okay. You'll be hearing from our lawyers." He cursed and slammed the receiver into the cradle.

"Another one?" Julie's stomach tightened.

Derek's frown deepened as he waved message slips at Julie. "Yeah. That's the fifth canceled order this week. Leanne left notes on the other four. I haven't called them back yet. I don't want to hear their lame excuses. Gus, for Christ sake. He carried our line before anyone else in Ohio," he lamented, scattering the paper slips across his desk.

Julie set her purse and the portfolio on the floor and sat across from Derek. "Why are they canceling?"

"His purchasing agent wasn't *authorized* to order our merchandise."

Julie winced at his sarcasm.

"Gus claims he fired her and if we want to come after him, we can have at it."

"I'm guessing that a purchasing agreement signed by an ex-employee won't hold up well in court," Julie said.

Derek pounded his desk. "Burnside's got some balls!"

She gathered the message slips. "These are small orders from independent stores. Separately they don't hurt us. Altogether, they're maybe six percent of our business."

"Six percent is a lot. Burnside is sending a message." Derek rubbed his eyes and then stared into space.

"The way Ray Bolley claimed he would," Julie recalled before briefly outlining her meeting with the man.

"Damn Gary."

"Stop blaming Gary. Game Masters, not your friend, put a target on us. In fact, he may have helped us. Because of him, the red flags came out sooner. And that might be Burnside's undoing. In the meantime, we need to keep operating as usual." She picked up her portfolio and pulled out an art board. "Here are Kelly's drawings for the Christmas campaign. Let me know what you think by noon."

A light knock sounded at the door. "Excuse me," Leanne said. "Gary's in the lobby. He knows you don't want to talk to him, but he claims to have some information. He says it's important."

"Tell Mr. Carlson thanks, but no thanks."

"Wait." Julie turned to Derek. "Let's hear what he has to say."

Derek glared. "Are you kidding? He sold us out."

"Maybe he has a guilty conscience. You guys are old college pals and all."

"If Gary's coming clean, he's figured out another angle he can profit from."

Julie glanced at Leanne still standing in the doorway. "We need to know what's going on. We can't keep guessing. If Gary has information—good or bad—we should know. Wait about twenty minutes, Leanne, then show Gary to the conference room. Buzz us once he's in there."

***

As soon as Julie and Derek walked through the conference room doors, Gary rushed to where they stood. "They're taking me off your account," he said "They haven't told me yet, but I know they are. They'll leave me alone for a day or two until they can transition a new attorney to represent you."

Gary sported a wrinkled shirt, sleeves rolled to his elbows, no tie. The bags under his eyes made Julie wonder if he went without sleep. For a second, she felt a twinge of sympathy. Clearly, he paddled in water way over his head, but she couldn't let Gary's failings draw her company into the abyss.

"Did you tell them we're hiring another attorney?" she asked, noting Gary's uneven breathing.

"Yeah. That's what got this thing going. Look, the reason I'm here is to take one more shot at brokering this deal. If they move Fulton Rush in, there's no telling what will happen."

"We're firing you, Gary. That means we're firing your firm." Julie took her seat alongside Derek. "I don't care who they assign to my account. There is no account."

"Burnside isn't a regular guy," Gary said, still standing, desperation weighing on every word.

Derek barked a laugh. "No kidding. You just figured that out?"

"Derek. Julie, listen—"

"Not to you, we won't. We've done your job, Gary. We researched Burnside. We know we're in for a fight."

"That's what I'm trying to tell you. Stop fighting. Stop researching. Stop making waves. You can't win. Sell FunWorks while there's something left to sell."

Julie stepped back, shocked at the truth in Gary's words. Now she and Derek were the ones out of their league.

They would never beat Burnside at a game he invented. Chalk this one up to experience and move on. Derek certainly couldn't withstand another attempt on his life. Julie wouldn't risk their futures; his with Leanne, and hers, even though less certain, with Trevor. No matter; her children needed her, and she needed them even more.

Julie rubbed her hands together, eyeing Gary now hunched against the wall. "That might be the smart thing to do, but I won't sell. Not to him. Not to anyone."

"You heard the lady." Derek walked to the door and made a sweeping motion with his arm. "You can leave now."

"You've got to believe me. You are in danger."

Julie joined Derek near the doorway and anchored her hands on her hips. "More danger than having Derek's air tank malfunction sixty feet under water?"

"That wasn't me. I swear. I saved Derek's life. If I hadn't been there…"

"What?" Derek asked, closing the space between them. "What would have happened?"

"I don't know." Gary yanked at his shirt as though the collar closed off his own air supply.

Derek's face reddened. "Did you know that guy was near our tanks before we took our dive?"

"I never saw him before that day."

"Did Burnside send him?" Julie asked.

Derek continued peppering Gary with questions. "How did they know where we'd be? Well?" He waited for an answer.

None came.

Julie watched Gary slowly shuffle out. A deep uneasiness planted itself inside her core.

First me. Then Derek. Would Trevor or Leanne be next? Who else's life would Burnside put in jeopardy?

Chapter Fifteen

Julie entered a quiet house and headed to the kitchen. An early evening spray of sunlight dusted the room, heralding daylight savings time, still weeks away.

Teresa, standing at the sink, turned to busy herself washing dishes. Nicole and Emily sat at opposite ends of the kitchen table. Nicole gnawed the end of a pencil, staring past the math book propped open. Emily's backpack, discarded on the floor near her feet, untouched.

Julie dropped her purse and briefcase on the counter. She smiled, knowing the effect rivaled any bright red grin painted on a circus clown. Now standing in the center ring, her troupe appeared to be deserting. "Hey, guys, what's going on?"

"Your dinner's in the oven, girlie," Teresa said.

"Oh, thanks but I had a late lunch. I'm not the least bit hungry." Julie held out her arms. "Anyone got a hug for a weary mom?"

Emily scooted away. Julie's heart dipped a little.

Nicole accepted Julie's embrace but didn't return her squeeze. "I've got to finish this worksheet on fractions, Mom." She pulled away. "Why are you so late? Have to work with Derek again?"

Julie stepped back, an intense sickness sweeping through her. "Wow, why the inquisition, Nic? I thought we worked through all this a week ago when we went out to dinner with your dad."

When neither daughter responded, Julie continued. "Don't you think I'd rather be here with you than at the office?"

"No, I don't." Nicole slammed her book closed and put her head down.

Except for the sound of her daughter's sniffles, a thick silence hung in the air. Teresa motioned Julie to the other side of the sink.

"It's been a hard day," Teresa whispered. "All this crazy stuff with their dad is taking a toll."

Julie crossed her arms and stared at her daughters, who were straining to hear. After spending every waking moment working to keep her family together and a roof over their heads, her children still blamed her for their dad leaving, for the family falling apart. The fear and anger stenciled on their faces couldn't match the volcano gathering strength inside Julie's stomach, on the verge of erupting.

"You think I'm the one who needs to get her act together?" The girls looked away. "Well answer me, damn it, do you?" Her voice was now bellowing through the kitchen.

"I…I…" Nicole said.

Julie had taken all the abuse she could handle, from bankers, manufacturers, clients. From Trevor, from Derek, from Bennett Burnside. This final mutiny by her daughters quickly put her over the top, stripping her of the last strand of patience.

"You what?" Julie stormed to where Nicole sat, yanked her textbook and flung it across the room. Both girls and Teresa jumped at the thud of the book bouncing off the refrigerator, finally landing somewhere near the dog's water bowl.

"You ungrateful little…" Julie stopped before cruel words slipped out. "You have no clue about what I'm going through. How hard I work to keep food on the table and clothes on your back."

"Julie, calm down," Teresa said.

"Seriously, you think I need to calm down?" Julie took a deep breath and turned back to her daughters. "I didn't ask to be sued. I'm not the one who left. I'm here, day in and day out. I'm the one you can count on, not your father." She put her hand up to her mouth, regretting the words as soon as they spilled out. "You know I didn't mean that. Your dad loves you very much."

"He loves you very much, too," Emily said.

"Not anymore." She hurried to wipe a tear wetting her cheek. "I'd crawl back if he'd have me, but he's found someone…" The words caught in her throat.

"Daddy's not seeing anybody else." Nicole stood, hands on her hips. "You're the one with the boyfriend. And we hate Derek. He's a twerp."

"Derek? What does he have to do with this?"

"Isn't he your boyfriend?" Emily asked. "Don't you love Derek now?"

Julie blinked away more tears and took in a gulp of air. "Whoa, hold on a minute. Is that why you two look like someone just canceled Christmas?"

Emily nodded.

"Oh, baby, come here." She cradled her youngest daughter's face in her palms.

"Well, is he?" Emily asked.

"I'm not in love with Derek. We work together. That's all. Girls, I love your dad. I always have, and I always will. Whatever gave you the idea I liked Derek?"

She motioned for Nicole to join them, but she remained planted where she stood, staring at the floor. Finally, she said, "Jason saw you holding hands."

"And that made you think I'm in love with Derek?"

"That's what Dad thinks, too," Emily added.

"We all do," Nicole said.

The words pummeled Julie like acid-filled paintballs, each one hitting its target and destroying a piece of her.

"Jason said Teresa's our real mom now. All you care about is Derek and your stupid paper dolls." Emily cried.

"Jason's really mad, but he won't talk to you about it," added Nicole.

"Derek comforted me because of what's going on with your dad and me. How could you even think...?" She waited for Teresa to return her gaze. "Even you, Teresa? This is madness. Where is Jason? I want to straighten this out."

"He's not here," Nicole said. "He went to Dad's."

Julie reached for the kitchen counter to steady herself.

Teresa stepped closer to Julie. "I need to talk to you about that after you settle in and get some food in your stomach. He packed his duffel bag after school and moved to Trevor's apartment."

"He what?" Her voice returned to the decibel level of moments ago. "Did Trevor have anything to do with this?"

"Trevor didn't know until I called him." Teresa pulled out a chair and guided Julie to sit. "We both thought we should let Jason's decision play out."

Julie's voice rose uncontrollably. "You and Trevor discussed what's best for my son? No one thought I should be included?"

"You didn't see the look on his face. He needed to cool off a little."

"You should have called." Julie waited for a response. None came. "But you didn't because you thought he was right."

Nicole hugged her mother. "This is just a big misunderstanding."

"Which I will fix right now. Starting with Jason getting his butt back home or he'll be grounded so long, he'll have time to grow a beard."

Julie jumped in the car and sped away. Within minutes she shifted the Volvo into park and turned off the ignition.

The glimmer of a street lamp illuminated the front seat about as thin as her patience. She inhaled deeply and released the breath, gazing up at Trevor's apartment.

Her heart, throbbing like a teenager going on her first date with the prom king, reminded her of how her chest pounded the night she saw Trevor's band. Naïvely, she appeared dressed to the nines, never imagining the real reason behind Trevor's invitation.

Her heart had split open watching him move in on a frizzy blonde barely old enough to pass the ID check. *I'm twice as old as her bust size.*

She wiped tears away with the back of her hand, then reached for her purse. That didn't matter now.

Nothing mattered except bringing Jason home.

***

Trevor peered out of the apartment window and watched Julie park. An eternity passed waiting for her since Teresa's call.

"Listen, Trevor. You got this whole Derek thing wrong, wrong, wrong," Teresa said minutes before. "I'll let Julie tell you herself, but I know for a fact that she's not interested in that wimp. Not when she's married to a real man."

Trevor smiled. For the first time in months, he felt hopeful. Waiting for Julie to come through the door, he paced back and forth like a schoolboy waiting to sneak a peek at his high-school crush.

What's taking so long?

Jason huddled on the second-hand couch, channel-surfing between a baseball game and MTV. "I heard you talking to Teresa about Mom. I'm not going back home. I don't want to be there watching her and that guy."

Teresa had better be right. Trevor didn't dare discuss Derek with his son. He walked to the kitchen and grabbed a bottle of water.

"Jason, this isn't about you. It's about your mom and me," he hollered through the doorway, not wanting his son to see the hurt on his face. "I want you back home, with your

144

sisters, taking care of things until Mom and I straighten our stuff out."

"Whatever," Jason snapped in that annoying teenage tone. "It's just not right. Mom's not right. This FunWorks thing has messed everything up, and—"

Julie knocked. "Your mother's here," he said, attempting a casual tone. "Open the door."

Jason turned back to the television. "You open it. I don't want to talk to her."

***

Julie stood on the doorstep for what seemed like an eternity, waiting for her legs to stop shaking. *Trevor better not fight me on this. We must keep the kids living under one roof.*

She finally heard the knob turn and looked up to see her husband dressed in a light blue T-shirt tucked into well-fitting jeans. His smile deepened the crow's-feet around his eyes. Gray dotted his five-o'clock shadow blending with the gray hair feathered around his ears. She thought his eyes sparkled when he saw her.

"Hi, Jules." He raised his eyebrows and gestured for her to come in.

She scooted past him. "I'm rounding up a missing child. You don't happen to have one handy, do you?" Julie glanced around the apartment. The space was clean and sparsely furnished. She could see where the kitchen began, but she didn't detect a table and chairs. Jason curled on the couch in a familiar position: remote in one hand, soda can in the other.

"Jason."

He flipped through the channels. "Hi, Mom."

Julie wanted to yell at him and hug him at the same time. Instead, she decided to talk him through this. "What are you watching?"

"Nothing."

Julie studied her son, amazed at how much he resembled his father. He had Trevor's build, mannerisms, and an unruly clump of hair that constantly fell into his eyes. When he finally glanced her way, her heart sank at the determination in his eyes.

"I don't want to hear it, Mom. I know what's going on and I don't want to be at the house when your *friend* comes over."

Julie fought the overwhelming impulse to grab him by the hair and drag him home. *Don't make this any worse.* She bent toward him, her hands curled into fists. "Jason, you have to understand, there is nothing going on between me and Derek. Look, I'm sorry you got the wrong impression. I guess I've given everyone the wrong idea."

She glanced toward Trevor positioned in the archway, his body halfway in the kitchen. *Preparing for a quick exit?*

Jason scooted toward the end of the couch. "I'm supposed to believe you, just because you say so? I saw you. Right there in our house."

"You saw wrong." Julie grabbed Jason by the shoulder. "I know things haven't been easy lately, but the one thing that will never change—can never change—is how much I love you and your sisters. I am always here for you, no matter what."

"So that's why you miss my games to play kissy-face with Derek?"

"That's not true. I missed one game. I've been so absorbed with these damn lawsuits…" Julie sucked in an extra-large amount of air.

Jason pulled farther away. "Do what you've got to do." He clicked the remote.

"Listen carefully because I'm only going to say this once. I'm not in love with Derek. We don't think of each other that way. We never have. He's my employee. That's the only relationship I'm interested in having with him. In fact, he's dating Leanne, my assistant."

"So why was your employee at our house? Holding your hand, Mom?" Jason demanded, anger and fear dancing in his eyes.

"Derek and I are trying to figure out how to save the company. I hadn't slept all night, worried about losing everything." Her voice caught in her throat as she stole a glance at Trevor.

"Yeah. Right. Those paper dolls put food on the table."

Julie froze at the vitriol dripping from Jason's words. He had never missed a meal or watched his mother struggle to pay the electric bill. He had never known poverty. How could he possibly understand her fears or her need to be independent?

"Jason, " Trevor commanded. "Show your mother some respect. She's worked hard. You can't know all she's going through."

Julie steadied herself, surprised at Trevor's validation. "Our family is all that matters to me. Yes, I spent a lot of hours at FunWorks. That business pays the bills. And your dad and I are having a tough time. But Derek's not the cause."

She wanted to look at Trevor but kept her gaze on Jason. "Daddy and I will figure out our problems. We'll do what's best for our family, because no matter what, son, we *are* a family." She manufactured a smile, but he still wouldn't meet her eyes.

Julie stood. "I want you to come home. It's better if you and your sisters are together." Julie motioned for Trevor's agreement.

"Mom's right, buddy. You need to be home with the girls right now." Trevor shot Julie a look. "We talked about that before you got here."

At last, Jason unfolded slowly and stood to his full height.

"Be the man of the house." Trevor hugged him.

"Yeah, sure." Jason grabbed his duffel bag. Not waiting for his mother, he trudged out the door.

Julie swung around to face Trevor. "I can't believe you let him move in."

"I didn't let him. He's a teenager and a guy. He had to have his say."

Julie rubbed her forehead. "So, this little act was for my benefit? Did you believe that I was sleeping with Derek, too?"

"I didn't know what to believe," Trevor said as though challenging Julie to deny his suspicions.

"Well, I don't sleep around." Julie strode out, slamming the door behind, her heart pounding so hard, she gasped for air.

She wasn't the cheater in this family, but that truth didn't relieve her pain or help her regain Jason's trust. With her marriage crumbling, how could she defend the assault?

She took another big breath before entering the car. Jason, now engaged on his cell phone, didn't acknowledge her. They drove in silence, Julie mentally rehearsing what she would say to him once they reached home.

Julie opened the front door and Jason trudged past her. Standing awkwardly in the entryway were Nicole, Emily, and Teresa, an ad hoc welcome wagon, waiting to greet him.

"I let the girls stay up," Teresa admitted. "They wanted to see their brother."

"Okay, everybody." Julie spread her arms, hurrying everyone along. "We all have to be someplace early tomorrow morning. Give your brother a hug, then go brush your teeth and get ready for bed."

After the girls left, Julie steered Jason to the couch. "Sit."

He reluctantly plopped down as though girding for his punishment.

Julie slipped in alongside him. "You and I will talk more after school tomorrow, but I hope you learned tonight what happens when you jump to conclusions."

"Seriously, Mom. Even Teresa thought you and Derek—"

"It's late. We'll talk more tomorrow."

"But me and the girls saw what we saw."

"What you *thought* you saw. Things aren't always as they seem," Julie said, her thoughts skipping back to her night at

Mulvaney's. Perhaps she should follow her own advice. "It's always better to ask questions. Don't guess."

"Okay. Next time I'll ask."

She tipped his chin toward her. "And I'll do my best to give you a straight answer. I'm hoping your dad and I can work things out. I love him very much. I know it's hard for you to understand, but you have to trust us."

Jason nodded yes, as though a springy bobblehead replaced his own. Julie garnered his agreement at the touch of a finger, but Jason held no passion behind his assent.

"But no matter how things turn out, Jason, he's still your dad. And I'm still your M-O-M."

Jason smiled. "I'm sorry but, geez, it really looked like that Derek dude moved in. I like the guy all right, but he's not Dad."

No kidding. Julie kissed the top of Jason's head before he stood to go.

Despite their disagreements, no one could ever replace Trevor. As reliable as the sun rising in the morning, he withstood the test of time.

Why, then, did she allow her fears to overcome her heart? Why had she traded her true love for financial security? If Julie could answer those questions, then maybe her marriage would survive.

Chapter Sixteen

Images of Trevor and that willowy blonde looped through Julie's mind the next day as she shuffled spreadsheets and three-ring binders on her desk. She grimaced, recalling the tender way Trevor had touched that woman's shoulder.

That's the way he used to touch me.

She willed the thought to vanish, secretly taking pride in compartmentalizing her emotions like men did. If her mother could have mastered that skill, her childhood wouldn't have ended in shambles.

Julie's professional success hinged on the ability to seamlessly suppress her deepest fears and paralyzing worries to focus on the work at hand. But Trevor's leaving had knocked the scaffolding out from under her, allowing reality that lurked in the dark corners to come to light.

Derek's voice interrupted her thoughts "You have your notes from your meeting with Ray? They might give Vincent Williams a head start."

He and Leanne sat at a small conference table in Julie's office preparing for their two-thirty appointment with the new attorney.

"Yeah, and copies of the newspaper accounts of the lawsuit," Julie replied, pointing to a file in front of her.

"Should I have sent them by messenger before our meeting?" Leanne asked.

"No, I want to hand them to him personally. There's too much at stake. I'm hoping he'll see some way out of this mess." Julie shifted her eyes to Derek. "But after that nightmare with your buddy, I'm not expecting miracles."

"Was he honest in college?" Leanne asked.

Derek raked his fingers through his short hair. "Are you kidding? The Gary Carlson I knew wouldn't even use other students' notes to study for a test. I hate to say it, but I think he got in over his head. It's going to be tough to trust a new attorney after the one I've known most of my adult life hosed us."

Julie shifted toward Leanne. "How far did you get on the background check on Vincent?"

Leanne opened a thick file filled with notes and newspaper clippings. "I ran him through the State Bar attorney search. His membership record showed no complaints, no disciplinary actions, or anything else that would affect his eligibility to practice law in California."

Leanne flipped through more pages. "He was a Yolo County assistant DA in northern California for a couple of years before starting his own practice, twelve years ago. At first, he specialized in estate planning and probate. I'm still working on why he switched to intellectual property law and patents."

"Anything else?" Julie asked.

Leanne reached for another document. "Married for fifteen years and has two kids, a girl and a boy. The wife's a teacher."

"Did you talk to any of his former clients?" Derek asked.

"His office supplied three references. They all gave him glowing reviews."

"Keep checking records at the courthouse for other cases he's handled," Julie said. "I want to talk to clients who weren't handpicked."

Derek took the last swallow of coffee and shot his paper cup into a nearby trash can. "Maybe we're being too paranoid. Ray recommended this guy. We should let him do his job."

"We're not imagining things. Just this morning I received an email from Butterspring Animation, a formal letter to follow. They're putting our film on hold. They claimed a shortage of studio time."

"They'll come back around," Leanne said.

"Maybe." Julie stood and crossed her arms. How much longer could she cope with the constant anxiety, the rocks of uncertainty pressing heavy against her gut? She longed for the days when a supply chain boondoggle or a product recall constituted the major causes of her grief. She had counted on FunWorks' percentage of the movie's box office, and the spike in demand for PlaytimePals to pay the bank and fund future development.

No doubt Burnside's tentacles snaked their way to a film producer, causing the delay and possible cancellation. Another closing revenue stream.

"On a happier note, our market share grew by four percent over last year's projections. Can you believe it? With all this legal craziness and buyers canceling holiday orders, kids still want PlaytimePals." Derek laughed. "If this keeps up, demand will exceed our current supply."

Julie raised an eyebrow at Derek's insincere chuckle. She picked up the computer printouts and leafed through them. Everything was trending the way Burnside planned.

Leanne set another report on the corner of Julie's desk. "Here are the quarterly sales figures."

"Without cancellations, holiday sales would have increased our profits by fifteen percent."

Julie nodded. "That's why we're in this situation. Burnside is choking off the supply so that by the time Game Masters owns FunWorks, there will be pent-up demand and they can easily increase the price."

She noticed Derek's bloodshot eyes. His normally clean-shaven face was camouflaged by several days of stubble. He rarely spoke of the diving accident; still, she wondered if the strain surged deeper, affecting his health.

"Hey guys, we've been at the grindstone all morning." Julie reached for her wallet. "Let's break for lunch."

"I'll treat," Derek volunteered.

"How about that new sandwich shop that just opened two blocks away? I hear they have a BLT to die for. You want to join us, Julie?" Leanne asked.

"No, thanks." She pointed to her report-strewn desk. "I want to get a better handle on these numbers. You two go. Bring me back a tuna salad."

Derek and Leanne shared an intimate glance. Julie hurriedly removed a pencil tucked behind her ear, put her head down and made notes. Their love was beginning to flame as hers was burning out.

"Okay boss. Wheat or white?"

"What?"

"The sandwich?"

"On lettuce. They have salads, don't they?" Julie snapped.

"Yeah, I'm sure they do. We'll come back with something good," Leanne promised.

Julie watched her grab Derek by the wrist and guide him out of the room.

"I'm capable of leaving an office," she heard him complain as Leanne pulled the door closed.

Julie ran to the hallway to apologize for snapping but stopped when she heard their voices near the elevator.

"What was that about?" Derek asked.

"Sshhh. She needs some time alone," Leanne whispered. "She's worried about this lawsuit, but her bigger problem is with Trevor. He has a girlfriend."

"She told me, but I think she's mistaken. She's been wrong about a lot of things these days," Derek retorted. "Frankly, I'm having a tough time trusting her judgment."

"She's under a lot of pressure," Leanne scolded.

"It's ironic. If this litigation goes badly, Trevor will have deserted his wife for no reason."

"Oh, there's a reason. And from what I hear, she's about five-foot-eight and has long blonde hair."

Julie crept back unnoticed, her heart pounding and she lowered her head on to the desk. Time for a minor meltdown, tears and all.

***

Julie stabbed at the tuna salad, but her appetite, like everything else, had abandoned her.

She wished Trevor had suggested some solutions to the lawsuit, but she really hadn't given him much of a chance to volunteer an opinion. Still, since they lived in a community property state, FunWorks belonged to him, too. But he didn't seem to be interested in offering any help. He clammed up every time she mentioned FunWorks or Derek.

"This is stupid." She slammed her plastic fork against the desk and reached for her cell phone. "I have to know where I stand and who that woman is."

As Julie dialed Trevor's office, Leanne tapped on the door frame. "Mr. Williams is here."

Julie pushed the end call button.

"He's waiting in the conference room with Derek." Leanne moved toward Julie's desk. "Do you need help carrying these files?"

"No, thanks." Julie placed a hand on top of the pile. "I'll be right in."

As soon as Leanne disappeared, Julie hit redial. When she heard his voice mail greeting, her throat tightened. "Trevor… I've been thinking about things and…I don't want to lose you. If you feel the same, call me as soon as you get this message."

She clicked the screen lock button, stashed the phone in her jacket pocket and grabbed the files. For the first time in weeks, relief instead of despair coursed through her mind as she headed into the meeting.

"The way I see your case," Vincent Williams said minutes later, "Game Masters targeted a small successful business operated by a woman and found out you're represented by a Ryder lawyer. They teamed with them, threw in a few legal scare tactics, and thought you'd cave. Slam. Bam." He brushed his palms together. "Quick and dirty, end of the story."

"Trying to kill me is hardly a simple legal tactic," Derek complained.

"There is no real proof that Game Masters caused your accident. Still, with everything else that's been happening, I'd be hard pressed to believe otherwise." Vincent stared at Julie.

As though caught not paying attention in class, Julie stopped doodling in her day planner and nodded for him to continue. She needed to be fully engaged in what Vincent said; however, thoughts of Trevor seeped into her mind, muddling her thinking. She questioned her goals. What good was her success without the man she loved?

"Almost every acquisition to their toy company 'family of fun'—as Game Masters refers to themselves," he raised his eyebrows, "has been under questionable circumstances. I spoke last week to the former owner of Solar Wheels. He held the patent on a remote-control car powered by the sun. The guy claimed working with Game Masters is like making an expensive dinner: you buy the groceries, cook the food, and set the table. Then they eat the meal. Worse, they expect you to say thank you for the opportunity."

"So how do we fight back?" Julie asked.

He reached for his legal pad and peeled back a few pages. "Since I received your call, I've thought of little else. I stood on the sidelines and watched what happened to Ray. I won't let that happen again. I have a strategy to give us a greater chance of prevailing at the patent hearing. Maybe even put an end to Game Masters' duplicitous business practices for good."

Julie locked eyes with Vincent. "If you put a stop to Bennett Burnside and Game Masters, all the better. Just remember, that's not my primary goal. I'm paying you to protect *my* business."

"I understand."

"We haven't stolen anyone's idea. I created our products. Derek markets them. We've worked our butts off to keep the line fresh. That's why it's popular." Julie took a deep breath and let the air out slowly. "Frankly, I don't understand how we live in a country where anyone with deep pockets can cherry-pick companies and litigate them into selling."

Leanne crossed her arms. "How does that happen? I mean, how can Julie get sued for selling her own product?"

"Sadly, the law isn't always about what's legal or fair. It's about what you can prove." Vincent tossed his yellow legal pad on the table. "Big corporations like Game Masters take advantage of what's intended to be an equitable balance of justice and use the law for their own purposes and ultimate gain."

"What's next?" Julie said.

"The way I see things—"

All eyes turned as the door to the conference room pushed open.

"Ah, sorry to bust in on your meeting." Trevor carefully closed the door behind him. Julie watched as he moved toward her. "Can I speak to you for a minute?"

"We're in the middle of something really important," Derek admonished. "Can it wait?"

Julie recognized the flash in Trevor's eyes. The same furious expression she saw displayed that Saturday morning when he found her in the kitchen with Derek.

"No, Derek." Trevor's clipped tone brought Julie to her feet. He reached for Julie's hand. "This really can't wait."

"Who's this?" Vincent asked no one in particular.

"My husband." Julie quickly introduced the two men. "Excuse us for a minute."

***

"When Rick told me that you were at Mulvaney's that night, I couldn't believe it," Trevor said, standing in the hallway outside the conference room. "Why didn't you let me know you were there?"

"I wanted to surprise you," Julie motioned him to follow her further away from the door.

Trevor's heart pounded.

"I sat in a dark corner, dressed as sexy as I could manage. Even ordered you a drink. I thought you'd see me and sneak back."

"I never got a drink from you."

"Well, I ordered one. A bottle of water."

His eyes widened. "There's always water by the stage, compliments of the house. Why didn't you just come up and say hi?"

She licked her lips. "I wanted to be mysterious and alluring. It had been a long time since you invited me to see you play."

Trevor smiled. "Believe me, if I had seen you looking mysterious and alluring, I would have been all over you. Fact is, I figured you didn't care enough to show. And I felt pretty crappy about that."

"I watched you hang with the band and that girl. I thought you wanted me to see you with another woman."

His chest tightened. "I sat with Russ's sister, hoping you would show up."

Julie leaned against the wall and let out a sigh. "That was *Valerie Wheeler?* The last time I saw her, she weighed about a hundred and sixty pounds and had a pimple problem. Now she looks more like a Miss California contestant."

Trevor tilted forward and gently kissed her lips. "I wanted to spend some time with you, away from the kids." He reached for her hand and Julie's eyes slid to his wedding ring. "People kept asking us to play 'smoke on the Water,' but I wouldn't until you showed up. I even asked Val to keep an eye out for you. She said you never came."

"When did Rick tell you he ran into me?"

"Today. I got your phone message during a late lunch with him and Russ. That's when Rick told me you were leaving as he arrived. He said you acted weird. You barely said hello, even though you hadn't seen him in three years."

Julie bit her lower lip. "I was a little upset."

"I got to thinking about what Teresa said about you and Derek. Then today when Rick told me you were crying that night, everything clicked. I left them at the restaurant and drove here like a maniac."

"I'm so glad you did." She flashed a smile, her eyes dancing with relief and love.

Trevor wrapped his arms around Julie's waist, soaking in the tingle of excitement in her embrace. He pulled her to him for another kiss.

"I've missed you," she said when they finally separated.

"Me, too. I love you."

She reached for him, her touch sending a shudder down his spine. "Everything is my fault. I didn't realize—"

"Shhh. There's plenty of time for that." They had both made mistakes. He was willing to change. He hoped Julie was, too.

***

Julie and Trevor finished the meeting with Vincent Williams, and then drove to a nearby hotel. The next morning, they awoke in a jumble of sheets. Her business suit and his boxers lay crumpled in a pile on the floor.

Their hours of heartfelt confessions, followed by a night of lovemaking, reenergized Julie. She rubbed the base of her neck more out of habit than necessity. The tightness had melted away. Trevor, her antidote to the constant tension residing in her head and her heart. She reached to where her husband lay satisfied and stroked his back.

"Teresa must think we're nuts."

"I'll bet she's relieved." Trevor reached into the nightstand for the room service menu and turned onto his back. "She's been working behind the scenes to get things back to normal."

"Well, she did sound more happy than surprised when I told her I wouldn't be home last night." Julie climbed out of bed and headed to the bathroom. "At first, she sounded ticked off, but when I explained that we were ironing out some misunderstandings, she wanted us to take the entire weekend."

"Sounds good to me," Trevor said.

Julie peeked from the bathroom and smiled at Trevor, now propped on his side, still wrapped in blankets. "She wants to talk about cosigning a loan when we get home."

"I forgot about that. Can we help her now, with everything going on?"

"I'm not sure."

"How much does she need?"

"About ten thousand."

"Wow. I sure hope she's not asking for Zeke."

"She mentioned a plumbing problem, something about a leak at her house," Julie said, not convinced Teresa was telling the truth.

"That doesn't sound likely," Trevor said. "Room service or do you want to go out?"

"Huh?" Julie grunted from the bathroom, glad the hotel provided toothbrushes and miniature shampoos.

"Breakfast. Do you want me to call room service or should we hit the nearest IHOP?"

She leaned against the bathroom door, wiping toothpaste foam from her mouth. "Let's savor this morning before we head home."

"When this mess gets straightened out, we're taking a real second honeymoon. Someplace exotic like Kauai, Bali, or maybe St. Thomas. Let's stay for two weeks. Leave the kids with Teresa. You can trust Derek to handle FunWorks while you're gone, right?"

"The real question is; do *you* trust Derek?"

Trevor moved out of bed and patted her on the butt. "I do now." He leaned against the doorjamb and made a fist with his right hand. "He's lucky I didn't pound him into ground meat."

Julie moved past him to the clothes piled on the floor. "I was just as crazy to think you were interested in some sexy groupie who's half your age."

Trevor grimaced. "Seriously. We're talking about Russ and Rick's baby sister. You've known her since she wore braces."

Julie shook the wrinkles out of yesterday's wool skirt. "Well, she's not wearing braces now."

He reached over and kissed her. "You're the only beauty queen in my life. The only groupie I'm interested in. Do me a favor, though. From now on, sit in front."

"And the next time you think about leaving me—don't." She reached for his hand and squeezed. "Don't ever leave me again."

Trevor dropped his head and took a deep breath. "I didn't know how else to get your attention, baby. You are like a runaway train, always traveling on a new track. I don't want to be the caboose."

She frowned, regretting the part she'd played in their breakup and vowing to make everything up to him.

"From now on I'll be riding in the front cabin next to the world's sexiest conductor." He traced his finger along Julie's lips. "You'd look hot in one of those engineer hats."

Julie glanced at the clock radio on the nightstand. School wouldn't let out for five hours. "We have time to get this locomotive back on track."

Trevor grabbed Julie's waist and pulled her into him. "All aboard!"

Chapter Seventeen

Teresa Desmond took a sip of ice water and winced at the coldness against her teeth.

She wondered if her lunch date with Zeke caused her shudder. Her son expected cash and would be angry once he realized she had none to give. The restaurant, American casual, was nearly full. She hoped having so many people around would make Zeke think twice about creating a scene.

She inhaled sharply when she saw him approaching, wearing the same faded T-shirt and torn jeans he had donned days before. His whiskery face, still unshaven, seemed to blend into his shoulder-length unruly hair matted behind his ears.

Teresa tugged her sweater and pulled her handbag closer, preparing to deliver the bad news.

Zeke spotted his mother and trudged toward her, shoulders slumped. Sliding into the booth, he reached over and pecked her cheek.

"I didn't get the loan." She said the words quickly, as though ripping a bandage from her skin. She glanced up to assess his reaction. This time she couldn't fix things.

His eyes flashed hard and unresponsive.

Zeke reached for a menu. "What happened?" he asked, his voice barely a whisper.

Teresa could feel his anger rising. "The bank said no. There's not enough equity in the house."

"What about Julie and Trevor?"

"I asked. Things aren't going well for them."

Zeke pressed. "Well, ask again."

"I will, but I can't promise anything." Teresa fiddled with the clasp on her purse, clicking it open and closed. The melodic snapping helped calm her nerves to cope with Zeke.

There was no way to tell how her son would take this news. He might storm out after throwing the salt-and-pepper shakers across the restaurant. Or, he could get very quiet, contemplating his next move. Both options terrified Teresa.

"I need the money in the next three days, or—"

"I know." Teresa put her hand up to stop Zeke from continuing. She had listened to this conversation too many times. Too many bad guys threatening to pound her son into a bloody pulp, or some other descriptive beating. She wondered what she'd done to merit such a deadbeat for a son. He was a grown man and he still couldn't take care of himself. The thought of him being hurt by some unknown thugs turned her stomach, but so did the vision of the man her little boy never became.

"They mean to hurt me this time."

"I'll get the money," Teresa said, having no idea how she would keep this promise.

He lowered the menu. "Thanks, Mom."

"I won't bail you out again. Not after this."

He shifted in his seat.

"Do you hear me, son? This is the last time. You need help. Professional help."

"I know, I know. That's what Marilyn said. She's mad because I quit GA. But I won't hang with a bunch of losers who can't control their gambling."

"I spoke with Marilyn yesterday."

"Really." He paused and closed the menu.

Teresa blinked back the tears forming in her eyes. "She's worried and she loves you. When you moved back you promised to get help. It's been three weeks."

"I've got to do this my way. Don't you understand? I'll fix everything. I just need to get these guys off my back first."

Teresa pulled away, alarmed at the wildness in Zeke's eyes.

He grabbed his mother's hands. "Once everything is settled, I can move back home with Marilyn and the girls. You coming through with this money means I have a second chance to make things right for me and my family."

"I know, son." Teresa's voice softened. "But you've got to quit the gambling."

"I already have." He opened the menu again and waved to the waitress.

She knew better.

***

Julie removed the towel covering a mixture inside her orange Pyrex bowl setting on the kitchen counter. She lifted a baseball-sized clump of dough into the air. "Okay, who's going first?"

"Me. Me." Jason cupped his hands together as a target for his mother.

"Nice catch." She laughed as his fingers closed around the orb, oozing dough through his fingers.

For years, nothing preempted this Rafferty ritual. With sauce, cheese and pepperoni as their paint and brushes, Grandma Bridget's family bread recipe was transformed into edible canvases. Competition between siblings grew for bragging rights for the craziest, funniest, most off-beat designs. But for Julie, the laughter and love filling her kitchen became her secret topping.

Then FunWorks took off, changing her priorities. Prebaked pizza shells replaced homemade dough and eventually, pizza night became a distant memory. With Teresa away visiting her sister, Julie and Trevor reinstituted do-it-yourself pizzas, the perfect way to celebrate their reunion.

Pizza pans clattered as Trevor arranged them alongside each other on the table. "I think tonight's shapes should have a theme. How about favorite storybook characters?"

"Are you kidding me?" Jason rolled his eyes. "I don't have a favorite storybook character."

"What are you reading at school?" Julie asked, now standing by the stove.

"*Across Five Aprils.*"

Trevor winked at Julie. "I guess a Civil War soldier pizza doesn't sound too tasty."

Jason stretched his dough into a long rope. "I'll do mine in the shape of a comic book character. Maybe an S for Superman. The storybook thing should work for Nicole, though. She can do Wilbur from *Charlotte's Web.* She's got a lot of experience making pigs."

Nicole punched Jason's arm.

"What's the pig thing?" Emily asked, grabbing her share of the pizza dough.

"A long time ago, he said my pizza looked like a pig snout. And he should know since he's a pig."

"Knock it off, you two." Julie turned to Emily. "What character are you going to do?"

"Horace Hardbuckle, Superhound. He's my favorite."

"You know he's not real, right?" Nicole said. "Dad made him up."

Jason cocked his head and stared at Nicole. "Storybook characters aren't real either, stupid."

Julie stirred a pot of marinara sauce and lifted the wooden spoon to her lips for a taste. "Don't listen to them, Emily. They're as real as your imagination wants them to be. Horace is as important as any Mother Goose story."

Emily smiled, then stuck out her tongue at Nicole.

Nicole turned away. "Whatever."

"Isn't it about time for another installment of Horace's adventures as Superhound?" Julie asked, breathing in the strong garlic scent permeating the room.

"Probably long overdue." Trevor pointed toward Julie's ringing cell phone.

"I hear it." Julie glanced up, her kids now statues in front of their pizzas, their chiding voices trailed to a halt.

Trevor's eyes asked the question, would she let FunWorks interrupt their lives again?

The call had to be from the office, probably something important about the lawsuit, but Julie didn't want this moment to end. She couldn't let anything interfere with this critical rebuilding of her family's trust. Their relationships might not withstand the strain.

She raised the spoon, now coated a saucy red, into the air like the starting flag at a car race. "Whoever it is can wait. On with Build-Your-Own Pizza Night." She returned to stirring the simmering pot. The room seemed once again filled with air and light.

"We bought red onions at the farmers' market. And some precooked chicken, too. Jason, you still want to make a barbecued chicken pizza?"

"Yeah."

"That sounds good," Trevor said. "Is there enough for me, too?"

"You bet." Julie retrieved the chicken chunks from the fridge and handed a scoop to both Jason and Trevor.

"Super Barbecued Chickenman," Jason declared moments later, flying his tray around the kitchen.

Julie ducked out of his way. "Chickenman can be Horace's sidekick, like Batman and Robin, or Shrek and Donkey, except that your characters fight the evil pepperoni cartel."

"Don't forget the anchovies," Trevor added, wrinkling his nose.

"What do you have against anchovies?" Julie asked.

"The aftertaste when I'm kissing you." He winked and dropped a chunk of chicken into his mouth.

She reached for him and they shared a deep kiss. This was the success Julie sought, the security that somehow always eluded her mother. Simple moments shared by a family. Owning a business could never match the safety and joy of being loved by Trevor, of raising their children together.

***

Julie nursed a nearly empty glass of Merlot, legs curled beneath her, listening to the rumble of Trevor's voice from upstairs as he tucked Emily into bed. She closed her eyes and willed her brain to slow down, if only for a minute.

"Need a refill?"

Julie's eyes popped open. Her heart lurched. Trevor stood a few feet away, cradling an open bottle. She recognized the amorous twinkle in his eye and his come-on smile.

She held out a glass, admiring his hands, the same hands that caressed her last night with a tenderness she craved. "Sure, but just half. I have to get up early."

"What's on your mind?" Trevor tossed a throw pillow to the floor and scooted alongside.

"Us. You and me. The future, I guess." She waited for his response but instead, he filled a wineglass and took a taste.

Julie continued. "Seems I'm clocking more hours doing legal work than I am designing toys these days."

"Cheers." He tapped his glass against hers in a mock toast, then took a swallow.

"I wouldn't mind a fifty-fifty split," she continued. "You know, half-time lawyer and half-time toy mogul. But these last couple of days have forced me into full-time legal-eagle status."

Trevor took another swallow. "How's the background check going? Have you arranged another meeting with Williams?"

"Not yet." A sexy smile danced across her lips. "You've been keeping me a bit preoccupied." She took another sip and set the glass on the coffee table.

"What's this?" Trevor pulled her left hand to his lips and kissed her ring finger.

"You know."

"Yes, I recognize it, even in this bad light. But where's the two-carat headlight I bought you for our tenth anniversary?"

"The headlight is safe and sound in my jewelry box. I haven't hocked it if that's what you're worried about."

He laughed and playfully intertwined his fingers in hers. "Why are you wearing the beginner ring?"

"Don't call it that." She held the tiny diamond, barely a fifth of a carat, to the lamplight. "It reminds me of simpler times. This ring will bring me luck. Already has." She held his hand tighter. "You're home and we're alone sharing a bottle of wine at ten o'clock at night."

He kissed the tips of her fingers. "I am your good luck charm, baby."

She nestled her head on his chest.

He tilted her face toward his. "You aren't going to fight this battle without me. Rickman knows I won't be in for a few days. Tell me when and where you're meeting with Williams and I'll be there."

The gnawing tension deep inside in her stomach subsided slightly as she fingered his strong hands. Julie willed his clear-thinking decisiveness to transfer to her brain. Trevor, she could trust.

"Besides, you and your office cohorts aren't the only amateur detectives around. I've logged a lot of hours watching reruns of *The Rockford Files*. I know how to track down a clue."

Julie laughed and met his lips. The urgency of his kiss sent delicious shock waves through every nerve, a welcome replacement for the snarled tension that had become part of her days. She closed her eyes, savoring the trail of butterfly kisses he planted along her neck.

Why did I deny myself this joy?

She took a deep breath, satisfied about recommitting herself to Trevor. No matter what happened with FunWorks, they would get through this—and any other challenges—together.

Julie pulled him from the couch. "I love you."

"I thought so." Trevor followed as she led the way to the bedroom.

***

Long after the kids left for school, Julie and Trevor lingered over breakfast the next day, hoping toast and two pots of coffee would offset the sleep they'd lost.

Trevor outlined possible defenses against Burnside. "There must be a way to slow this process down and get FunWorks on more solid financial footing."

Julie yawned and wiped a kernel of sleep out of her eye. "If only."

Trevor stirred sugar into his cup. "They caught you off-guard. We need to correct that."

"Vincent has some new ideas. I'm supposed to meet with him today." She fished her cell phone out of her purse. The screen showed one missed call and one voice mail message.

Both from Gary Carlson.

"Julie, I know I'm the last person you expected to hear from and I'm probably the last person you want to talk to. Please give me a call, no matter how late. I've learned something that will help get Game Masters out of the picture. Call me. Please."

"Trevor." She shoved the phone at him. "Listen to this."

Chapter Eighteen

Leanne's voice bounced against the hallway walls as Julie walked toward her office.

"I'll give Ms. Rafferty your message as soon as she comes in. I realize it's important," Leanne replied as Julie approached her desk. "Oh, Mr. Bolley, just a minute." She put the call on hold. "Am I glad to see you! It's been a nuthouse around here. Didn't you get my calls?"

"Sorry." Julie smiled, not regretting turning off her phone, and the lovemaking that made her late to work that morning. "Ray Bolley?"

"He wants to talk to you. I'll transfer him to your office line."

Leanne called after Julie hurrying down the hall. "You've got two messages from a woman in the court clerk's office. Cases you were asking about. I left the notes on top of your inbox. They didn't make a lick of sense to me."

After being so eager to talk with her a few days ago, Ray had suddenly become hard to reach. The causes of his inaccessibility piled on like football players scurrying after a fumbled snap. This conversation wouldn't be good.

Julie rounded her desk and picked up the phone. "Hi, Ray. I'm glad to hear from you." She heard what sounded like a bus or train station noise in the background.

"Are you somewhere you can talk?"

"In my office. Why?"

"Because I'm only going to say this once and I want to make sure you understand."

"Is everything okay?" she asked, afraid of what the answer might be.

"With me, yeah. I'm just not sure how things are going to be after you hear what's been happening."

"What?" The sereneness of the morning was now compromised by anxiety.

"I ran into Bennett Burnside. Or I should say, he ran into me."

Julie held the receiver closer to her ear. "I can hardly hear you. Where are you?"

"A phone booth. I've used all my change. Got a pencil? I'm at 843-555-8687."

She repeated the number.

"Call me back from a landline, not a cell phone."

Julie disconnected and dialed. Ray owned a cell phone. He had her cell number. Why was he calling the office and why from a phone booth?

Julie licked her lips and redialed for the tenth time in as many minutes. Each ring amped up her pulse rate.

Answer, damn it, Ray. Answer the phone.

"Are you sure you wrote the number correctly?"

Julie's gaze sliced to Derek, who had walked in after hearing Julie yell in frustration. "Pretty sure. We had a bad connection and he hurried me off the line."

"Why the hell did you hang up on him?" Derek shouted in that condescending tone that caused Julie to grit her teeth.

She glared. "Calm down. He hung up on me."

"Do we have another number for him?"

"Only his cell."

"Call anyway."

The man she met days earlier didn't do drama. He wouldn't run scared. If Ray left the phone booth, there was a good reason. "No, we have to wait."

170

She waited five minutes before dialing again. This time the phone was answered.

"Hello. Ray?" Julie heard the panic in her own voice. "No, I understand. Thank you." She slowly put the receiver in its cradle. "Ray's not there. Someone walking by said it's a pay phone outside the Charleston Maritime Center."

Derek put his hands on his head and stared into space. "This isn't happening. Should we call the Charleston cops?"

Julie imagined Ray hurt—or worse. "I don't know. What would we say? The company that's suing me may have gotten to Ray?"

"This is so messed up," Derek said.

Messed up didn't even begin to cover this debacle. Burnside wanted her to panic but she wouldn't give him the satisfaction.

Julie folded her hands to keep them from shaking. The impending threat seeping in from all sides eroded her ability to think straight. Might everyone she loved be in danger?

***

"It's noon already?" Julie checked her watch.

Trevor slid into a chair opposite her. He'd come right away when she relayed the latest about Ray.

Leanne followed Derek into the office, toting a bag from the corner deli.

Derek placed the sack on the table and unloaded sandwiches and cookies. "Still no word?"

"Nope. Julie even tried his cell phone. The calls go straight to voice mail." Trevor said, grabbing a sandwich.

"Seems like we follow the trail of one case and the door opens to a dozen more," Derek said, as they all gathered around the conference table to eat.

"Burnside is the prince of patent law. So what?" Trevor snapped. "If I'm as big as Game Masters, I'd want the best. That's why we hired Vincent, isn't it? To give us our own edge."

"True," Derek answered.

Julie pointed to a pile of papers on the credenza. "I've been on the phone with the clerk in Douglas County in Nevada. That's the jurisdiction where they filed the lawsuit against Ray Bolley. When I asked her about the final determination of Ray's case, she told me about three other cases in their system." Julie looked at her spiral notebook. "Cell phone software, the solar-powered toys case Vincent mentioned, and the third company made a lightweight backpack. The products and the companies involved are from different parts of the country, but they used the same attorney. The clerk thought that was odd, so she directed me to the public record for more information."

"New Tech made the cell phone. Solar Wheels designed the toys and School Sensations made the backpacks," Trevor said. "All three are now subsidiaries of a Nevada company— BAB Enterprises."

"And BAB Enterprises owns Game Masters," Julie said.

"We've found Burnside's name tied to twelve similar cases dating back about twenty years. Some were filed before Bolley's, but most of the lawsuits began after Burnside forced Ray to sell his water company," Julie said.

"Think about it," Trevor prodded. "After a few years as a struggling patent attorney, Burnside figures the real money is in finding mom-and-pop operations with a marketable product. Then he sues because they can't afford to pay the big bucks to fight his type of litigation."

"It's brilliant," Derek said. "No one would expect an upstanding philanthropist to mastermind small companies out of business. Maybe we should go to the feds."

"With what proof?" Trevor asked.

"BAB has to stand for something," Leanne said.

"Bennett Burnside, but what's the A for?" Derek asked.

"Alberto!" The name exploded from Julie's mouth like a cork popping from a champagne bottle. She frantically searched her papers. "Bennett Alberto Burnside. Says so right here." Julie handed the business card to Derek. "That's who owns BAB Enterprises."

Julie jumped at the ring from her desktop phone. "Hello." A smile spread across her face. "Ray. It's really you."

Julie pushed the speakerphone button. "We've been trying to reach you."

"Sorry, things got a little weird around here. Too many old skeletons coming out of my closet, if you know what I mean. I had to move," Ray said. "This is the first chance I've had to call back."

"When we couldn't reach you, we got concerned."

"Don't worry. I'm an old coot who can take care of himself. In fact, I should have done this while Myra was still alive."

"Ray, this is Trevor, Julie's husband. She's put you on speaker. Man, you scared the hell out of us."

"Funny thing about fear. It's powerful." Ray's voice softened and slurred. "It makes you do things you really shouldn't. Fear makes you agree to deals you don't want and, if you're not careful, you turn into someone you don't want to be."

Julie thought she heard ice clinking against a glass. "Are you okay? Should we call the police?"

"Nah. Listen," Ray said. "You have a lot of life ahead of you. And your youth showed me I don't have to be afraid of Burnside. I'm too old and tired to live in his shadow."

Julie heard him take a gulp. "Ray?"

"I'm still here. Anyway, I can't change what's happened to me, but maybe I can help change your future."

Julie leaned forward, her elbows on her knees. They had already hurt Derek. She had no doubt Burnside wouldn't hesitate to harm a doddering plumber if he thought Ray would get in his way. "Not if helping us puts you in danger. I won't let you risk your life."

Ray chortled. "The good Lord will take this ol' life whenever he's ready. In the meanwhile, I aim to do something worthy of my time on this here earth."

"If you can safely give us some information that will help, we're all for that," Trevor said.

"Here's the thing. They want PlaytimePals. Just as much as they wanted my water saver company. The difference is, this time Burnside and his goons know it's not a slam-dunk. He knew you flew all the way to South Carolina to talk to me. That got him a bit nervous." Ray let out a loud guffaw. "Did my heart good to see that buzzard jumpy."

"Did Burnside threaten you?" Julie waited for a response but heard only labored breathing. "You still there, Ray?"

"I'm here. Me and my bottle of Bushmills."

Julie's chest tightened. "Why did you call earlier?"

"I held back a few things when I talked to you." He cleared his throat. "I'm ready to tell you now."

The tension in the room released slightly and Julie grinned at Trevor. "We're going to tape-record this call, okay, Ray?"

"Sure thing. I've got nothing to hide."

Leanne turned on the audio recorder. "What's a water-saver?" she asked.

Julie heard a sneer in Ray's voice "It's a gizmo that saves folks a bunch of water every time they flush. Everyone said it'd be worth millions. As things ended up, I got a big runaround, not much else to show for my efforts. Hey, I'm not complaining. I'd been living the quiet life here in Bluffton. Things were good until Burnside's ugly face turned up."

Julie heard another liquid pour and swallow.

"Anyway, after the usual chitchat, he got to the real reason. Somehow, he knew I had met with you, Julie, and he wasn't happy. He didn't say so outright, but he made his meaning clear: If I talk to you or see you ever again, there'll be hell to pay."

The line went silent for a time.

"After all these years that guy has the brass balls to tell me who I can talk to. And this after the way he put my poor Myra through the meat grinder. That sorry cuss don't care about nobody but himself." Ray blew his nose.

"Where are you? How can we help?"

"I wanted to let the past stay in the past, not get involved. But Burnside's little visit made me mad. Someone's got to stop that sorry son-of-a-bitch, and I think you might be smart enough to catch him."

"We're already meeting with the attorney you recommended. What else should we do?"

"I got a couple of ideas."

Ray spent the next twenty minutes telling them about a small Texas company that had become very successful producing flavored salsas. The owner patented his grandmother's recipe. Some years later, he turned his popular salsa fresca into a product line of novelty salsas, like Some Like It Lemon and Salsa Popper. Ray's favorite was Muy Hot Chocolate.

"A well-known food manufacturer tried a knock-off version, but failed," Ray said. "Guess who owns that food company? Our old buddy Burnside. He tried to sue them, claiming his company invented the chocolate salsa, but Texas courts are friendly toward patent holders."

"That's true," Trevor said. "Where I work, we've had some of our patents upheld in Texas. The state is very responsive to intellectual property claims."

"Do you think we should file our paperwork in Texas?" Julie asked.

"I wouldn't know about that," Ray said. "But here's something I do know. Burnside won't like two of his conquests teaming up on him. Get ahold of the salsa folks. Maybe you can learn something. Their name is Sals-A-Fire."

"I've heard of them," Trevor said. "We have two bottles of their sauce in the fridge."

"They're headquartered in Dickinson, Texas, south a' Houston. Here's the number."

Julie scribbled the number in a spiral notebook. "Who do I ask for?"

"Esteban Becerra. Do you need me to spell the name?"

"No, I got it."

"Good. He'll be expecting your call."

Trevor raised an eyebrow. "Huh?"

"Ray, how do you know all this?" Julie asked.

"Let's just say, I've been doing a bit of poking around myself."

Chapter Nineteen

Julie yawned and twisted her body gently. Her eyes wanted to cross after sitting for hours, poring over documents. She knew the right path lay before her. She just needed to dig a little harder.

"Vincent should be able to enlighten us on Texas patent law when he gets here," she said to Trevor and Derek. The trio clustered around Julie's office conference table.

"That's not for four more hours," Derek muttered, looking at his watch. "What should we be doing now?"

"Before we expose ourselves to this Esteban guy, we need to do a little research on Sals-A-Fire," Julie said. "He might work for Burnside, too. Leanne, get your hands on everything you can about the company and its owner."

"On it," Leanne said and hurried out.

Moments later Leanne tapped on Julie's partially closed door before stepping inside the office. "Sorry to interrupt, but guess who's wearing out the soles of his Hush Puppies on our new carpeting?"

"Beats me," Julie said.

"Gary Carlson."

Derek turned to Julie. "Why is he here?"

"Maybe he finally realized he was being used."

"Time for atonement?" Trevor asked.

Derek rocked back in his chair. "I doubt he can spell atonement."

"He was your friend," Julie pointed out. "Maybe he made a mistake, a really bad one. Maybe he's trying to correct that now."

"That's a pretty forgiving attitude," Trevor said, standing. "He might cost you—us—the company."

Julie frowned. Perhaps she was being too forgiving. Still, she didn't believe Gary orchestrated Derek's accident. Her intuition told her he wasn't in on the plot. Guilty of being gullible—now, that was a different story. Not a good quality in an attorney.

"If I hadn't suggested Gary represent you as your corporate attorney, none of this would be happening." Derek rolled a pen between his thumb and forefinger. "All this is my fault."

Trevor moved away from the table and paced. "And if I was more involved, none of this might have happened, either. There's enough blame to go around. We all screwed up."

Trevor touched Derek's shoulder. "It's time to let go of being angry at Gary and stay focused on our problems. People do all sorts of things when they're mad or hurt or don't understand all the facts." Trevor's eyes darted to Julie. "Second chances are a good thing."

Julie shook her head to clear her thoughts. Trevor's words sounded like an apology; but for what?

"In a weird way, Gary actually helped us. Because of his inept handling of the case, we started asking our own questions."

Julie turned to Leanne, still standing in the doorway. "Show him in."

***

"There is something I need to tell you, Julie. Can we have a moment alone?" Trevor cleared his throat. "It concerns the lawsuit and where Game Masters got the idea that FunWorks might have infringed on their software patents."

Julie gathered her notes and slid them inside a manila folder. "What are you talking about?"

Before Trevor could answer, Gary Carlson entered the room.

Julie stood and pointed him to a leather club chair at the far end of the table. "You know Leanne. I don't believe you've met my husband, Trevor Rafferty."

"Yes, we've met." Gary shook Trevor's hand. "He's been to the office a couple of times. I'm a little surprised to see you here."

"Why would you be surprised?" Julie asked.

Gary hesitated.

Julie narrowed her eyes. "Cook's Finest retains Ryder, Rush & Ryder? That's news to me."

"What's Cook's Finest?" Derek asked.

"The company I work for," Trevor answered, a knot forming in his stomach. "And no, they're not the reason Gary saw me at the Ryder offices. That's what I wanted to tell you, Julie. I've met Gary's employers."

"Former employers," Gary corrected him. "I'm quitting. Handing in my resignation tomorrow and moving back east to start my own practice. But before I go, I want to straighten out a lot of misinformation."

Julie put her hands on her hips and turned to Trevor. "You two have met? How? When? Why?"

Trevor's pulse quickened, a sick feeling of betrayal increasing with each beat. "Maybe ten months ago…" Trevor exhaled. "I got a call from one of their paralegals."

"Who?" Julie's voice rose and nearly cracked. "What did you tell them?"

Trevor hung his head, staring at the floor. He knew this day would come. All the deception and maneuvering he'd hidden, now exposed. "I don't remember. Gary might know her name," he said. "Doesn't matter. She said something about preliminary research for a client. Since my name is on the FunWorks ownership papers, she thought I'd be interested in a buyer for the company."

Trevor paused and glanced at Julie. "I told her I'm a silent partner, that I didn't have any decision-making authority. If she had a serious buyer, she should contact you."

"The conversation ended there?" Julie asked.

"That day. But she called back about six weeks later." He paused, recalling the moment. "We'd fought the night before, Jules. A real blowout. I wanted you to spend less time at the office and more time with me and the kids."

Julie shifted in her chair, obviously uncomfortable at airing their dirty laundry in public, but it was too late to ask the others to leave. "I remember. I'd just found out FunWorks won Best New Toy Manufacturer at the New York Toy Fair. We were finally a player. You said you were proud of me."

"I am very proud. But when she called, I thought I'd found an answer to my prayers."

"You talked to them again, after we were finally reaching our goals?"

He reached for Julie's hands, but she pulled back and folded them across her chest.

"You could've sold the company, made a big profit and our lives could've gone back to normal. I never agreed to a takeover plan. You have to believe me," Trevor pleaded.

Julie pushed back from the table. "I can't believe you talked to these crooks and didn't tell me."

The tsunami of rage bursting through Julie's words caused the room's temperature to rise.

"I meant to, baby, I really did. But then things started unraveling between us and I got to thinking the best thing that could happen for our family would be for you to sell the company." He let out a big sigh. "Then you'd need me again."

Gary interrupted. "I don't mean to defend Trevor. Lord knows I have enough trouble defending myself. But these guys are polished. They're so smooth you'd sell your own mother for a pack of hot dogs and a can of beans."

Gary reached into his briefcase and pulled out some documents. "I don't know the details of your personal life, but I do know that Bennett Burnside can find a chink in anyone's armor and turn that into a chasm by spinning information in a way that makes sense at the time."

Gary spread papers on Julie's desk. "Ray Bolley's wife's illness triggered that takeover. With you guys, a neglected husband." Gary turned to Trevor. "Sorry, man."

Trevor nodded. He couldn't believe what had just happened. He had painted himself as a liar and a traitor. He needed to fix this. Somehow, he would make this right.

"But that's what they do. They find a wedge and use it. In a blink, you go from president of a company to a memory. Happens all the time."

"Not this time." Trevor straightened. "I have no idea how they found out about our problems or how a paralegal called the day after our last big fight. I realize now they used me to get to you. Can you forgive me?"

***

Julie moved farther away from Trevor, exposed as her Judas.

She'd been stupid for trusting him again. Maybe he hadn't cheated on her with another woman, but somehow this deception registered far worse.

Trevor followed her to a corner across the room. "Jules, those jerks made a big mistake when they picked on you. You and FunWorks are a package deal. I know that now." He grasped her shoulder. "I'll find a way to fix this. FunWorks can succeed, and our marriage will, too."

Julie didn't answer. Instead, she turned to Gary. "Why are you so eager to help us now?"

Gary stood. "I'm no hero, but I'm not a thief, either. I've never knowingly cheated or misrepresented anything in my life. Remember that poli-sci test you wanted to give me the answers for, Derek? I didn't take them, right?"

"That was a long time ago."

"But I'm still the same guy. Burnside robbed me, too. He stole my good name and self-respect." Gary glanced at Trevor. "Like with you, the short-term goals enticed me. Now I see the bigger picture. I'm hoping it's not too late to change things."

Julie's head spun as the truth sank in. The only person she could count on was herself. "I've got to trust you too?" she snapped. "Not happening."

"I have some information that may help. And maybe, just maybe, send Burnside on his slimy way. Let me tell you about this family from Georgia who sued MaxOut Toys." Gary raised a coil of papers loosely rolled into a shape resembling a torch.

"We already know about the suit," Julie said, exasperated at Gary's big discovery. "Their son was injured while playing a video game."

"Did you know they never got a penny in settlement money?"

"Sort of." Leanne frantically turned the pages of her notepad. "They received a judgment but never collected any money. Newspaper accounts referred to them as a family from Georgia. Coverage disappeared after the jury found the toy manufacturer liable. They never discovered their name or where in Georgia all this happened."

"Their last name is Thorson. Dale, Janet, and their son Ben."

"Is that Thorson with an o or an e?" Leanne asked, writing furiously.

"An O. I'm not surprised you weren't able to find out anything else. Part of Burnside's ploy involves having journalists in his pocket."

"One of them wouldn't be Roberta Perkins, would it? She's been doing a hatchet job on me," Julie mused.

"There's a crew of them. Small-time writers who can spin stories in any direction that benefits Burnside. Anyway, about the time the $9.9 million judgment was handed down, the county DA got a manila envelope full of goodies in his morning mail from an anonymous source."

"About the Thorsons?" Julie asked.

"Oh, yeah. The envelope contained a video of young Ben playing in a Little League game the month before. He pitched, threw strikes, too." Gary's mouth twisted in disgust. "The coach who testified during the trial disappeared and the new coach didn't know anything about Ben's disability."

Julie surveyed the faces around the room. The term *setup* came to mind.

Gary paced around the office. "Turns out the boy's hand was fully operational. No paralysis. The kid gripped the ball like a future Cy Young winner. More documentation proved the doctor had forged his reports. And a rap sheet for Dale and Janet outlined their history as con artists." Gary laid the documents on the corner of Julie's desk. "As far as the DA could tell, the Thorsons had bamboozled people for years. This was their biggest score, though, and apparently, that caught the attention of some community-minded citizen who wanted to remain nameless."

"The DA bought that anonymous tip story?" Julie asked.

Derek scowled. "Seems a little thin to me."

"Ben's folks claimed Game Masters invented the idea. Dale said he'd been approached by a man who asked him to sue MaxOut. The go-between promised that their case would be easy to win because he'd provide everything—expert witnesses, doctors, and any medical proof necessary. A physical therapist came to the Thorsons' house for weeks before the trial and coached young Ben on how to hold his *paralyzed* hand."

Gary tapped his forefinger on the pile of papers on Julie's desk. "Everything's in here. How Ben learned words to use to describe his pain, what to point to when asked where it hurt the most. These guys numbed his hand with Novocain to ensure a convincing performance."

Julie slowly paged through the documents. "They thought of every angle," Julie said minutes later, finding proof of Gary's word in the pages.

"As long as Ben could act, there would be lots of money to go around. When the time came to collect their winnings, they got arrested instead."

"And defending themselves proved harder than they thought," Trevor surmised.

Gary continued. "First, the man who contacted them couldn't be found. Then the therapist and anyone else who had testified disappeared. All the paperwork pointed to a dead end. Dale showed a business card and some other official-looking records, but they were fakes. The address didn't exist. The phone numbers—no longer in service. They probably used burner cells that expired after a certain date and were virtually untraceable." He sighed. "Ben's counsel, Wallace and Weinstein, is the only thing real about the case."

Trevor pulled a discarded envelope from a nearby trashcan to write on. "Give me that name again."

"Wallace and Weinstein. The same firm that filed the lawsuit against FunWorks. They've been in Atlanta for nearly thirty years. Since the judgment was so large, it became a capital case and the DA went after the parents for fraud. That DA is the state attorney general now."

Julie nodded. "What happened to the Thorsons?"

"It was the third strike for Dale, so he received the maximum sentence. He's eligible for parole at the Georgia State Prison in about four years. Janet will be out in February. Ben lives with his grandmother in Prescott, Arizona."

Julie handed the documents to Derek. "According to these, Game Masters won the rights to sell BlastAway in time for the holidays. Poor Mort Gunther. Burnside claimed his dream toy for a song."

"And that's what they're trying to do with us," Derek said. "Only they've been more transparent, not so many backdoor dealings."

"They've gotten cocky over the years," Julie agreed. "They don't cover their tracks like they used to. That's why they went after Trevor, hurt Derek, and used Gary. They didn't have a terminally ill wife or low-life parents to barter with."

"They thought they scored a reliable mole." Trevor's voice quivered, each syllable a pebble of remorse, dropping hard onto a suffocating mound of regret. "An unhappy husband who wanted his wife to sell and an eager, naïve attorney. The rest should have been easy."

"Not as easy as they think. Can you stay for our meeting with Vincent Williams? He should be here soon."

"Tell him everything you've told us, Gare," Derek said.

"Gare? That's an improvement over what you've been calling me recently. Yeah, I'll stay."

Derek smiled. "It's not because I'm happy with you. I'm just getting good vibes about our chances."

Julie shifted to her desk and spread the documents out in front of her. "Burnside's bunch never planned to make money for the Thorsons. They wanted MaxOut Toys for cheap."

"That's what they're hoping to do with us." Trevor turned from the window and crossed his arms.

Us? There is no us anymore, Julie wanted to yell.

Derek pointed to a stack of canceled invoices. "They might still succeed."

"Seems to me we've spent a lot of time counteracting their moves. Trying to figure out what they're going to do next," Julie said, aware that Trevor stood next to her.

"Let's make some moves of our own," he said.

That's what needs to happen, but you, my soon-to-be ex-husband, have surrendered your spot on this team.

Julie took a sip of water to quench her dry mouth. An ache in her heart replaced the tenseness in her stomach. She could overcome anything but betrayal. She could not stay married to a liar and that would break her children's hearts—and her own.

"Excuse me." Vincent Williams stood at the door. "There's no one out front, so I just walked in. Hope that's okay."

"Please come in," Julie said. "We have a lot to talk about."

***

After their meeting ended, Trevor hurried to Julie's side. He needed a moment to explain. Again.

Instead, she nearly bowled him over, rushing to her office and slamming the door.

He knocked and didn't wait for a response before entering. "Are you about done for today?" He moved closer to where she sat, jangling his car keys in his pocket, waiting for an answer.

"I'll be along in an hour or so," Julie replied after what seemed like an eternity. "I want to review my notes from meeting with Williams, and I have a sales report I have to go over."

"I'll wait."

She lifted her head for a moment. "No. You go on. Teresa has dinner waiting."

"Let's talk about this," Trevor said.

"Not now. I can't think." Traces of tears pooled in Julie's eyes.

"I never intended—"

She waved her hand. "Just go."

He kissed the top of Julie's head. Her hair smelled like lavender. "Okay. I'll see you at home." He lingered, breathing in her scent before leaving.

A mixture of anger and self-loathing coursed through his veins as he made his way toward the parking lot.

He thought he and Julie had finally gotten their life back. Sharing stolen moments like impetuous lovers, her laughter and spontaneity filling their bedroom. He was once again taking care of his wife, the role he craved. And now this. How could he have been so stupid? He had to rectify the hurt he caused and win back Julie's love and trust. But how?

"Can you wait a minute?" Trevor hurried toward Gary, unlocking his car.

"Sure, man. Sorry about what happened back there. I didn't mean to out you."

Trevor grimaced. "I should have told Julie myself. I just couldn't find the right time. It's better that she knows."

Gary nodded. "The air was cleared on a lot of fronts."

Trevor pulled a paper and pen out of his pocket. "What can you tell me about Julie's patent on PlaytimePals?"

"It's like I said at the meeting. We filed her computer software patent four years ago. It's valid for another sixteen years."

"No other company can produce PlaytimePals or anything resembling the product without Julie's approval?"

"That's right. As far as I'm concerned, she has strong legal standing to retain her design patent. You should prevail in court if you can afford to fight that long."

Trevor inhaled. In the software market, even sixteen weeks equaled an eternity. No wonder Game Masters didn't want to wait that long. "I'm still confused. How can they sue us?"

"They're claiming FunWorks overstepped the extent of their patent and infringed on their intellectual property rights," Gary said. "It's a ploy to run you around until you sell, at a discount."

Trevor shifted his weight, thinking. "Why FunWorks?"

"It possessed all the ingredients Burnside wants, like a healthy P&L. It's expanding into an older demographic by using the licensed images of popular teenage singers and actors. Heck, there's a film scheduled to come out next year."

"Julie never told me about a movie possibility." Trevor sighed.

"Probably slipped her mind," Gary added quickly. "With all the interest in computer-driven designs for kids, PlaytimePals has an unlimited future. Your wife is sitting on a goldmine."

"Before you go, what can you tell me about Water Saver?"

Trevor listened to Gary describe another of Burnside's cases. A recurring theme played out in Trevor's mind: Personal turmoil equaled business opportunity. Damn Burnside. The old SOB had a penchant for nudging people's misery along. Trevor had to find a way to make Burnside the miserable one this time around.

Trevor shook Gary's hand and headed for his car, wondering how Burnside learned so much about their private lives. He slid behind the wheel of his Highlander and slipped the key into the ignition.

In his rearview mirror, he spotted a man standing in a doorway across the street. The silhouetted figure made no attempt to hide.

Is he spying on me? Trevor wondered. He quickly dismissed the idea, not wanting to add paranoia to his pile of problems. He put the car in reverse and pulled out of the parking slot. A second later, he glanced over his shoulder and the man had disappeared.

Chapter Twenty

"Is there anything else you need?" Leanne asked, her purse on her shoulder.

"Oh." Julie blinked. "I thought you left."

"Vincent called. Burnside will be served the countersuit tomorrow."

Julie shuffled through folders, pondering how Burnside would react to her suit seeking eight million dollars in actual damages for loss of current and future income and $250 million in punitive damages for Game Masters knowingly filing a false lawsuit.

"We have a little reprieve, so what are you still working on?"

Julie motioned for Leanne to sit. "When we started digging around, I never thought a plumber, a game manufacturer and software paper dolls would have so much in common."

"It is surprising."

"Yeah, a lot of surprises today." Julie slumped and put her hands in her lap. Terror of the unknown leached into her heart, sending waves of nervous energy through her body. She lived with the anxiety from Burnside's tightening vise but the deeper hurt, the one she couldn't reason away, was Trevor's deception.

"It's funny. I thought even in the worst of times, we could talk. We might not always agree, but we'd talk." She closed her eyes. "Hash the problem out. When we dated, Trevor would call every night after his last class. We'd talk so long. I'd fall asleep holding the receiver to my ear. We communicated—twenty years ago."

"You still do." Leanne uncrossed her legs and leaned forward. "He told you what happened, and he confessed in front of everyone. That couldn't have been easy."

"Yeah, maybe this is my fault," she retorted.

"That's not what I meant."

Julie pushed away from her desk with both hands. "Even Teresa told me to slow down and see what I was doing to my family. But..." she stabbed her chest with her thumb, "...this girl knew better. Maybe going back to being a regular mom is the best thing." Tears welled in her eyes.

Leanne handed her a tissue. "Even if you decide to sell the company, you don't want to sell your life's work to these lowlifes."

Julie half-smiled and wiped a tear away before others followed. "Funny how life is. Just when you think you're in control, what you love most is snatched away."

"You can't love both your marriage and the company equally. One has to come first," Leanne said. "Which one can't you live without?"

Julie closed the file and glanced at her watch. "Doesn't matter."

They're both being stripped away.

"I'm worried about you. That's why I stayed."

"I'm a tough girl, don't you know that by now? I'll land on my feet." Julie winked sending a tear splashing on to the folder. "Go home, Leanne. Derek's waiting for you."

After Leanne left, Julie sat in the quiet of her office, with the realization she couldn't love Trevor and FunWorks equally quaking through her.

Leanne was right.

Her choice made, Julie twisted off her wedding rings and dropped them inside her handbag.

***

Trevor pulled into the driveway, turned off the ignition, and let his forehead fall onto the steering wheel. He stayed that way for several minutes, his mind swimming.

Teresa called his cell an hour ago to ask when he and Julie would be home for dinner. Odd of her to check on them, but with their schedules so erratic lately, perhaps she wanted to make certain they were coming home.

As he approached the house, he saw Nicole through the living room window, tottering on a kitchen chair stretching to reach the other side of the dining room archway. A crinkled poster-paper banner spanned the space between her and Jason.

"Now that side is crooked," he heard Emily moan through the open window a few feet away. "Get your side higher, Jason."

"My side is fine. Nicole can't get hers straight."

Trevor jiggled his keys loud enough for them to hear.

"Dad, you're home already." Jason held one hand against the banner to keep the paper from falling. "Is Mom with you?"

"What's all this?" He read *Hurray for Mom and Dad!* painted on a banner in the dining room. "Who made the sign?"

"We all worked on it," Jason boasted.

"We wanted to surprise you and Mom."

"So, Mom gets top billing?" Trevor nudged Emily. "Well done. She deserves it."

"Where is she?" Jason asked.

Trevor helped Nicole with the sagging end of the sign. "She'll be home in about thirty minutes. When she gets here, I can walk in again, and we'll both be surprised together."

"Nah," Jason said. "As long as we surprised you once, that's good enough."

"We've made dinner, and we're going to have a party," Emily said.

"Teresa let us bake a chocolate cake with white icing." Nicole's excited speech matched Emily's.

"And the cause for celebration?"

"Things are back to normal," Jason said.

"That's great of you guys to throw us a party." Trevor measured his words, reluctant to join their optimism.

They hadn't seen their mother's face after he'd confessed about speaking to the Ryder lawyers.

***

"What I can't accept is why you never told me. How could you think so little of me?" Julie shouted, her fists balled as though ready to strike. "Or of our marriage to go behind my back and sell me out to those crooks?"

Trevor hated that shrillness in Julie's voice. He had fallen victim to her accusatory derision too many times, but today he deserved every word she yelled. An hour earlier, they played the happy guests-of-honor at dinner.

Now she stood in their bedroom, Trevor the target of her wrath.

He wished she would calm down, or cry, or something. Any break in her tirade that might give him a chance to make his case. Nearly twenty years of marriage had taught him better, though. When Julie careened off the rails, he stood silently and took the punishing jabs.

Once the verbal fireworks ended, he stepped toward his wife and started to wipe a stray tear from her cheek. She batted his hand away.

"If I could take back what I did, I would. All I can do now is try to fix my miserable mistake." He leaned his hip against her dresser. A sparkle gleamed from a tray near Julie's jewelry box where her wedding ring now lay. She made her decision. With the pad of his forefinger, he wiped a tear from his own eye.

"I can't talk to you right now." Julie moved quickly to the far side of the room.

Trevor didn't dare follow. Instead, he picked up Julie's wedding ring as though the last vestige of their marriage had surrendered. "I don't blame you for being angry."

"Isn't that big of you?" she answered, now turning to meet his gaze. "This isn't a game. My career, this company—they aren't games to be played."

"I'm not playing games. I... I just—"

"Yes, you are, and you have been. Our marriage is one long board game. We outmaneuver each other, strategizing where to place our token. And bam! Tonight, I win. Tomorrow, you're the victor. Whatever the outcome, our kids always lose."

Trevor hung his head. Julie spoke the truth. For years he competed with a business, not a person, but to Julie, there was no difference.

"Why aren't we ever on the same side, playing for the same team?" Her voice softened. "Striving for the same goals?"

"We are a team." Trevor stepped closer, knowing words would not make his case. He needed to do something, something real, to convince her.

"Not today. Today the fix was in. You played for the other guy, and all because—"

"I know I screwed up, big time," he defended. "All I'm asking is a chance to fix things."

"I want to believe you, really I do. That would be the easy, orderly thing to do," Julie huffed, her arms folded tightly around her chest.

Trevor wondered if she was cutting off all circulation to her hands.

She turned to face him. "But I can't. A voice inside of me keeps saying I'd be a fool if I did. I want you to move out."

Her words hit Trevor as though the bottom of a heavy bag of groceries split, sending the contents crashing to the floor. Everything that mattered to Trevor, now lay shattered, irreparable.

"Move out?" he shouted, tossing Julie's ring back into the jewelry tray. "You're joking, right?"

"Do I look like I'm laughing?"

"The kids just threw us a party. They'd be heartbroken if I left. I'll do anything to make things right. I love you."

A veil of steel overtook her face. "It's too late."

Trevor punched the bedroom wall and instinctively grabbed his knuckles, rubbing where the pain now emanated. "For God's sake, you can't be serious."

"You're the one who's not serious. You've never taken me seriously."

Trevor closed the space between them in a single bound. "Hell, I'm just trying to catch up with you."

"Catch up, huh?" Julie squinted so hard, Trevor cringed.

"Take a minute and think about what you're saying. You want to tear our family apart, again."

"I'm not the bad guy here," Julie said, a new calm now coloring her tone. "You tried to coerce me into selling, and when that didn't work, you left me. And our kids."

"I never really left. I just wanted you to—"

"Anybody but you, Trevor. I could have taken anyone but you as Burnside's stoolie."

"I'm not Burnside's anything!" Trevor shouted, knowing he was losing the battle. "I'm not working for him. I just want things back the way they were. Back to when you counted on me." Julie showed no sign of forgiveness, sending a wave of hopelessness crashing over him.

"Give me two weeks," he said. "If I haven't convinced you by then, I'll explain everything to the kids and move out. I can't go now, just when we're starting to rebuild our life together."

She stared, her lips pursed tightly in a straight line. Her eyes narrowed suspiciously. Trevor couldn't tell if she was considering his offer or looking around the room for something to throw at his head.

"Well, what do you say, Jules? One more shot. You trusted me at the college Book Barn all those years ago," he said, hoping to soften her resolve. "The only thing that has changed for me is how much more I love you and our kids."

She stormed to his side of the room. "You can stay for two weeks. The clock starts right now. I need that much time to sort things out. But you're not sleeping in my bed." She threw a blanket and his pillow at him. "Take the floor or the recliner."

Chapter Twenty-One

Julie spent most of her sleepless night running the names of those small companies through her mind. None were big enough to be on anyone's radar, except Bennett Burnside's. Why? She rolled over and punched her pillow. What was the connection?

She took satisfaction knowing Trevor's rest had been equally disturbed. The bedroom recliner creaked throughout the night, his body continuously moving in search of a comfortable position. Finally, she heard him throw off the blankets and pad to the en-suite bathroom. She glanced at the clock. Five-seventeen.

Twenty minutes later, she pretended to be asleep while he riffled through the closet, hangers clanking against the wardrobe rod. Curious, she peeked from under the covers and watched as he removed a case from the top shelf. He shoved something into his jacket pocket and crept out of the room.

She tossed and turned for another sixty minutes before giving in to the sliver of sunshine slicing through the bedroom window. Birds in the distance welcomed the morning with cheerful tunes, but their melodic inspiration skipped by Julie. She couldn't imagine ever again enjoying the sunny promise of God's new day.

Yawning, Julie swung her legs out of bed.

I can't worry about Trevor now. Burnside is coming after me with a vengeance. I need to prepare.

When she arrived at the office an hour later, those six companies and their products were still bouncing inside her head like balls in a bingo cage. Toilets, backpacks, cell phones, solar cars, video games, and salsa, for God's sake. What thread tied them together? If she could figure that out, she'd know what Bennett Burnside was really after. It certainly wasn't hoping for a spot on the *Forbes* List of Richest People. The return for making paper dolls wasn't all that much.

She cleared her desk, leaving in place the research on Burnside's past takeovers. She pulled out a tablet and drew five vertical lines on the sheet. At the top of each column, she wrote the company name and briefly noted the facts of each case. Except for the salsa company, after the cases settled, BAB Enterprises owned all assets, including intellectual property rights.

Julie paged through her day planner. Burnside had first approached her at the toy fair, about six weeks after FunWorks received the 3D paper dolls patent. Vast improvements in digital technology pushed the price tag for 3D printers down, Julie read in a *Wall Street Journal* article touting the emerging market. In fact, increased sales last year topped $2.2 billion worldwide, improving nearly thirty percent from the previous year. She had brought the idea to Derek and he quickly agreed. FunWorks' next frontier included three-dimensional products. They could expand into more toy categories than paper dolls.

She tapped her pencil against her lips. That was the connection! She flicked the intercom button. "Leanne. Please bring all the files relating to our patents. And get Vincent Williams on the phone." She clicked off, realizing she would have to contact the former owners to learn what proprietary information they'd lost when Burnside cannibalized their companies if, in fact, they knew.

A satisfied smile formed on her face. *I'm going to learn your true motive, Burnside, not what you want me to believe.*

***

Trevor sat in the parking lot and checked the slip of paper again: 4721 Carriage Center Way. He surveyed a nail salon, an ice cream parlor, a postal store and a dry cleaner. Where are the corporate offices?

He had left the house early after retrieving his Smith & Wesson pistol from the locked box in the bedroom closet and slipping a handful of cartridges into his pocket. Not that he expected anything bad to go down, but Trevor liked to be prepared. Well before the rest of the world took their places at work, he had driven six hours across the Nevada border to Harpersville, a small town a few miles outside of Carson City.

Trevor shook his head and pushed open the door of *We've Got Your Mail.* He scanned the postal store, empty except for a heavily-pierced clerk deeply engaged in a phone conversation. He waited, hoping the chat would wind down. After five minutes, he shoved the slip of paper with BAB Enterprises information in front of the clerk. "Where is Suite 343 located?

"Hang on, Dirk. Someone's here." She placed her hand over the phone, clearly annoyed at Trevor. "Are you looking for box 343?" she asked, cracking her gum between each word.

"No. Suite 343. It's a corporate office."

"Well, not here it ain't." She handed back the scrap of paper, still holding the cell phone in her other hand. "There are no suites here, as you can see. We just call 'em suites." The clerk rolled her eyes and then returned to her conversation.

His search for the corporate offices of BAB Enterprises led to a dingy post office box in a rundown strip mall in the western corner of Nevada. No conglomerate held board meetings in this place. It was solely a street address to put on their letterhead.

Trevor started to leave, then stopped. "When is the manager in?"

"Hang on again," she said into the phone. "Tomorrow morning, but Earl's not going to know anything either. People have their mail delivered here because they want to do things privately. Know what I mean?"

Trevor left, making certain the bells hanging from the door rail jingled loudly as he slammed the door behind him. Apparently, Earl and his clerk didn't like surprises either.

He stuffed the crumpled paper into his jeans pocket. *What do I do now?* Tracking down this lead had seemed like a good idea at four this morning. Now, not so much.

The 210-mile drive to Harpersville took longer than expected. The small town, accessible by winding roads and one-lane highways, made the journey nearly twice as long as he'd estimated. The day, quickly evaporating into night, left Trevor with nothing to show for his efforts. Nothing to prove his sincerity to Julie. No breakthrough to combat Game Masters.

He glanced at his watch. Three-fifteen. *Crap, I should be on my way home, but I can't face Julie empty-handed. Gotta wait for Earl.* He stifled a yawn and stretched, hoping to ease the ache across his lower back.

He dialed Julie. Nothing.

Can this day possibly get any worse?

He banged the heel of his hand against the screen displaying an empty battery icon and tossed the phone on the seat. Trevor slowly rolled his neck and then his shoulders producing a series of cracks and pops emanating through the car. *Ahh. Ouch.*

Sleeping—or rather, *not* sleeping—in a slipcovered recliner tweaked his muscles, leaving behind radiating tenseness for a travel companion. No way could he make that drive tonight. Better to check into a cheap hotel, get a good night's sleep, and start over in the morning.

I'll call Julie from the room. Maybe she's cooled down a little and will talk to me. Maybe.

***

While the kids and Teresa slept, Julie paced the living room, waiting to hear from Trevor. The steady *tick* of the mantel clock and an occasional creak from the wall heater kept her company.

She listened again to Trevor's message from several hours earlier. "Hi, baby, I'm still in Harpersville, Nevada. Just wanted to check in. I'll call in the morning…I love you." As soon as Julie heard Trevor's voice, she regretted sending the call from a blocked number to her voice mail.

At midnight, Julie sat on the edge of her couch and hit the call button again.

This is Trevor. Leave a message.

"Where are you?" Julie bit her lower lip. "Why won't you answer?" She set the phone down and unzipped her briefcase, revealing the patent documents Leanne retrieved before Julie left the office—PlaytimePals, PlaytimePals hologram, and PlaytimePals 3D. Julie pushed aside the linen tablecloth to make room for the three legal-length manila folders. She set them side by side on the dining room table, pulled a cap off her pen and propped her chin on an elbow.

The answer was in here, somewhere. She just wished she knew what to look for.

She opened a file and lifted a diploma-type certificate embossed with a seal and blue ribbon granting the first PlaytimePals patent. The following page listed the patent number again, her name as inventor and owner, and the date her legal rights began.

She hoisted a thicker packet—an abstract summary with figures, drawings, and explanations. This pictorial labeled key elements of PlaytimePals software. The last pages provided a detailed description of the software and a list of claims describing the invention, how it worked, its scope and limitations.

Julie rubbed her eyes to keep them from glazing over. Why did they write this stuff in another language? Everything appeared in order as far as she could tell. But then again, she never went to law school. Other folks did that sort of work and she happily paid for their expertise. Since dealing with Gary, though, trust-but-verify had become her mantra.

She pored over the remaining files, forcing herself to read each page, jotting notes about confusing sections. This could be a waste of time, busy work to keep her focused until she heard from Trevor.

Where is he? An uneasiness crept along her temples and intensified.

She realized that Trevor had taken their gun across state lines. What was he expecting to find? If harm came to him, if Burnside hurt him, she would be totally to blame. The fight last night practically forced him to prove himself.

Trevor accepted Julie's anger, rage, and hurt. He understood and continued explaining, but the devastating news overwhelmed her every sense. Listening to any rationalization Trevor contrived became impossible.

Instead, she wallowed in her own pain, dictating the rules and setting in motion a self-fulfilling prophecy—that her husband was no better than her father.

Still, she would never intentionally put Trevor, her children's father, in danger. Despite his betrayal, she loved him.

Please call, Trevor. Please.

She blinked quickly, refocusing on the files. "This all seems fairly normal, boilerplate legalese," she said aloud, hoping some irregularity would pop out.

Excitement had swirled throughout FunWorks for the 3D expansion. For a toymaker, the applications of 3D printing technology reached the moon. Clothes, accessories, even doll houses would be a few creative clicks away. For the past year, Julie followed the pricing of 3D printers. The costs were curving down and soon they would be affordable for families. Her product would be ready when the 3D printer market exploded.

Many companies experimented with 3D product lines, but as far as Julie knew, her patent applied only to toy software. The 3D PlaytimePals file, thicker than the others, held paperwork for two patents, a design patent, and a utility patent.

Julie closed the file. She blew out a long breath and hit the redial button on her cell phone. "Trevor, it's me. Again. Call please."

She disconnected and dialed Gary. He answered after several rings.

"Did I wake you?"

"Is everything okay?" He sounded groggy.

"I'm not sure. Have you talked to my husband today?"

"Trevor? We spoke for a couple of minutes after the meeting yesterday. Why? What's happened?"

Julie shifted the phone to her left hand and grabbed a pen. "What did you talk about?"

"He wanted to know more about the plumber's case. He asked if I'd found out anything else about Water Saver."

"Well, did you?"

"Only that it's now owned by the same company that sued Ray Bolley. Then he asked me about the Thorson case again. He said he was in a hurry and would explain later. What's going on?"

"What did you tell him?"

"All the stuff we went over in our meeting."

"That's all?"

"Pretty much," Gary said. "Except—"

"Except what?"

"He asked about Wallace and Weinstein."

The knot in Julie's neck tightened as though Gary had turned a ratchet. "Why? What's the connection?"

"I don't know. He insisted on me giving him their contact information. Why aren't you asking Trevor these questions?"

She swallowed against a dry throat. "Because I can't find him. He's not answering his phone. He left me a message several hours ago from Nevada. I haven't heard from him since." She paused. "Should I be worried?"

Gary exhaled. "I don't want to overreact, but we both know it's not beyond Burnside to do something crazy."

Dread crept through Julie's veins like kudzu, spreading its tentacles around her limbs and crushing her airway. She recalled the Gunther boy's overdose and near-death, Derek's near-drowning, Ray's wife.

Julie took in a measured breath before asking, "Do you think he would hurt Trevor?"

"I don't know of anyone being physically injured unless you count what happened to Derek, but we can't prove that. Usually, Burnside takes people down in other ways. Ways you can't trace. The Thorsons are in jail. Bolley abandoned his dream. The guy who invented the solar toys is in bankruptcy."

Julie sucked in air, hoping the influx of oxygen would quell the fright mounting inside her. "I have another question. I'm going through the paperwork for my three patents. You handled all of my filings, right?"

"Sorta," Gary said.

"What does that mean?"

"Most of that stuff is routine. Paralegals do the grunt work. The client gets billed under the attorney's name at the higher per-hour rate."

"Nice."

"It's common practice. The supervising attorney is ultimately responsible, so that's how we rationalize the higher fee. Why do you ask?"

"We filed for both a design and a utility patent on the 3D products. The others were just design patents. Why?"

"I don't understand."

"PlaytimePals and the hologram version are both listed as design patents, but the 3D version has both a design and a utility patent." Julie heard nothing but Gary's breathing. "Well?"

"I'm thinking. A design patent protects the product's design, in PlaytimePals case, a unique external appearance," Gary said. "A utility patent protects the article's function and other elements a design patent doesn't cover. Things like processes, chemical compounds. You should have both patents on all your products."

"According to these files, I only have the utility patent on the 3D products."

"That has to be it," Gary said slowly, hard reality painting his voice. "You own the utility rights to that software. That's where the real money is."

"You think he's not after the entire PlaytimePals line?"

"I'd bet money on it. You're using that patent for toy software. Burnside must have other ideas—more lucrative ones—in mind."

Julie tossed her pen on the table. "That makes more sense than anything I've heard recently. Now what?"

Gary took a shaky breath. "We have to be careful. This sheds a new light on Burnside. As soon as you hear from Trevor, tell him to come home." Julie's heart ceased, realizing Gary's panic at the growing threat.

"And Julie, keep those files someplace safe where only you can get to them."

Her temples pounded against another wave of nausea creeping inside her throat. She disconnected the call and prayed.

Please, God, keep Trevor safe.

***

Trevor checked out of the Easy Times Motel before seven the next morning, eager to talk with the mail store manager. He opened the glove box, laid his revolver inside, and fished out the car charger for his phone. With the cord plugged into the cigarette lighter, he made certain the battery charge light flashed.

Earl the manager should be there by now, Trevor thought, driving to the strip mall. He hoped so, and he hoped the guy would know something so this trip wouldn't turn out to be a wild goose chase.

He parked in front of the dry cleaners adjacent to the mail store and looked for signs of life as he checked his cell phone screen. Seven missed calls and five voice mail messages—all from Julie. Trevor let out a long breath and dialed.

"Trevor, for the love of God, where are you? Everyone's worried sick."

"I'm sorry."

"I've been calling nearly every hour." Julie's anxiety surged through the phone line.

"My battery died. That's why I called from the motel. I left a message on your cell phone."

"You didn't leave a number."

"Didn't it come through on the caller ID?"

"No. I haven't slept, worried sick that something bad happened to you."

He took a sip of motel coffee and scowled. "So…you missed me?"

"Missed you? I've been so afraid, I could hardly breathe. Where the hell is Harpersville, Nevada? And what are you doing there?"

Trevor explained.

"You drove all that way yesterday to follow a lead?"

He flinched at the anxiety in Julie's voice. "Seemed like a good idea. I thought I'd discover something important, something to tie Burnside to this. But all I've managed to uncover is Rocky Road at the ice cream parlor."

"You're not making any sense."

"I know. Sorry. Listen. I called Weinstein and Wallace and tricked someone in their office into giving me the address of BAB Enterprises—in Harpersville, Nevada. I tried to poke around and find out how they operate so I could surprise you by figuring out how Burnside swindles small businesses."

He let out a sigh. "But it's only a mail stop. There're no corporate offices here. This is a front for something, but I don't know what. And I don't know why it's in Po-Dunk, Nevada."

"Po-Dunk. I thought you said Harpersville."

"Same difference. If you saw this place, you'd understand. Gary said nailing Burnside would be tough and he was right. So far, all I've done is waste twenty-five gallons of gas and a lot of time."

"Are you on your way home?"

"Not yet. I'm going to hang out to talk to the day manager before I leave."

"We think Burnside is after my utility patent on the 3D PlaytimePals. I want you to drive home right now. We'll figure out another way to fight."

"I can't leave yet."

"You know what he did to Mort Gunther's kid. We think he sabotaged Derek's air supply." Julie's voice cracked. "I couldn't bear life if something happened to you. Please come home."

He heard her sniffle. "Ah, honey. Don't cry. I won't take any chances."

"I'm scared. This isn't worth it, Trevor."

"It's worth everything if you trust me again. I'll be home in a few hours. Plump the bedroom chair for me."

"This isn't funny."

He paused. "I know. I'll be home soon."

"Hurry. And this time, keep your cell phone charged."

Chapter Twenty-Two

The trill of voices competing for attention at the Papaya Juice Bar comforted Julie. Not wanting to be alone, she lingered in the building lobby, clutching a paper cup and attempting to meld into the scene. The backdrop of various conversations confirmed that the world still turned and after last night, Julie craved that message.

She sipped green tea, feeling a little guilty about leaving the house early to dodge questions the children would surely have about their dad's whereabouts. Julie closed her eyes and prayed again, beseeching St. Jude, the patron saint of hopeless causes, for an answer, knowing there wouldn't be an easy, safe way out of this mess.

Getting her husband back unharmed was the best she could hope for.

She opened her eyes and spotted Derek and Gary standing at the ordering counter. She waved the duo, both clad in jeans and T-shirts, to her table. They were encouraged by Gary's revelation about MaxOut Toys and the Thorson family. Since their meeting in Julie's office, however, their sources had dried up, with phone calls no longer being returned. Every promising lead had turned into a dead end.

Every lead except the one Trevor insisted on tracking down.

"Thanks for meeting me here, guys." Julie forced a smile.

"I caught this dude packing his suitcases." Derek tipped his cup at Gary. "I won't let him take off until this mess is straightened out, though."

Gary let out a *harrumph*. "After talking with you last night, or should I say early this morning, I knew I couldn't stay in my apartment, but I couldn't leave town, either. Not until Burnside is caught."

"I'm worried about Trevor," Julie said. "He's still in Nevada, trying to get a line on BAB's headquarters."

Gary's eyebrows shot up in alarm. "Didn't you tell him to come back?"

"Of course I did, but he has to be the knight in shining armor, riding in to rescue his damsel in distress." She swallowed, both horrified and flattered by Trevor's actions. "I'm the one who put him in this situation, telling him he's never been there for me. Forcing him to prove his love."

"Where is he exactly?" Derek asked.

"Staked outside a postal store known to be BAB corporate offices."

"You mean they don't have an actual headquarters?"

"Apparently not," Julie said. "Trevor's waiting to talk to the store manager."

Gary twisted the cap off his water bottle and took a drink. "How did he learn about the post office box address?"

"From you," Julie said.

"Me? I gave him a phone number for Wallace and Weinstein."

"He got lucky, I guess," Julie said, now fidgeting with a plastic spoon.

Derek grinned. "That husband of yours is a pretty resourceful guy."

"If we can trace these companies back to Burnside through BAB, then a lot of our questions will be answered," Gary said.

Julie no longer wanted answers, especially any that might put her and those she loved in danger. All she cared about was Trevor coming home alive.

"Where can we get a copy of BAB's ownership papers?" Derek asked.

Gary's eyes shifted from Julie to Derek.

"Well?" Derek said.

Gary wrinkled his forehead. "I'm thinking. How would Wallace and Weinstein know where the headquarters of BAB Enterprises are located? They were the counsel of record for the Thorson boy. They had no reason to contact BAB, unless…"

"Unless what?" Derek asked.

"…unless BAB paid their bills. Did Trevor use his real name?"

"I don't know," Julie said, as a sinking feeling churned against the tea barely settling in her stomach. "Why?"

"If they're a part of this, if they figure out Trevor made the connection, then he might be in real danger. Can you reach him?"

Julie's fingers shook so violently she could barely dial.

"Tell him to leave right now."

"I already told him." Julie heard Trevor's voice say *Hello.*

"Honey. Listen—" A beep cut her off.

This is Trevor. Leave a message.

***

An hour later, Julie set aside the sales reports she haphazardly reviewed and drummed her fingers against the desk blotter, waiting for Trevor to call.

"How long have you been standing there, Derek?" Her voice was barely above a whisper.

"A second or two." He crossed from the doorway and stood near the bank of filing cabinets. "No word yet?"

Julie glanced at her cell, willing the phone to ring. "Not since the early morning call I told you about."

"I'm sure he's okay."

She picked up a pencil and rolled it between her fingers, offering another silent prayer to St. Jude. "Yeah, you're right. He'll call as soon as he knows something."

Derek opened a manila folder. "Well, I have some good news for you. The documents from Vincent are here. We have Burnside by the cojones."

"Cojones?" For the first time that day, a smile teased the corners of Julie's mouth. "You speak Spanish now."

"This should give barrister Burnside something to think about."

Julie scanned the pages for several minutes, sighed, and rubbed the bridge of her nose. "Well, it's a start." *I'd feel better if Trevor were here instead of in Harpersville, though.*

"Maybe we can slow things a bit by hauling Burnside's butt into court."

Julie pushed her chair away from the desk and faced Derek. "The coward never picks on someone his own size. I wish we could nail him for that, too."

Derek rubbed his chin. "He lost once. Sals-A-Fire won the suit and he paid their court costs."

"Yeah. One for our side." Julie licked her finger and traced a number one in the air.

Derek slammed his fist against the palm of his other hand. "I'd love to take Burnside down in one big bash, rather than piece by piece."

Julie let Derek's words sink in. "Can we do that? Sue him on behalf of Ray and the other companies?"

"Nah, Vincent says we don't have the standing to initiate a class action suit yet. Once we beat him, he can solicit those other companies individually, and tell them how we prevailed," Derek said.

Julie lowered her voice. "When Trevor gets back, I'm going to talk to him about selling the company."

"What?"

"I don't want to fight anymore. I'm scared, Derek, for all of us."

"Burnside won't quit. We have to stop him."

Julie didn't reply. The threats to her family and to Derek made beating Burnside no longer important. She sympathized for those companies that would be his future conquests, but they weren't her problem.

Julie held only one wish—to make her family whole. Once Trevor returned, Burnside and FunWorks could rot in hell as far as she was concerned.

"I still think we stand a better chance if there are lots of enemies coming at him," Derek said. "It's easier to pick off your enemies one at a time."

"I can't deal with any of that now."

"Our win, combined with the salsa folks, gives legal precedence for those other small businesses."

Julie pondered the impossible. "That jerk would fall apart like a cheap paper kite in a Chicago wind if lawsuits were being fired at him from all sides. Even the mighty Bennett Burnside couldn't withstand that kind of attack."

Derek flicked his eyes at Julie. "Most of the companies were wiped out years ago. Remember, you really worked to get Ray Bolley to talk."

"He wanted to leave the past in the past." That seemed like sound advice. Soon all of this would be a distant memory and her family would be whole again.

"And now that we're involved, Ray wants to fight back." Derek sounded a bit like a braggart. "Vincent is working on that list of the companies you uncovered. He's starting with Ray's and researching every patent infringement case filed in the last ten years."

Julie nodded and moved her cell phone closer.

"Vincent spoke with Ray and the guy who used to own New Tech," Derek said. "They're both interested in reopening their cases, but neither will be ready in time."

"What about a continuance?" Julie asked automatically, not really listening, still focused on Trevor's whereabouts.

"Vincent thinks it's best to hit Burnside quick. The longer we take to prepare, the more time he has to devise a defense."

"True."

"He's already lost his attempt to be king of the flavored salsa world. As soon as Vincent gets the other cases up and running, Burnside will see nothing but lawsuit after lawsuit." Derek smirked, his voice rising with excitement. "They'll stretch across his future like fence posts."

Julie swept a few stray hairs from her forehead. "Let's not get cocky."

"Why? Are you having second thoughts?"

"Burnside isn't going to give in. And I can't risk my family.

"What else can he do? He's sued us. He has our customers afraid to do business with us. The DA is investigating you for money laundering. What's left?"

Julie made a scoffing sound. "Don't ask. The good thing is we know his real motivation—the 3D patent, not the toy company. Maybe that gives us an edge."

Derek tossed his tablet on Julie's desk. "Who knows how many more companies he's cheated? If we can get access to the BAB records, we may find out this is just the beginning."

"That's what Trevor thinks. But if BAB is only smoke and mirrors, there might not be any real records to get hold of."

Julie eyed her silent phone. She wished Trevor would call. *Damn...*

***

Trevor visited a nearby sandwich shop, preparing for a long afternoon of waiting. Five minutes before one o'clock and still no signal from the manager.

As he headed back with food, he heard his phone ringing through the closed car door. Probably Julie, he thought, sliding in behind the wheel.

"Trevor, thank God," Julie's voice boomed through the receiver, a mixture of relief and anger pouring out. "Are you all right?"

"I'm fine, baby." The fast-food wrapper crinkled as he bit through layers of turkey and cheese bookended in sourdough.

"I've been going out of my mind with worry. Where are you?"

"Still in the parking lot of the Carriage Center."

"You're not still in Nevada, are you?

"Would you be mad if I said yes?"

"Mad? Trevor, it's not safe for you to be there. I told you that this morning." Her voice cracked. "I'm worried about you."

"Does that mean you love me, too?"

"Of course, I love you."

"Enough to restore my bedroom privileges? Sleeping in the chair hurts my back and my neck. My pride isn't happy either."

"You can sleep in our bed. You can have your marital privileges reinstated. But you've got to be alive to enjoy them."

He laughed, his attempt at levity ringing hollow. "Thank you." In truth, he worried that Burnside or one of his minions could get a bit out of line, but after their discussion, bringing his gun seemed like a brilliant move.

"Please tell me you're driving home."

"I spoke with the day shift manager this morning," Trevor said, diverting the conversation. "Some guy comes in between six and seven to collect what's in that post office box. It's about one-thirty now. I'm going to hang out for a couple more hours and see who turns up."

"Trevor!"

"Honey, it makes no sense to leave now. I won't do anything crazy. I'm not going to put myself in front of a bullet." He heard Julie's deep gasp.

"You don't have to prove anything to me. I know you love me and you'd never intentionally hurt me."

"That's not what you said the other night."

"But, Trevor—

"Listen, my phone is charged. Call every five minutes if you're worried. Right now, I'm going to finish my lunch and wait for a guy who's about six feet tall and balding."

"Okay, but the first time you don't answer, I'm calling the police."

"Fair enough. Hey, I have a bunch of missed calls from Gary. What's that about?"

Julie explained.

"If Burnside is worried, that's good."

"I'm not so sure. I'm going to tell him I'm ready to sell."

"No. Don't. Not yet." Trevor couldn't be the reason Julie abandoned her dream. He'd never be able to live with himself knowing she sold out because of his foolish decisions. "Trust me, please. I'm going to check this out and then I'll be on my way."

"I don't want you facing off against some hoodlums."

"This isn't the gunfight at the OK Corral. I just want to talk to the guy who gets the mail. Then I'll head home."

He ended the call, hoping this wasn't the last time he'd talk to his wife.

On the other hand, where was the danger in asking a few questions?

***

It was hard for Julie to understand what Leung Jun said. The phone connection from China was scratchy, but not because of the whir of machinery. She heard drawers slam, metal containers scrape against concrete floors.

"They close us because of you," Jun shouted in broken English. "I don' know why. Stipends are pay."

Stipend, Julie mused. A euphemism for bribe. It was a little after two in California. Early morning in Shenzhen.

"The labor minister say they receive complaint. Say we don't pay overtime. We always pay overtime."

Julie heard the panic in his voice. "Jun, what's going on? Who complained?"

"He shut everything down. Say there'll be fair labor audit."

"Who wants an audit?" Julie asked recalling the horror stories she'd heard from other manufacturers including investigations for unsafe working conditions, excessive recruitment fees, and underage workers. She and Derek picked Jun's company as their contractor because of his good labor rating and consistent on-time delivery record. Only one person could be behind these trumped-up charges.

"The labor minister. The employees. I not know. Someone call labor watch hotline."

Julie didn't want to believe what she heard. "It was an anonymous complaint?"

"Guess so. I can no fill any electronics orders." Jun's frustration escalated with each word before reaching full panic mode. "All customers have to wait. I miss their deadlines."

"When did this happen?"

"Just now. They still here, walking about, talking to employees. Ask if I'm bad boss." Julie thought she heard Jun sob. "You fix this. Please, Miss Julie, fix this."

"But how?" Julie asked. "I'm in California."

"Agent say you know what to do. Hurry, please. Other customers take their orders to another factory if I not operating in twenty-four hours. Workers leave, too, even though they don't want to go back to garment factory."

"Don't worry, Jun. I'll take care of everything," Julie lied. "This is a mix-up. I'll make a few calls and get the matter straightened out."

"Need to hang up now, Miss Julie. The minister wants to talk to me." Jun disconnected.

Julie stood, her spine steel straight, for the first time fully realizing the massive scope of Bennett Burnside's reach. The torment he was capable of inflicting stretched to the other side of the world. Innocent Jun was now caught in the crosshairs of her battle.

She would make things right—she *had* to make things right—as soon as she figured out how.

Chapter Twenty-Three

Trevor watched as someone jogged up to the mail center. After the man entered, the clerk waved from the storefront doorway.

Trevor straightened. That was his signal. At that moment, his cell began ringing. He pushed the *I'll call you back* auto-message reply, slid the phone into his pocket, and hurried through the entrance toward the clerk.

Trevor glanced around. "Well, where'd he go?"

"Where'd who go?" Earl, the day manager, said.

"The guy who just came in."

"You mean Jasper?" He pointed his heavily-tattooed arm to a man hanging his jacket in the backroom. "He works here."

Trevor sighed. "Did anyone collect the mail for box 343?"

"Not that I know of," Earl said.

"Then why did you wave to me to come in?"

He held out the receiver. "Because there's a call for you."

Trevor's stomach lurched as though a truck dumped its load of stones. "A call for me? No one knows I'm here."

"Apparently, somebody does. He wants to talk to the guy sitting in the dark blue Toyota Highlander. That's you, dude. Do you want the call or not?"

Trevor grabbed the receiver. "Hello."

"Rafferty. We've got Emily."

A cold edge of terror sliced through Trevor's body. There had to be a mistake. "What? Who is this? What are you talking about?"

"If you want your little girl back, stop asking questions and go home."

"Who the hell is this?"

"Your daughter's safe. If you want her to stay that way, you and your wife better do what you're told."

"Let me talk to her!" Trevor ordered. His stomach roiled. He fought to keep the vile taste of lunch down.

"Call your wife." The line went dead.

Trevor shoved the receiver at the clerk, narrowly missing his face.

They've taken Emily.

"Dude. Don't take your stuff out on me."

Trevor ran back to his car, wondering how he could make the seven-hour drive to San Marcel in less time.

The tires squealed as he drove out of the parking lot, waiting for his call to Julie to connect.

"They took Emily!" she shouted, panic in her voice.

Trevor clicked on the speakerphone and Julie's terror flooded the car. "I know, honey. It's going to be all right." He panted. Sweat poured down his face, over his body. "I'm on my way home now. They won't hurt her."

"How do you know?" she screamed. "Anybody who'd kidnap a child will do anything!"

Trevor swallowed hard. His wild-goose chase gave Burnside more time to plot. And now the man had made the ultimate move. He'd taken the one thing they could never live without—their child.

"They can have anything they want. Just give Emily back." Ragged sobs smothered Julie's words.

"I know, honey, I know." Trevor fought to keep his voice calm. "I feel the same way. Hey, we can't fall apart."

"None of this is worth what's happening to my baby girl."

Trevor wiped his eyes. "Have you called the cops?"

"He warned me not to."

"Call the police, Julie. Right now!"

"No," she replied through a torrent of tears. "He said if the police get involved, we'll never see Emily again."

"Did you recognize the voice?"

"No," Julie yelped.

Her tone ran an icy finger along Trevor's spine. "Who else is at the house?" he asked.

"Jason, Nicole, and Teresa."

"No one else?" He merged onto the freeway.

"No, why?"

"Just making sure everyone is accounted for."

"You don't think they'd come after Jason or Nicole, too?

"Obviously, we are way out of our league. I never in a million years thought…"

Trevor pushed the gas pedal harder, his leg jerking with tension. While he'd been playing private eye, someone had lured Emily away. A thug hired by Burnside stole his baby daughter. What kind of father let that happen? What kind of father didn't protect his family?

"Teresa was supposed to pick her up from school."

His speedometer needle moved past eighty. "They knew I was in Harpersville. One of Burnside's goons called me at the mailbox store. What did your guy say?"

"Emily is fine," Julie answered between sobs. "She'll stay safe if I withdraw my countersuit and sell FunWorks to Game Masters."

"You spoke to her?"

"For a second. They were on their way to the movies."

The veins in Trevor's neck bulged, working to contain his pulsating heartbeat. "The kidnapper is entertaining her?"

"That's what it sounded like. He told her to hang up because the movie was about to start and they had to get popcorn."

"Popcorn?" Trevor's voice thundered through the empty car.

"He wanted off the phone before she panicked." Julie's tone softened.

"Honey, I know you're worried, but think. They don't want Emily. They want FunWorks." Trevor exhaled sharply, hoping that was the truth. "As long as you don't sign anything, Emily will be safe. And at least she's not scared."

"Not yet. I want her home. She needs to be home."

"I'll be there as fast as I can."

"They're going to call in the morning and give me instructions." Julie sobbed again. "I don't know what to do."

Trevor's hands trembled but he kept his voice steady. "She'll be home soon. I'll call you in an hour to see if anything has changed." He hit disconnect, then dialed another number and pressed harder on the gas pedal.

Why hadn't Teresa picked up Emily?

"They have Emily," Trevor shouted into the phone. "Burnside knew I was in Nevada."

"How?" Gary asked.

"Doesn't matter. They've crossed a line. We can't trust their word." *Including their promise to keep Emily safe.*

"I'll get hold of Vincent and cancel our plan," Gary said. "This might be for the best. Sell and get out of Dodge."

"Wrong." The word shot from Trevor's belly as though propelled from a slingshot. He knew the countersuit had pushed Burnside to take this horrific, desperate step. They caught him off-guard and couldn't reel back the only offense they had. "Then we have no guarantee they'll return Emily. FunWorks is our only leverage."

"I guess, but Trevor…*kidnapping*, for God's sake. That's a felony."

"So was trying to drown Derek."

"We can't prove that," Gary countered in his strongest lawyer voice.

"Doesn't make it any less true."

"Have you notified the authorities?"

"No, and we won't until we have something to give them."

"I don't know about this," Gary said, the words rattled out as though tumbling from a salt shaker.

"We have no choice."

For the next several minutes Gary listened as Trevor outlined a new strategy.

"Watch your back," Trevor warned. "If they know you're talking to me, who knows what will happen. I'll call you when I can."

Trevor disconnected, confident he was doing the only thing he could to save his family. Still, he prayed. *Dear Lord, keep Emily safe. Give me Your vision*, he sobbed. *I need You, God. I need You now.*

Chapter Twenty-Four

Julie slammed closed the scrapbook album from Emily's last birthday party and hugged the book to her chest. "It's been hours!"

Earlier she had taken up her First Communion rosary and led the family, bead by bead, in a series of Our Fathers and Hail Marys. Relief didn't arrive, and she wondered why she turned to God when her prayers continued to go unanswered. She dropped the album onto the coffee table and instinctively reached for the silver cross dangling at her neck.

Jason scooted to the edge of his chair, closer to his mother. "When's Dad supposed to get here?"

"Around one, he thinks." Julie fingered the medal as though rubbing a prayer stone with the power to soothe and calm. She wanted to believe the cross could grant her plea: bring Emily home safe. Surely God would send her a sign, a ribbon of light to reassure her that Emily would be home soon. But as the minutes slipped away, so did her faith.

Nicole spent most of the night curled in a chair near the bay window, waiting to see Trevor's headlights pull into the driveway. Jason alternated between sitting close to his mother and peering out the window.

"Do you want me to put on a pot of coffee?" Teresa asked standing on the far side of the living room.

"Yes, please," Julie said as the mantel clock chimed midnight. Time crawled. She slumped onto the couch.

Teresa leaned against the brick fireplace and stared at the floor. "We could order pizzas."

Julie clapped her hands, infusing fake enthusiasm for the idea. "Yes, pizza. That's what we need. Who can we call this late?"

"Palermo's, I think." Jason opened a desk drawer and retrieved a takeout menu. "They stay open until two."

"I'll call." Julie stood but her knees buckled. She fell on the couch, buried her face in her hands and sobbed.

Teresa hurried to Julie and rubbed her shoulders. "Nothing's going to happen to Emily," she said. "I promise."

"How do you know?" Julie barked.

"Our Emily is one tough cookie." Teresa's face creased in pain. "I love these kids like they were my own grandchildren." She swiped a tear from the corner of her eye. "If only I hadn't stopped at the market…"

"Even if you'd been on time, Burnside and his goons would have found another way to take Emily, and they might have hurt you in the process." Julie sniffed back tears. "They were sending a message I was going to get, one way or another."

"Well, they went too far when they messed with my baby sister." Jason stood beside his mother and Julie reached for his hand.

"I put you all in danger." Tears flowed. "And for what?"

Jason patted her hand. "You didn't do anything wrong, Mom."

Julie sucked in some air and released the breath slowly. "That's not entirely true. Emily would be upstairs right now, asleep in her bed, if I hadn't been so stubborn. Instead…" Julie glanced toward the windows. "I don't know where she's sleeping or what's happening to her. Or if they're hurting her."

"She's fine," Teresa repeated. "Once you give them what they want, they'll return her."

Julie turned to Teresa and gripped her hands. "I pray you're right. But these people are ruthless. They tried to kill Derek. They've shut down my manufacturing plant in China. And now they've taken Emily." Julie shook her head and released her grasp on Teresa. "This is going to stop and I'm going to stop it. As soon as they call."

Nicole jumped from her chair. "Dad's home." She bounded toward the door.

Julie threw herself at Trevor as he stepped inside. Cradled in his arms, the shudder enveloping her body calmed for a fleeting moment.

***

Julie thought she heard the beginnings of a Hail Mary as Teresa headed toward the kitchen. Her housekeeper and true friend couldn't hide her worry for Emily's safety. Teresa faulted herself for this misery, but Bennett Burnside, not Teresa, held the blame.

Julie followed Teresa to tell her so, but Teresa's voice stopped her before entering. Instead, she stood silent and tilted her ear toward the kitchen door.

"Bring her back right now. This isn't what I agreed to…Zeke, this is getting out of hand," she overheard Teresa beg. Fright caught in her throat.

"Let me talk to Emily." Teresa's plea sounded as fragile as toppling crystal. "Okay, then don't wake her. Zeke, if anything…Zeke?"

Julie pushed open the door. Teresa quickly slid her cell phone into her jacket pocket. "Who was that?" Julie asked, her voice gravely and accusatory, even to her own ears.

Teresa swung around and placed the carafe on a tray alongside a few mugs. "Just finished brewing the coffee. Trevor looks like he needs a cup. We're in for a long night." She lifted the tray and moved toward the living room.

Julie shifted to block the exit, hands balled into fists. She was sure of what she'd heard. Dread crawled along her spine, tightened her throat. "Who was on the phone?"

"Huh?" The tray rattled as Teresa tried to maneuver around, but Julie wouldn't budge.

"You asked to talk to Emily," Julie said, her patience quickly uncoiling.

Teresa sidestepped. "How could I talk to Emily? I don't know where she is."

"Then who were you talking to at nearly one o'clock in the morning?" Julie shifted too, still standing with her arms folded across her chest and her lips tight. Her face hardened with anger.

Teresa stared through Julie. "No one. The coffee's set. I was heading back to the living room."

Julie stepped closer. "Not until you tell me who you were talking to."

Teresa backed away. "You're upset, honey. I don't know anything more than the rest of you." She charged toward the doorway, using the tray as a barrier, but Julie blocked her exit again.

Julie held out her palm. "Let me see your cell. I'll redial the last number you called and we'll straighten out this whole misunderstanding."

Cups and spoons clanked as Teresa plunked the tray on the kitchen table. She crumpled into a nearby chair. Her aging hands covered her face, muffling her wails. "Oh, Zeke, what have we done?"

"Zeke's involved?"

Teresa's sobs overwhelmed her mumbled reply.

Julie seized Teresa by the shoulders, shook her. "Did Zeke take Emily? Tell me, Teresa! Does he have my baby?"

Teresa cringed.

"Where is she?" Julie screamed and jerked Teresa harder. "Is she with Zeke? Damn it, Teresa, you better tell me what you know." Julie slammed her hand on the kitchen table. "And I mean right now."

Teresa flinched, looking away. "You'll never forgive me."

Julie's heart pounded so hard her vision blurred. "What have you done?"

"I gave them Emily."

"What? Trevor, get in here!" she yelled.

"What's the screaming about?" Trevor asked, barreling into the kitchen seconds later. "What happened?"

Teresa grabbed a dish towel, wiped her eyes, and began twisting the cloth.

"Teresa and Zeke kidnapped Emily." Julie pointed, her voice cracking. "She's in on it."

Trevor shook his head in amazement. "The kidnapping? Are you sure?" He shifted his eyes to Teresa but she wouldn't lift her head to meet his gaze.

"I heard her talking to him a minute ago," Julie snapped.

"Is Zeke in trouble again?" Trevor demanded, yanking Teresa to her feet. He tilted her chin to face him. "What's Zeke have to do with Emily?"

Julie stood next to Trevor. "There's a frightened little girl out there, wondering where her mom and dad are."

Teresa gulped in a breath. "She's not frightened. She's asleep." Her voice fell to a whisper. "Zeke told me she's asleep."

***

Trevor glimpsed his reflection in the mirror above the sink. Frightened, bloodshot eyes and a five-o'clock shadow stared back. Knowing Zeke perpetrated the kidnapping didn't instill relief. Instead, Trevor's anger grew.

Someone he didn't trust had Emily, leaving Burnside still in control.

"He owed twenty thousand dollars," Teresa sobbed.

"To Burnside?" he asked, staring at the woman who had once offered his children warm homemade oatmeal cookies after school. The truth crushed him. Teresa sacrificed Emily for her own son's safety.

"No, to his bookie. I don't know how Burnside got involved." Teresa shrugged. "Zeke couldn't raise that kind of money. I tried to borrow some, but… The idea didn't seem so wrong at the time."

"Didn't seem wrong?" Trevor fought to keep control.

Harming Teresa wouldn't bring Emily home. He rubbed his aching temples as though the increased blood flow would help him think. "If these guys scared Zeke, don't you think they'd scare Emily?"

"What else could I do? They were going to hurt him, bad."

Julie stepped toward Teresa. "All right, your little confession time is over. Take us to Zeke so we can end this."

Teresa twisted the dish towel tighter. "I don't know where they are. And I don't think he's alone."

"Call then. Pretend you have the wrong number. Maybe we'll hear something in the background," Julie said.

"What will that get us? It's 1:30 in the morning. They'll know something's up."

"Trevor's right. They promised nothing would happen to her," Teresa reminded. "They'd forgive Zeke's gambling debts if we took Emily for a little overnight. Emily would be returned as soon as Julie signed the paperwork."

Trevor shook his head, mystified. "And you believed them? You used a seven-year-old baby as a bargaining chip." The words caught in his throat. "She trusted you. I trusted you. You betrayed all of us."

Teresa squirmed in her chair. "They threatened to break both his legs this time." Teresa's voice broke. "Trevor, you know how hard life's been for Zeke."

"I know how hard he's made life for himself," Trevor said, no remorse in his voice. Teresa had been bailing Zeke out of scrapes since middle school and that's when their boyhood friendship began to fray.

The last straw came in their senior year when Zeke borrowed Trevor's pickup and rolled the truck on the highway. Zeke, high on meth, walked away unscathed. The truck was totaled.

"She's with a man who owes thousands to a bookie." Julie wailed. "Worse, he's working for a criminal who thinks nothing of destroying people. You must be out of your mind."

"I wasn't thinking straight."

Trevor slammed the wall with the flat of his hand. "Yeah, cash can change a lot of straight thoughts into crooked ones."

"It wasn't just the money. I hoped you two would get back together," Teresa cried.

Julie stared. "Back together? Why was that your responsibility?"

"If you had listened to Emily's bedtime prayers—"

"This is *our* fault?" Trevor's voice went up an octave. He threw his mug against the wall, sending ceramic shards and coffee exploding across the room. "What a load of crap."

"It's just that…when you moved out, Emily took it hard."

"She's seven. She's going to be upset to see her parents fighting," Trevor yelled.

Teresa dropped her head. "She wanted her family back the way things used to be. There were days when I was the only adult here. But that's not my only reason for agreeing to do this." Teresa turned to face Julie. "You'd have more time to take care of your family once the business was sold."

"You can't possibly rationalize your way out of this," Julie bellowed.

"You've got to understand. He's my only child. I had to help him get out from under before they hurt him again."

"You've been bailing Zeke's ass out for years," Trevor argued. "It never helped him, Teresa. Never. If anything, you coming to his rescue only made things worse."

Teresa stood and touched Julie's arm. "Emily's not afraid. She thinks she's helping you and her dad. This was God's answer to her prayers. That's why I know she's not frightened."

Julie shoved Teresa and moved closer to Trevor. "And what about tomorrow? Will she be frightened when she wakes up and we're not there?"

"Will Zeke keep her safe?" Trevor prodded, then shook his head in disgust. "Of course not. He can't even keep himself out of trouble."

"How could you give our baby to these people? How could you?" Julie's slap landed hard on Teresa's cheek, knocking Teresa back on to her chair.

Trevor stared at the red mark on his wife's palm, his thoughts exploding through the top of his head.

Where are You, God? Where are You now?

***

Julie hadn't slept in forty-eight hours. She sat on the couch, cradling Nicole's head on her lap with one hand resting on her oldest daughter's cheek and the other on her cell phone. Trevor and Jason were still asleep in the recliners.

Teresa sat in a ladder-back dining room chair, alternating between staring out the window and at her folded hands.

Julie jumped at the bell tower ringtone. The loud chiming woke everyone.

"Hello." Julie's shoulders tensed and she struggled for air. "Yes, I understand." Her eyes darted to Trevor now sitting next to her. Nicole, Jason, and Teresa clustered around them like starving puppies.

"Just let me talk to Emily. I want to make sure... Yes, I know, but... Wait!" She slumped. "He hung up." The words choked in her throat. "I can't stand this waiting." She buried her face against Trevor's chest.

Jason moved closer. "What else did they say?"

She used her hands to swipe tears away. "A messenger will be here in fifteen minutes with buyout papers. They'll hurt Emily if I don't sign them."

Trevor rubbed Julie's back. "After you sign those papers, they'll have the company and Emily."

"What else can we do? The woman will notarize my signature and give me a check. Once she leaves, they'll tell us where to pick up Emily."

"They have to make this appear to be on the up-and-up. I'm sure the amount is nowhere near market value," Trevor said.

Julie's voice deadened. "Two million dollars."

"That's less than a third of the company's worth."

Julie collapsed on the sofa. "I don't care. I'll sign the papers. We'll get Emily back and move on with our lives." Her lips formed a straight line.

"Just like Bolley."

"Yes, exactly like Ray Bolley. He was the smart one. He got out when he and his wife still had a life together. And that's what I'm going to do."

Julie's phone rang again. "I understand. Yes, I will be at the law offices at ten. When do we get Emily back? No, that's not good enough. I want to talk to her now." Julie listened and then hung up. "They've changed their minds. They're not sending a messenger. Too many people around. They want me at the Ryder offices in forty-five minutes."

"Where's Emily? Why won't they let us talk to her?" Trevor asked.

Julie lifted a framed family photo and traced a finger across Emily's smile. "He said we could call her in five minutes on Teresa's cell phone." Julie stared at the housekeeper. "He says she has the number."

"How could they know Teresa talked?" Jason asked.

"I told you these guys are for real." Teresa squirmed. "They find out things...like how Zeke owed money to a bookie."

Trevor nodded. "And how they knew about—"

Julie put a finger to her lips and set the photo frame facedown on the coffee table. She grabbed a pen and wrote frantically on the corner of a newspaper:

THE HOUSE IS BUGGED.

Trevor's puzzled eyes scanned the room.

Julie pointed to a small wireless transmitter stuck to the back of the photo frame. "I don't know how they're finding stuff out," Julie stammered. "And I don't care. All I care about is Emily coming home safely."

Trevor put his arm around his wife. "Then you better leave if you plan to get to their offices by ten."

Julie narrowed her eyes. "Not until I talk to my daughter. Teresa, dial the damn number."

Chapter Twenty-Five

Time moved in slow-motion for Julie on the twenty-minute ride to the attorney's office. She struggled to keep her focus on the road, a nervous vibration radiating through her body. She clicked off the radio and let Emily's sweet voice replay in her mind.

"I'm fine, Mommy," her precious daughter had said minutes ago. "Why didn't you get me last night, like Uncle Zeke said you would? Are you with Daddy?"

"Not right now, sweetie. I have to sign some papers first, and then Daddy, Jason, Nicole, and I will come get you."

"They get to miss school today?"

Julie couldn't help grinning at Emily's whiny tone. "Just this one time. It's a special occasion. So special we're going to celebrate with breakfast at Louise's Café."

"Yum-mee," Emily said. "I ate a donut and some milk, but I'm still hungry."

A man's voice interrupted. "We have to go, honey."

"Where are we going? Where's Uncle Zeke?" Emily asked the man.

"Go wash your hands. They're all sticky. I'll tell you when you get back." He cleared his throat. "Okay, Mom, you've talked to your girl. She's not scared, and I know you want her to stay that way."

"Who is this?" Julie asked.

"Go sign the papers." He clicked off.

Julie's mother had endured insurmountable struggles raising three daughters alone. But in all those years, Bridget Jameson never put her children at risk. Julie, Monica, and Kate remained safe and secure despite the numerous gray hairs they'd caused their mother.

What would Bridget think of Julie now...

"Momma," Julie said into the quietness, wishing her mother was still alive. "I've been praying like I saw you do all those years, but prayers don't help. Not the way you promised they would." She sucked in a tear. "They have Emily Bridget, the granddaughter you never met. Did you know she's named after you? She's so much like you. Inquisitive. Trusting. Generous. Faithful. Please ask God to keep her safe. I haven't been able to."

Julie pulled into the parking lot and gazed at the marble and glass building. Burnside's people had arranged the takeover like an ordinary business transaction, camouflaged among mahogany desks and thick pile carpeting.

Where's the seedy B-rated movie ending I deserve? Julie thought. If there was any poetic justice, I'd be signing papers in some dank, dark back alley under the watchful eye of a tobacco-chewing thug named Rocco.

Standing on shaky legs, Julie slammed the car door and turned toward the entrance.

Mom, you always taught your daughters that all things are in God's hands. Ask Him to open them wide to hold Emily. And me.

***

Gary Carlson greeted Julie as soon as she entered the conference room.

"You're here?" She spat the words.

Gary ignored her insult. "Hi, Julie. Nice to see you again."

"You're the last person I expected to see," she said, giving him a limp handshake.

He held her grasp. "I'm your attorney of record."

She pulled her hand away, noticing a bruised swelling on his cheek.

"Remember? You refused to let Fulton Rush take over." Gary nodded toward a man seated at the far end of the conference table sitting next to Bennett Burnside. "I'm glad you've accepted Game Masters' generous offer."

Julie tightened her fists.

Fulton Rush crossed the room to wedge himself between Gary and Julie. "Please sit. We'll explain the process, and then you can sign the papers and be on your way, with a nice-sized check." His condescending grin sent a chill along Julie's spine.

"Look, the only reason I'm here is because you've kidnapped my daughter. Otherwise, I'd never be in the same room with pond-sucking scum like you. Where is Emily?"

Burnside stood and bowed half-heartedly. "That's no way to talk. It's nice to see you again, Ms. Rafferty."

"He's facilitating this transaction," Fulton added.

Julie scowled. "Facilitating? It feels more like a fu—"

"Ms. Rafferty, it's my understanding your daughter is voluntarily spending time with your housekeeper's son," Burnside said.

"You kidnapped her!" Julie shouted.

Burnside let go of the formalities. "Calm down, Julie. No one's been kidnapped. Now take your seat so we can get on with this."

Gary pointed to a chair. His hand brushed the bruised area of his face in a soothing motion.

"You're wise to take advantage of this opportunity," Burnside said to her.

He sounds like a general, commanding the troops to victory, Julie thought. She sat next to Gary, on the opposite side of Fulton Rush, leaving them both with a clear view of Burnside.

"I'm referring to the very generous offer Game Masters has made to purchase FunWorks." He pointed to the files placed in front of them.

"I know why I'm here. I want to get this done so I can get my daughter back."

"We're eager to finalize, too." Burnside's smile eerily reinforced what Julie already knew.

"Your attorney has reviewed the documents and agreed in principle on the matter," Fulton said, changing the direction of the conversation.

"My attorney is Vincent Williams," Julie reminded.

"Unfortunately, before you hired Mr. Williams, you didn't release Mr. Carlson of his duties," Burnside shot back. "Gary obtained Williams's signed affidavit relinquishing his position as your counsel an hour ago. A copy of the paperwork is in the file."

Gary cleared his throat. "A standard RR&R contract prohibits the client from retaining additional representation without first getting approval from us. Williams concurred that his agreement was invalid."

Gary fished the document out of the file folder. "He asked me to offer his congratulations for settling the matter expeditiously and profitably."

"You guys got to Williams, too?" Julie folded her arms, hoping that would quell their shaking.

There really was only one way out. Trading a toy company for Emily.

Julie would make that deal every day of the week.

She looked at the three men in the room. Their arrogance made her stomach churn. In another place, in another time, she would take them on and win. But not today.

"The entire agreement is spelled out in the file in front of you. I think you'll be pleased with what we're offering. Once you sign," Burnside held an oblong slip of paper in his right hand, "I'll hand you this cashier's check."

He displayed the check. "Two million dollars." He lingered over the words, as though they were drops of brandy.

Julie put her elbows on top of the unopened file and kept her gaze on Burnside.

"In exchange, Game Masters acquires all interest in your company. That means, intellectual property rights, sole ownership of all contracts with celebrity endorsements and…"

Julie stopped listening as Burnside droned on. Instead, she prayed a silent Hail Mary for Emily's safety and drummed her nails on top of the manila folder.

Trevor had said to stall.

She took a deep breath, hoping to slow her rapid pulse. She straightened in her chair, her heart stopping for a moment. "My life has been stretched beyond normal boundaries ever since I met you at the Toy Fair. Last night was especially stressful. I haven't slept in two days." She waited for Burnside's reaction. None came. "Regardless, I still need to read the paperwork before I sign anything."

Burnside's scowl added to Julie's mounting anxiety, but she continued. She flicked her eyes from Burnside to Gary. "Give me a few minutes to review this with my counsel, such as he is."

"Review it? Why, of course, Ms. Rafferty, you can review the offer."

She winced at the sudden stiffness in Burnside's tone.

"Perhaps you want us to read along with you, page by page?" Fulton said.

Julie allowed a slight grin at the sarcasm. "No. That won't be necessary. I'm able to read. What I want is some time to understand these contracts…and maybe a cup of coffee."

Burnside's eyebrows arched. "You want a cup of coffee? You were so eager to get this deal over and done with. You said the sooner, the better."

"I'm not in a hurry to get the deal done." She stood. "What you heard me say was I'm in a hurry to get my daughter back."

"Delaying signing the papers isn't in the best interest of your family."

Neither is selling my business to a creep like you.

"I need to know what I'm signing, even under these extreme circumstances." *Trevor, you better know what you're doing.*

"Margie." Burnside directed his words to the secretary sitting in the corner of the room. "Bring coffee and whatever else Ms. Rafferty requests. Maybe you'd like a muffin or fresh fruit, too?"

"No, thank you."

Burnside waited until Margie left the room. "We'll come back in thirty minutes. Is that enough time for your consultation?"

"Yes, that's fine." Julie took a deep breath, trying to move the rock-heavy lump that lay in her chest. *It had better be.*

"If these papers aren't signed when we return, then this deal will be off the table...and so will any other agreement we've made." He waited long enough for his threat to sink in before he strode out with Fulton tailing behind.

Julie stared into the space vacated by Burnside, her heart thumping so loudly in her ears she couldn't think.

So help me God, if you've done anything to hurt my daughter, you will never have another moment's peace. I'll spend the rest of my life guaranteeing that.

***

Trevor watched a plumber's truck drive by and park a few doors down. He moved from the window and sat on the arm of the couch, like a panther waiting to pounce. At the sound of a knock, he flew across the living room in two strides and had the front door opened before anyone else had a chance to move.

Ray Bolley stood on the doorstep. Without speaking, Trevor gestured him to the front lawn. Jason, Nicole, and Teresa followed them to the side yard where they'd be less visible to passing cars and formed a loose circle around Ray.

"Mr. Rafferty, nice to meet you." Ray extended his hand.

He gave Ray's hand a strong pump. "Call me Trevor."

"I can't thank you enough for what you're doing."

"We don't have a lot of time. Julie's at the attorney's office right now," Trevor said. "I'm worried Burnside's watching the house too, so we have to make this fast. Kids, I'm going with Ray. Go back inside and act like nothing's changed. Watch TV, play a board game or something." He brushed Nicole's cheek with his finger. "And don't say anything about me not being here."

Jason and Nicole nodded.

"Write down what you need to communicate. Don't say anything out loud."

"I want to go with you guys and help," Jason stammered.

"The best way you can help is to wait. Stay with your sister and keep an eye on Teresa." Trevor placed his hands on Jason's shoulders. "I know it's hard, son, but we need Burnside to believe everyone's still in the house. They can't know I'm gone."

Jason nodded slowly, his sun-streaked hair moving with his answer.

"Your dad knows what he's doing," Ray said in a grandfatherly way. "I wish I'd known your mom and dad when I faced this SOB. Things might have turned out differently for me, boy."

Ray patted Jason's shoulder. "But that's another story for another day."

Jason kept his gaze on his sneakers.

Trevor tilted Jason's face to his. "Ace. Take care of the ladies until I get back."

"Yeah, Dad. Sure. I don't care what happens to stupid FunWorks, I want Emily back." He used his fists to wipe away tears that found their way into his eyes. "Even if she's the most annoying kid on earth."

***

The mahogany-paneled conference room featured a large gilded-framed mirror mounted on the wall across from where Julie sat. *He's watching me and, I bet, reveling in his genius.* She lifted her slouchy oversized purse, dug inside for a pen and set the bag on the table in front of her hoping to block his view.

Shifting closer to Gary, she slipped a note on top of the document. "Start with page one. I don't want you skipping any of the fine print you lawyers love to layer into these contracts."

Gary read her note: *They're listening. Don't say anything that will give us away.* He glanced at his wristwatch. "We have thirty minutes and the contract is sixty-five pages long."

Julie turned her chair sideways toward Gary to further block Burnside's view. "Tell me the most critical parts of what I'm signing away."

Gary moved away from the conference table and winced. He placed his hands on his sides.

They had punched him in the ribs, too.

"Do you want a more complete overview of what's stipulated in these pages?" Gary suggested. "Or, do you want to read through the agreement and ask questions as you go along?"

Julie rubbed her palms over her forearms, but the warmth she created did little to calm the fight-or-flight reflex prickling her body and her mind. Had Burnside intentionally amped up the air conditioning to add to Julie's anxiety?

"Which way makes more sense?" she prodded, wondering how much longer she could keep up the charade.

Gary shrugged. "It's really up to you."

Julie thumbed through a few pages. *How could Burnside expect her to agree to this?*

Minutes later, she pointed to a random section. "Explain this passage so I can understand."

Julie listened as Gary droned on, feigning attention. She needed to remain calm or appear serene even with her body's sympathetic nervous system flooding her blood with adrenaline, causing every tiny hair on her arms to stand at attention.

Less than an hour. You have less than an hour, Trevor, to find our daughter.

Chapter Twenty-Six

He's acting like he's in a scene from a John Wayne western, Trevor thought as Ray Bolley put his toolbox on the floor and climbed in on the passenger side of the truck.

The man had ridden in with both guns blazing, ready to shout, "Let's round up a posse, get a rope and hang them dang outlaws."

Trevor appreciated everything the old plumber had done. But if not for Ray, the takeover of FunWorks would have already happened and little Emily wouldn't have been kidnapped. That would have been a better outcome. But Trevor couldn't go back and ask for a do-over.

"These peckerheads don't got a soul." Ray's snarl compressed each wrinkle etched on his weathered face. "You can't trust 'em. Burnside will do anything to get what he's after."

Trevor was grateful for the old timer's tenacity. And for Teresa's courage. She had finally confessed that Zeke held Emily at her house. Having practically lived there through his teen years, Trevor knew every inch of the Desmond home. With that knowledge, their rescue plan came together easily.

"We have about forty-five minutes to pull this thing off. Julie and Gary are stalling for time, but if we don't move

quickly, we'll surrender our advantage and lose the company."
And maybe lose Emily.

"Is everything in place?"

"Damn right." Ray's grin revealed a few missing teeth. "I met Gary last night after you and he talked on the phone. Fulton Rush and his boys really put a beatin' on him. Not in places where you can see the damage, though."

Trevor turned the key in the ignition and the truck roared to life.

"He told me they physically outlined the short-term advantages of continuing as a junior partner with the firm," Ray quipped.

Trevor gunned the gas pedal, released the brake and pulled away from the curb a little faster than he wanted.

"Short-term, ha. They mean until the deal is done," Trevor added.

"Fulton Rush didn't realize that as far as the courts are concerned, Gary's still the FunWorks attorney. I would have loved to see the expression on Burnside's face when Fulton explained that screwup." Ray flashed a grin at Trevor.

"Even though we hired Vincent?"

"Yeah. There was some mumbo-jumbo legal reason."

"They cover every base, don't they?"

"Seem to. I never knowed Burnside to resort to violence, though," Ray said. "But I guess nobody ever fought back before."

"He wouldn't hurt Emily, would he?" Trevor asked.

"I'm sure Emily is safe with your friend...er, I guess ex-friend."

Trevor drove past Teresa's house and parked three doors down. "That's Zeke's old Impala parked in the driveway. They're in there."

He left the engine idling. The truck's vibration matched his shaking hands.

We *played wiffleball on this street. That tree was third base. We had some great times until Zeke traded street ball for street drugs.*

240

"When you knock on the front door, say you're checking for a sewer blockage," Trevor instructed. "Point to the house across the street and say they're having problems with their toilets backing up."

"I can BS my way through a clogged sewer line, no problem."

"While you divert Zeke's attention, I'll come through the rear door. I know a way into the backyard. We used to sneak in and out without Teresa ever knowing." Trevor turned off the engine. "That was long before Zeke changed."

"Are you calling Julie once Emily is safe?"

"That's the plan. Then we call the cops."

"I want to be there when they bust that jackass." Ray's smile deepened the arc of crow's-feet around his eyes.

"Nice of your former partner to loan us his truck," Trevor said.

"And the uniform?" Ray pointed to the *Friendly Plumbing* patch on his shirt. "Type casting. I get to play a plumber. Who'd a thought?" He grinned wider.

Trevor removed his revolver from underneath the seat, shoved the barrel into the waistband of his pants, and pulled out his shirttail.

"Does he have a gun?"

Trevor's lips parted in a worried smirk. "Not as far as I know, but I don't want to guess wrong. Just keep Zeke busy until you see me with Emily."

Ray lifted the toolbox and opened the door. "I'll give you a two-minute head start, then I'll hit the doorbell."

Moments later, from the rear entry, Trevor heard the chime. He touched the bulge at his waist and then unlocked the door with the key Teresa gave him. The door creaked open and he tiptoed through the kitchen to the living room. Traces of popcorn and sodas littered the coffee table.

The doorbell rang again.

Trevor ran into each of the bedrooms. They were empty.

Breathless, Trevor whipped open the front door. "They're gone."

"Gone?" Ray put the toolbox on the porch and scratched his head.

Trevor retrieved Horace Hardbuckle, Emily's stuffed dog, lying near the couch. "They knew we were coming."

***

Trevor stared out Teresa's living room window, his mind racing. Where had they taken her?

Ray did a slow jog in from the side yard. "No one's out back,"

"Emily was here, though." Trevor used the stuffed animal to point at the half-eaten bowl of popcorn and soda cans on the coffee table. Emily wouldn't have left Horace behind. He went everywhere she did. "I checked the closets. Found one of Burnside's cigars, stubbed out in the kitchen sink."

"How did they know we were coming?"

"No idea." Trevor sickened at the thought of anyone's hands on his daughter.

Ray scratched the stubble on his pointed chin. "Burnside has all the power now. Best Julie signs those papers and you guys move on."

"I'll text her." Trevor pulled out his phone and clicked a few keys. He prayed Burnside lived up to his word.

"I was a dang fool to think we'd catch him. I'm sorry I gave you kids hope."

Trevor sighed and jiggled Horace, his last link to Emily.

"What now?" Ray asked.

"Guess we go home and wait." Trevor headed across the driveway toward the truck with Ray following. Halfway there, he stopped.

If Zeke left with Emily, why was his car still here?

"Hold this." Trevor hit Ray in the stomach with Horace and trotted back to the driveway. He darted around the car, peering in the windows. The old car was clean, not even a food wrapper that might be a clue. Damn, couldn't they catch a break? Trevor slammed his fist down on the metal trunk.

Thunk. Thunk. Thunk.

Trevor froze. "Did you hear that?"

"Yeah," Ray said.

Thunk. Thunk.

"It's coming from in here." Trevor pointed to the back of the faded cranberry-colored Impala. He hit the trunk lid again with the palm of his hand. He heard and felt a series of short, faint thumps against the sidewall.

"We'll have to pry the lock. Give me something." Trevor pointed to Ray's toolbox, his heart pounding against his chest.

Ray handed him a small crowbar. "You got to insert the edge in there, just right. Get in between the gaskets."

"Emily, it's Dad. Don't worry. I'll have you out in a flash." Trevor jimmied the bar in the opening between the trunk latch and bumper and pushed. The trunk didn't budge.

Trevor grunted, twisting the crowbar for a better angle. "Hang on honey." He leveraged another shove and the latch popped. The tool clattered to the ground as he pushed the hatch up. Zeke lay in a fetal position; a pool of blood haloed his head. Duct tape secured his mouth, bound his feet and hands. Something more than a fistfight caused this much damage.

They'd left him for dead.

Trevor searched frantically, shoving Zeke out of the way to see if Emily lay behind him inside.

"She's not here!" he yelled to Ray.

Zeke groaned as Trevor ripped the duct tape from his mouth. "Where's Emily?"

Zeke stared with unfocused eyes.

Trevor shook him. "Come on, man. Where is she?"

"The guy's barely alive," Ray said. "We better call an ambulance."

"Not until he tells me where Emily is." Trevor reached for Zeke's shoulders. "Help me get him out."

"I don't think we should move him. Looks like he took a beatin' with a baseball bat, or worse."

"I don't care. He's going to talk. Where is she?" Trevor shouted. "Where did they take her?" He shook Zeke so hard his head bobbled as though held on with a rubber band. "Zeke!" Blood trickled down Zeke's chin onto Trevor's knuckles.

"Can you stand?" Ray asked, bracing his arm under Zeke's shoulder.

"Think so." Zeke laced his arm around Trevor's back and let himself be freed from the trunk.

"Where's Emily?" Trevor demanded.

Zeke coughed and spat. "Not sure."

"I'll get some water," Ray headed toward the truck.

Trevor propped Zeke's battered body against the fender. "You really screwed up this time. What did they do with my daughter?"

"I don't know." His voice was barely audible.

"Here." Ray handed Zeke a water bottle.

It took a moment for him to be able to swallow.

Ray pointed to a portion of the driveway out of street view. "Let's move him over there before someone walks by and starts asking questions."

Trevor nodded. "Grab him on that side."

The two men dragged Zeke toward the garage and propped against the door. "What'd he beat you with, boy?" Ray asked.

"Didn't see. Just felt it." He took another swallow of water, spat more blood and touched his teeth.

"Tell us what you do know," Trevor asked, his patience totally spent. "Where the hell is Emily."

"Everything happened kinda fast," Zeke recalled, rubbing his hand against his swollen face. "Bobby told her they were going to see her mom. Then Chuck jumped me."

Trevor stooped to Zeke's eye level, a resurgence of anger fired through him. "Bobby and Chuck? Your gambling pals?"

Zeke nodded. "They work for the bookie."

Trevor tapped the crowbar against his palm. "You must have some idea where they are. Think. Damn it! Think."

"I'd tell you if I knew. I'm sorry all this would happen. I was desperate."

"You've always been desperate, Zeke. Now you're just pathetic." Trevor squatted to eye level. Powerful waves of anger unleashed an intense hatred. "If they hadn't beat you to a pulp, I'd be pounding your ass into the ground."

"What can you tell us, boy?" Ray asked.

Zeke grabbed his chest and moaned.

Ray yanked Trevor to his feet. "He's bleeding pretty bad. We better call an ambulance. Won't do us no good if he dies."

"We'll call after he tells us where she is," Trevor barked, not relenting. He towered over Zeke and demanded answers again, this time a palpable threat permeated his voice. "You must know something, must've heard something."

Zeke took a ragged breath, then winced. "Burnside came last night and ordered us to move her. Said a car would pick us up early this morning. Never told me where."

"Guess, damn it. Where could they be?" Trevor's menacing tone turned into a plea.

"He don't know nothing. They was tying up loose ends. Zeke here was a loose end," Ray said.

Trevor shoved Zeke and heard him grunt.

"If I knew where they went, I'd tell you, man," Zeke said. "I should have known something went wrong when I saw Chuck get out of the car. I tried to warn you, but he took my phone."

"Took your phone? Who took your phone?"

"Chuck. He shoved it in his jacket. That's the last thing I remember. Then everything went dark."

Trevor turned to Ray. "We're gonna call for help. But first," Trevor tapped a few keys, "I'm texting Julie. I know exactly how to track these so-called bad-asses."

***

Julie glanced at the read-out on her cell phone. Fifteen minutes left before Burnside burst in and claimed his prize.

She'd extended the charade for as long as she could, using every delay tactic she could think of. Gary played along, making up legalese explanations to very elementary questions. Julie would sign on the dotted line and pray for Emily's safe return.

"And what's that?" Julie asked her final question, attempting to camouflage the phone with her shaking hands.

"Exclusivity clause," Gary answered. "You are prohibited from going into any similar business venture for the next five years."

"In this industry, five weeks is an eternity." The words scraped out like shards of broken glass. "Might as well be never," she said as her cell phone vibrated.

Worried Burnside could see her through a two-way mirror, she reached under the table and glanced at the screen.

Emily not at the house.

Her heart pounded.

Sign the papers.

"So, Julie, as I was saying," Gary's voice interrupted, "this provision clearly spells out one of the key conditions of the sale."

She nodded, frozen with panic while Gary mumbled something about her future rights to compete in the toy market. Julie returned her gaze to the sheaf of papers on the table.

He thumbed through the paperwork. "You're free to pursue other business opportunities, but for the next five years, BAB Enterprises will have first rights to purchase any products and or services you create or develop. You'll find that provision on page twenty-seven."

"Are you kidding? If I sign this, I pretty much lose my rights to make a living for the next five years. I thought California was a right-to-work state."

"This is different. You're not an employee of a company. You're selling intellectual property rights," Gary prattled on. "You won't be able to flood the market with infringing products, but you will pocket two million. You can hang out pretty easily for the next five years on that kind of money."

Julie rolled her eyes.

"I want to make sure you understand. Any new toys or software you create in the next five years will belong to Game Masters. Any patent you file for under your name will be null and void. Not valid. Understand?"

"Yes. Yes, I understand." *They take everything, including my brain. I can't stand another moment without Emily.*

Julie's phone vibrated again. She diverted her gaze from Gary to read the screen.

We know where she is. STALL.

Julie closed her eyes, the pressure choking her as though she were inside a trash compactor. Slowly the sides inched in, blocking every exit, restricting her oxygen.

"Tell me more about that provision," Julie said, her eyes still closed. "What would be considered an infringing product?"

Though Gary used his best legal terminology to explain, Julie wasn't paying attention. Her worry for Emily's safety ate through her like acid drops. This would likely be the last delay Burnside would allow.

"Hey, it's not a great deal, but considering all the facts, I think you should sign." Gary clicked a pen open. "We don't have a whole lot of time left to squabble about these small details."

Julie snatched the pen. "Where do I sign?"

"Full name here." Gary pointed. "And an initial here, and here and here. Great, all done." Gary sounded triumphant.

As if on cue, Bennett Burnside, Fulton and Margie returned. They had been watching and listening. Julie wished them endless misery for the rest of their lives.

"Nice work, Carlson." Burnside grabbed the contracts and handed them to his secretary. "Make two copies." He quickly dialed. "Bring the girl."

Julie's heart caught in her throat. *Emily was here.*

Burnside reached inside his coat pocket then turned his icy stare toward Julie. "While we're waiting, let's make this completely legal." He handed Julie a check and brushed his hands together.

"Game Masters now owns FunWorks."

Chapter Twenty-Seven

Julie fixed her gaze on the doorway, her heart thumping so violently her chest threatened to burst apart. When would Emily's sweet face appear? *Dear God, please let her be safe.*

The thought of Burnside's goons touching her daughter made Julie's stomach clench.

The conference room doorknob clicked and she jumped to her feet. Margie entered the room empty-handed, leaving the door open, her springy exit minutes ago, now reduced to a measured gait.

Julie's heart sank. "Where is my daughter?" The words tore from someplace deep inside. Julie steadied herself against the table.

Margie motioned with her chin to the doorway.

From a distance, Julie heard a little girl's voice. *Emily!* She raced to the door.

Trevor strode toward her, carrying their smiling daughter. On his heels came Ray Bolley and Vincent Williams, followed by two uniformed policemen.

Julie pulled Emily from Trevor and wrapped her arms tight around her daughter's waist. "Are you all right, baby?" She smothered Emily with a mixture of kisses and tears. "I'm so sorry."

Emily nuzzled against Julie's chest. "Mommy, I'm fine."

Julie tipped her daughter's face toward her. "You are, aren't you?"

Emily squealed. "You're hugging too tight."

Julie smiled and hugged even tighter. Now safe in her arms, Julie wouldn't let go.

"A mean man took me from Uncle Zeke. He said we were going to see you, but we just waited in a room." Emily held her tattered stuffed animal. "He made me leave Horace at Mrs. D's house. But Daddy brought him back."

Burnside's eyes darted to Trevor and then to the officers. He stepped toward the side door, but an older policeman blocked his path.

The officer unhooked the handcuffs from his belt and reached for Burnside. "Bennett Burnside. You're under arrest for the kidnapping of Emily Rafferty. And the attempted murder of Zeke Desmond."

He glared at Fulton as the officer pulled his hands behind him. "Do something," he growled.

"We got you, you greedy son of a bitch." Ray flashed a satisfied grin as the officer clicked the cuffs locked and read Burnside his Miranda rights.

Vincent handed Fulton an envelope. "This court order freezes all BAB Enterprises assets while the District Attorney's office conducts an investigation into unfair business practices. These officers are authorized to seize all the files here and at your home office."

Both Burnside's and Fulton's cell phones chimed in unison.

"You'd better answer that," Ray needled. "Might be more bad news."

Fulton's face reddened. Burnside averted Ray's gaze and clicked his cell off.

"Why didn't you come when Uncle Zeke said you would?" Emily asked, still wrapped in Julie's arms.

"We came as quickly as we could." Julie kissed both cheeks and rocked Emily back and forth.

Trevor squeezed Julie's shoulder. "You did great. I'm so proud of you."

"I've never been so scared in my life." Julie weaved her fingers through Emily's long hair. Her pulse still raced. She took a deep breath and let out a long exhale, wondering if her heart rate would ever return to normal. "I wanted to die when I read your first text." She swiped at a tear. "How did you know where to find her?"

"Zeke told us," Ray said walking up to the group. "Sorta."

"We found him locked in his car trunk, left for dead," Trevor said.

"Zeke?"

"Yeah, they thumped him worse than Gary," Ray said.

"Did Emily see that?" Julie asked, repulsed at the idea of her daughter witnessing a beating and now listening to this discussion.

"I don't think so."

"Is he alive?" Julie asked, afraid of the answer.

"Yeah, but barely," Trevor said. "The paramedics and the police arrived just as we were leaving. He's in the hospital now, but he's likely to go to jail, too."

Julie tightened her hug on Emily. "Does Teresa know?"

"When she confessed that they were holding Emily at her house, she gave up Zeke. My guess is, she is probably relieved. This ending is a long time coming." Trevor planted a quick kiss on Emily's forehead.

Julie sat, perching Emily on her lap, her arms entwined around her daughter. "But they moved her. How did you know where to look?"

"Remember Teresa complaining that Zeke kept losing his cell phone, and she'd buy him new ones? He'd forget them in some bar or under somebody's couch."

"Kinda," Julie said.

"Last month I suggested getting a phone-finding app," Trevor said. "When Zeke told us the goons took his phone, I knew we could track them, as long as they didn't turn the phone off."

Julie ran a finger along Emily's cheek. Was any of this nightmare real? The police had Burnside now, but could she get her life back? She doubted that. Nothing would ever be the same.

"Gary, are FunWorks assets frozen now that I signed?" she asked.

"Hardly." He turned to Burnside's secretary. "Margie, will you get those contracts you were about to copy?" Moments later Gary handed the packet of papers to Julie.

She paged through. "I know I signed this thing. I initialed my life away."

"That you did, but with *my* pen."

"Disappearing ink?" Julie asked, her tone incredulous.

Gary winked. "That was Trevor's idea."

"What old spy movie did you borrow that move from?"

"On my drive back from Harpersville, I called Gary. That's when we put this plan together."

As a police officer lead Burnside out the door, Fulton hurried behind, mumbling something about posting bail.

"They were watching us, but not Vincent," Trevor said. The adrenalin still pulsing through his veins made his words come out in rapid fire. "Gary emailed what we knew to Vincent and he passed everything on to a friend of his in the County DA's office."

Julie hugged the now-sleepy girl sitting on her lap, the horror of the crime still fresh. "They had Emily. How could you jeopardize her life?"

Trevor arched his brows. "If everything fell through, we had to hope Burnside would honor his promise of returning Emily. Once you signed away the company, we lost our leverage. Emily was their insurance policy. Burnside was arrogant enough to think that once he took her, we would fold. He never worried that we'd fight back."

Gary slapped Trevor on the back. "Burnside won. Or thought he did. Vincent linked eight or ten company takeovers to BAB. Separately, they were afraid to fight back, but as a group, they're ready to go after the guy."

"Might be years before all the facts come out, but there's a good chance many of those people will get their businesses back," Vincent added.

Trevor shook his hand. "You and Gary did some nice work. MaxOut Toys, New Tech, Solar Wheels. They're all ready to nail Burnside to the wall."

"Mort Gunther cooperated?" Julie asked.

Vincent grinned. "Reluctantly at first. Burnside put him and his family through major misery. Once we connected BAB Enterprises to Burnside, the rest came easy."

"He had a nice gig going, though. A couple of judges were on the take, but Del Evans was the centerpiece."

"The US District Attorney investigating me?" Julie sounded skeptical. "He was in on the scheme, too? Wow."

"The Justice Department had been covertly investigating him for several months. They were only too happy to hear our story," Vincent continued. "Evans is being relieved of his duties as we speak."

"After they go through Burnside's files, Justice might uncover more companies. Then we'll have a real class action suit," Gary stated.

"Don't forget Water Saver."

"There's no way to forget you, Ray." Vincent patted him on the shoulder, then turned to Gary. "I hear you're out of a job. I'm looking for an energetic, creative partner."

"Hey, what about me?" Ray said. "I'm pretty good at this detecting thing."

"True. But wouldn't you rather spend your days enjoying life knowing you helped put that creep behind bars?"

Ray nodded and tousled Emily's hair.

Emily squirmed on Julie's lap and finally scooted off. Julie stood and grabbed her daughter's hand, not wanting to let go…ever.

The two wandered to the window and watched the officers place Burnside into a patrol car. He yelled something at Fulton. Julie couldn't make out the words, but she suspected she knew what he said.

She should feel hatred for the man, but the only emotion pulsing through her body at that moment was relief. Julie squatted and peppered Emily with kisses, each one a confirmation that her daughter was safe, the nightmare finally over.

"Hey."

Julie stood, taking in Trevor's hazel green eyes, the twinkle in them unmistakable. An inner peace swept through her.

Burnside's threat was eliminated, and he didn't own FunWorks.

All because of Trevor.

"You did it," he said.

"*We* did it," she hugged him. "I'm sorry I didn't trust you. I should have—"

"We're together and safe. That's what matters. Let's head home." Trevor lifted Emily. "Jason and Nicole are waiting to see their sister."

Chapter Twenty-Eight

Sitting on a wooden bench outside the courtroom, Julie waited for the jury to return.

Headlines from the past eighteen months streamed through her mind like a news banner crawling across the bottom of a television screen. Her thoughts flashed to the rollercoaster of hardships she and Trevor overcame. Together. Could the misery be finally over?

Julie thanked God every day for Emily's safe return. She woke each morning offering a litany of gratitude for all the Lord gave her, savoring the most important blessing—her family whole again.

Still, nothing could truly end until Burnside received the punishment he deserved. Julie couldn't move past the horrors perpetrated on those she loved. She couldn't forget the haunting fear he instigated or forgive the terror he caused. Until justice had been fully served, she couldn't close this chapter and begin to rebuild her life.

Immediately after Burnside's arrest, the patent infringement lawsuit, along with the labor complaints at Leung Jun's plant, had disappeared. With Del Evans on his way to prison, the money laundering investigation dropped into an abyss. Bull's Eye doubled their original commitment for hologram PlaytimePals, sending FunWorks into a solid financial position.

Julie half smiled to herself, wondering when Roberta Perkins would be calling for a follow-up interview.

For months, along with Trevor and Ray, Julie had appeared at the San Marcel County Superior Courthouse to observe Burnside's trial for aggravated kidnapping and attempted murder. Today Derek, Leanne, Gary, and Vincent joined the trio, eager to hear the verdict.

"They're back. The jury is back," Leanne announced, excitement building in her voice. A mixture of dread and relief coursed through Julie's veins as she stood and followed the group back into the courtroom.

Bennett Burnside entered from the side door and took his place at the defendant's table, wearing his signature charcoal-colored suit, a silk crimson tie and matching handkerchief tucked neatly into his coat pocket. His hair seemed grayer. He fingered a cigar, occasionally lifting the unlit stogie to his mouth as though to puff.

Zeke's trial had concluded some eight months earlier with the state offering him a reduced sentence in exchange for testifying against Burnside, as well as his hired guns Bobby and Chuck.

Not having an appetite to send a sixty-five-year-old grandmother to prison, the DA recommended remanding Teresa to a women's halfway house. She lived there now, helping young women rebuild their lives while focusing on how to restore her own. The dozens of heartfelt apologies she wrote to Julie and Trevor, pleading for understanding and to see Jason, Nicole, and Emily, went unanswered.

"I've forgiven her," Julie had told Trevor on the drive home after one extremely long day at the courthouse. "I want Teresa to have a good life. I just don't want her anywhere near me or my family ever again."

Julie hurried to the courtroom and found a spot between Trevor and Ray in the gallery. The five women and seven men, sworn to uncover the truth, ambled into the jury box and took their seats. Julie sucked in a cleansing breath and reached for Trevor's hand. *They had to find him guilty. Guilty of everything.*

The unthinkable realization that Burnside might beat the charges sent quaking jolts through her stomach. That couldn't happen, could it? The jurors had to see the evil this man perpetrated on innocents, like Emily. Julie believed that. For weeks, she watched jurors' faces as they listened to testimony and nonverbally reacted to the merits of the evidence presented. There was only one conclusion. One verdict to be reached.

Burnside's guilt would send him to prison for a long, long time. And once he was behind bars, Julie could let go of the past and move ahead with her life.

Burnside and his attorney stood.

"Ladies and gentlemen of the jury, have you reached a verdict?"

The foreman rose. "We have, your honor. On count one, the members of the jury find the defendant, Bennett Burnside, guilty."

Julie held her breath as the foreman read each charge.

"Guilty on all counts," he finally said.

Julie let out a squeal of relief. Her eyes darted from the jury box to the defense table.

Burnside fell back into his chair as though his legs would not support him any longer. He bent over the defense table, crushing the panatela he still held, sending tobacco leaves cascading to the floor.

One Year Later

"She's lovely," Julie whispered in Trevor's ear, watching Derek and Leanne dance to "At Last."

Trevor handed Julie a half-filled champagne flute. "Never more beautiful."

Julie clinked her glass against Trevor's and took a sip. "That was some toast Gary made."

"Two years ago, this would have been the last place I thought we'd be. I was a fool then," Trevor said, his smile holding a devilish glint. "Now I'm a fool in love…and so is Derek."

They both watched Derek glide his bride across the dance floor, her white charmeuse gown swishing smoothly to Etta James's sultry voice.

Her eyes twinkled. "And to think Bennett Burnside brought us to this moment. We have so much to thank him for."

"Like meeting Ray Bolley." Trevor laughed. "Emily wants me to make up a Horace Hardbuckle story about him."

"I think that's a magnificent idea," Julie said, pleased Ray had moved back to San Marcel to begin a new life.

Emily ran from the dance floor toward Julie. "Mommy, these shoes hurt and this dress is itchy."

"That's the price you pay for being a flower girl." Julie reached under her chair. "Here. Leanne brought these for you."

Emily pulled off her patent leather dress shoes and swapped them for white sneakers before skipping off.

"She's having a ball." Julie closed her eyes. "Last night she asked me why she wasn't our flower girl."

"Maybe she can be." Trevor kissed Julie's lips. "We could renew our vows. Jason could be my best man, Nicole, your maid of honor and Emily, the flower girl.

Julie tilted her head toward Trevor. "And Ray could give me away."

"Hmmm. I like that idea. He's the true hero in this storybook ending. Of course, we'd have to go away on a honeymoon." He kissed Julie again.

"Naturally." Julie licked her lips slowly. "A really long honeymoon."

"With the kids, of course."

"Of course." Julie smiled. "Do you hear that?"

A grin spread across Trevor's face. "Sounds like 'We Are Family.'"

Julie stood and grabbed her husband's hand. "Care to dance? They're playing our song."

*

If you enjoyed this story by
Claire Yezbak Fadden, consider leaving a review on any online book site, review site, or social media outlet.

Chapter One

Kate Jameson took in the wide expanse of the Clearwater Crossing shopping complex and silently patted herself on the back. What she had originally thought would be a cookie-cutter strip mall with bean counters scrutinizing every dime spent against a balance sheet had become a community center. Her design had taken thirty-five acres of blighted brushland and transformed them into a community square, complete with a grocery store, a cinema, a neighborhood library and a walking trail. The finished result, a perfect mix of functionality and imagination, breathed bustling life into a forgotten corner of Phoenix.

Early on, Kate had pulled every move to get reassigned from the project, but Harry Mack, CEO of Mack & Partners Architects, had specifically requested her services. Seemed as though the development was financed by an old family friend of Harry's who had been impressed by Kate's work on the Ramble Hills Community College Library and Learning Hub.

Completing the local college's project filled Kate with pride and brought her notoriety among her peers. At twenty-eight she was named one of the state's architectural trendsetters, only to be rewarded by Harry with the Clearwater project. She protested, not wanting to be saddled with a life of plotting signage visibility from the I-10 freeway for strip malls.

As she watched the dignitaries, investors and shop employees, she sucked in the air of success. Clearwater Crossing now topped her short list of architectural accomplishments.

"Who's the tall guy on the end talking to the mayor?" Kate whispered to her boss, as she watched eight people, each holding a pair of scissors, nervously stand behind an oversized blue ribbon stretched across the anchoring store's entry.

"You mean Eric Wiley? He's the owners' son," Harry responded.

"Adele and Ben's? I don't recall him at the planning sessions or any of the follow-up meetings," Kate said, taking in Eric's strong build and blinding smile. She guessed he was close to her age and at least six feet tall. The group, poised to cut the ribbon, awaited the go-ahead as a series of photos were taken. From where Kate stood, she had an unobstructed view of Eric's left hand. No ring.

"You probably haven't," Harry stated. "He travels a lot for their company. But you will see more of him in the future. His folks are so pleased with how everything went on this project, that they want to build more of these across the southwest. Eric, their heir apparent, will be running these jobs going forward."

Kate smiled. Not the worst news she's heard today.

"All right everyone, get your scissors ready, but don't actually cut until I give the go ahead," the photographer directed. "Okay. On three. One. Two. Three."

Snip. Snip. The complex was officially opened for business. Kate grabbed a section of the ribbon that had fallen to the ground and tucked the souvenir into her handbag before following the group into the reception.

A small combo played big band music while the eight scissor-holders along with some fifty others mingled, eating shrimp puffs and chicken satay.

Kate understood that an important part of being an architect was ensuring satisfaction after the last tile was laid, the last shrub planted and the last set of keys handed over to the center manager. Still, these glad-handing events left her uncomfortable.

She glanced at her watch. Fifteen minutes more and then she could excuse herself without being reprimanded by Harry. She walked about the community room examining the string of framed photos hanging on the walls. Each offered a visual snapshot into the history of Maricopa County. Next to erecting buildings, history was Kate's passion. That is why she had insisted on the mini-museum exhibit as a design element.

Kate stopped at an enlarged black-and-white photo of four men wearing cowboy hats and read the engraved caption attached to the wall below: *Cotton harvest, circa 1888.* Kate leaned in closer to study the men's sun-weathered faces, their rudimentary farming tools and determined posture.

She turned to view the next photo and glimpsed Eric pushing his way through the crowd, carrying two glasses of champagne, one spilling as he bumped into Harry's back.

"Hello," he said extending a glass toward Kate. "Mom says you're the mastermind behind this concept. I thought you deserved a toast."

"Oh, thank you," Kate said, fighting a swarm of butterflies that arrived when Eric did, and now wanted to reside in her stomach. "This has been a fun project to work on. You're the Wileys' son?"

"Yes. I'm Eric," he introduced himself still holding both glasses. "I'm sorry we haven't actually met before. From what I'm told, your concept will be replicated across the southwest."

"I'm just very glad that everything worked out the way it did," Kate accepted the champagne flute, her fingers briefly brushing Eric's, causing the butterflies in her tummy to flap their wings faster.

"To Clearwater Crossing and its architect," Eric said, raising his glass before clinking it against Kate's.

Kate took a sip and got lost in Eric's brown eyes, strong and piercing.

"I thought we might talk more about the project, maybe over dinner," Eric suggested.

Kate closed her eyes, not believing that the man she drooled over moments before just asked her out. There was nothing she'd enjoy more than spending time with him. If only they weren't going to be working together.

"Are you okay?" Eric asked.

Kate blinked open her eyes. "I'm fine. I'm sorry I need to leave." She shoved the nearly full glass into Eric's hand.

"Did I say something wrong? If so, I apologize."

"It was very nice meeting you," Kate mumbled and headed for the exit.

Nope, not doing it again, she thought. Not dating anyone from work. After the last time, I'm keeping my professional life far away from my personal one.

*

Eric watched Kate scamper out the door without a backward glance.

What the hell just happened?

The way Adele and Ben, his adoptive parents, had spoken of their architect, you'd think the woman should be nominated for sainthood. "Why don't you go introduce yourself," Adele had instructed moments earlier. And Eric thought, *why not?* Enough time had passed since his divorce from Jenny. Maybe he was ready to start again. At thirty, he wasn't getting any younger, but even enticing a woman to have a drink with him proved impossible.

"I see you met Kate," Ben Wiley said, now standing near Eric.

"Just barely," Eric replied staring at the two glasses of scarcely touched champagne.

"Where did she go? The ladies room?" Ben asked.

"I don't think so, Dad. She ran out of here so fast, I thought maybe I'd grown a third eye during our short conversation. Here, drink this," Eric pushed a glass into Ben's hand. "To Dollar Deals."

"To Dollar Deals," Ben echoed, referring to their family business. "Your mother is chatting it up with the mayor. She loves these little soirees. Me, not so much."

Eric gulped his champagne and set the empty glass on a nearby tray. "Mom loves moving people around her chessboard, that's for sure."

"You sound bitter. What's wrong?"

"Nothing. Everything." Eric regretted starting this conversation but his frustration boiled over and he couldn't contain his anger. "I'm tired of these missions not turning up anything. I'm tired of chasing a man I may never find. A man who may not even exist anymore."

"Sssh. Someone might hear."

"You asked, so I'm telling you. Mostly, I'm tired of being alone. I want to have a real life. And the first time since Jenny and I broke up that I try to introduce myself to a girl, she runs away like I just peed in the punch bowl."

"You're being too hard on yourself. Kate probably had another business engagement. It probably has nothing to do with you," Ben said.

Eric scanned the room, searching for something, anything to look at besides the disappointment in his father's eyes. "I'm sure. She doesn't know enough about me and what I do to run away like Jenny did." To be fair, Jenny tried to make their marriage work, but Eric's obsession with his job prevented any chance of success. Kate's racing out the door before even the simplest of conversations just preempted the inevitable. She wouldn't stay around either once she found out he was an agent for the government.

Ben rested his hand on Eric's shoulder. "Son, you take everything so personal. Sometimes things are what they are."

"Sometimes." And sometimes you have to make things become what you want them to be. Eric gazed toward the doorway, recalling the image of Kate's shoulder-length auburn tresses flouncing with every stride against the back of her olive-green suit jacket. The scent of her perfume lingered in the air he breathed. She didn't have another appointment, still she left after they barely said two sentences to each other.

He wanted to spend time with this hazel-green-eyed woman. The woman Adele raved about for months. The young architect whose plans for Clearwater Crossing included a kiddie park, water fountains for dogs and special parking for pregnant women.

Eric didn't know why Kate left but he would find the reason. Because like in his professional life, Eric couldn't leave unanswered questions alone.

*

Get your copy of
Maybe This Time
today from any online retailer!

Join Claire's Mailing List

To get sneak peeks of upcoming stories
and to hear about giveaways Claire is sponsoring,
visit www.clairefadden.com.

Author Biography

When she's not playing with her grandchildren, Pennsylvania native Claire Yezbak Fadden is writing contemporary women's fiction. Her books feature strong women who overcome life's challenges, always putting their families first. She loves butterflies, ladybugs and holds a special affinity for carousel horses – quite possibly the result of watching "Mary Poppins" 13 times as a young girl.

The mother of three lives in Orange County, California with her husband, Nick and three spoiled dogs, Bandit, Jersey Girl and Bowie. Claire's work as an award-winning journalist, humor columnist and editor has appeared in 100 publications across the United States, Canada and Australia. Follow her @claireflaire, email her at claire@clairefadden.com or visit her at clairefadden.com.

Other Books by Claire Yezbak Fadden

Promises to Keep
A Corner of Her Heart
Maybe This Time